THE
PREACHER'S LETTER

Billy Beasley

eLectio Publishing

Little Elm, TX

The Preacher's Letter

By Billy Beasley

Copyright 2018 by Billy Beasley. All rights reserved.

Cover Design by eLectio Publishing

ISBN-13: 978-1-63213-464-6

Published by eLectio Publishing, LLC

Little Elm, Texas

http://www.eLectioPublishing.com

5 4 3 2 1 eLP 22 21 20 19 18

Printed in the United States of America.

The eLectio Publishing creative team is comprised of: Kaitlyn Campbell, Emily Certain, Lori Draft, Court Dudek, Jim Eccles, Sheldon James, and Christine LePorte.

Publisher's Note

The publisher does not have any control over and does not assume any responsibility for author or third-party websites or their content.

This is a work of fiction. Names, characters, businesses, places, events and incidents are either the products of the author's imagination or used in a fictitious manner. Any resemblance to actual persons, living or dead, or actual events is purely coincidental.

Merry Christmas

Micah 6:8

Billy Beasley

To my beautiful wife, Julie.
My singer in the storms.

Also in memory of Horace Hilton.
Shepherd, Pastor, Mentor and my friend.

Author's Note

Carolina Beach, NC is indeed a real place that we are blessed to call home. I did take some liberty in creating establishments that do not exist.

Portside Church, in Wilmington, NC, is mentioned throughout the story. It does not exist.

Acknowledgments

My sincere gratitude to the following:

My family, and a special thanks to my sisters, Pat, Kay, and Ada for your support and encouragement of your baby brother's writing journey.

Family comes in different shapes and I am most grateful for the Olivolo family, who took me into their wonderful loving family many years ago.

Jack and Kelly. Jack, I think of you when I hear the scripture, Proverbs 18:24, *There is a friend that sticks closer than a brother.*

Micah. Sharing this journey with you has been more fulfilling than I can put into words.

Kristy Huddle.

To Christopher Dixon and all the staff at eLectio Publishing.

1

THE REVEREND ALAN MATTHEWS towered over the clear acrylic showpiece that held his white, pristine Bible and the outline he worked from. He gazed out at *his* audience. There was not an empty seat to be found in the building that contained approximately eight hundred worshipers. He paused for several moments from his sermon for the intended dramatic effect. He had followed his script to the letter. After many years as a minister he was supremely confident that his routine was by now flawless. He opened with a brief scripture reading. Next, he instructed the choir to sing a traditional hymn that coincided with the message he would be bringing. After twenty minutes of lively praise songs it was a letdown to many in the congregation, but it was his routine. It was not to be deviated from. It also enhanced his standing with some of the more rigid, older members, who believed that church music should come only from a hymnbook, enhanced by an organ or piano at best. They found music fueled by guitars, trumpets, and thunderous drums, disrespectful.

Alan smiled at his captive listeners as he reached for the cup of water that was on the second shelf of the podium. He drank very little as he was not the least bit thirsty. It too was for effect. He self-consciously raised his hand, delicately parting his blond hair to make sure the receding hair line that disturbed him was concealed.

Buttoning his deep gray suit over his slightly protruding stomach he held his hands out to his side as if he wanted to embrace his people. His message today was about sex and the actuality that it would prove controversial stimulated him. He longed to converse about subjects that stirred the people from their well-padded pews.

He was an unconventional preacher, and he seldom referred to the Bible after the initial scripture reading. He told stories, quoted poets, musicians, and historical figures. Jesus was mentioned on occasion.

Oh, how he loved to perform. Every Easter he acted out a one-man play for the church. He was certain that if it were not for his higher calling that he would be earning his wages on stage, perhaps even under the bright lights of Broadway.

At one of his previous churches, one of his associate pastors once suggested during a staff meeting that after three consecutive years of his play that perhaps it was time to move in a new direction. That particular pastor was no longer with the church by the time the summer heat arrived.

It was of little concern to him if the parishioners, or for that matter the ruling board of elders disapproved of his techniques. After all, was it not these same elders that one year earlier implored him to leave his church of nine hundred members in Knoxville, Tennessee to become the spiritual leader of Portside Church, and its three thousand members?

Their salary offer when all the perks were totaled was in the neighborhood of two hundred thousand dollars annually. That surely didn't hurt their chances when they offered him the job. God's elite seldom left one church for another without God's spirit assuring them. The fact that larger salaries, houses, and better benefits almost always accompanied such moves, well, that only coincided nicely with God's plan.

He informed the elders shortly upon arrival that his calling was to preach. He would not visit the sick and afflicted in the hospitals or in their homes. The three associate ministers, and the elders and deacons of the church would serve those less important duties.

He was well versed in so many subjects but in his mind when it came to the uncomfortable topic of sex he believed he was an absolute authority on the matter. He loved visiting colleges and meeting with students to discuss the sexual issues facing them. Today's message contained a common theme. Abstain from premarital sex. He warned of the dangers of disease and unwanted pregnancies.

Now, forty minutes after he began speaking he stepped from behind the pulpit. He walked to the edge of the foundation that elevated him over his congregation. It was a calculated step--as were all of his movements.

"Now, brothers and sisters I would be remiss not to speak of forgiveness. God will forgive you of your sins."

"Thank God," Troy Dawkins said softly, but with biting sarcasm at the mention of forgiveness. The wife of an elder seated in the pew in front of him turned to see what voice so rudely intruded on the silence of the parishioners.

Troy's unflinching eyes met her look of disapproval, and she quickly turned around. He breathed deeply. So, that was it. Forty minutes of pointing fingers at the guilty and less than forty seconds spent telling them that God would forgive them.

He felt his mother, Ruth Dawkins, squirm beside him. She was the sole reason that he was in attendance today. He had promised her. He seldom made promises and he broke even less. His parents attended church regularly. His mom came to worship the God that she so dearly loved. His father, Tom, arrived each Sunday to claim his same seat and entertain those around him before the service. At the conclusion of the service he raced to the parking lot as briskly as a man nearing eighty years of age could in his attempt to be the first one freed from the congested parking lot. Once on the highway he let the old Buick roar at a top speed of thirty-five. He had always been that way as far back as Troy could recall.

He felt his mother grasp his hand and it amused him slightly. He was her little boy, always. The closeness he felt with his mother was equaled by the distance he shared with his father. Tom Dawkins loved to be the center of attention. He was clueless that people began rolling their eyes with a frozen smile upon their face as he would begin to repeat the same tired stories. He was a man with no filter and in Troy's eyes did not know enough to be embarrassed by his behavior. Ruth was often uncomfortable as well, but she loved Tom dearly and made excuses for him. She believed things about her husband that simply were not true. She refused to see him as self-centered and childish in his behavior. Maybe he wasn't the best father in the world but wasn't that because of the generation he was raised in? Big boys don't cry and they share little emotionally. The truth was Troy was certain that his dad had nothing to share emotionally, while his mom believed that one day, God would reach her husband, and this wealth of feelings stored up for a lifetime would come flowing out like the water at Linville Falls that Troy hiked to the previous New Year's Day.

The only emotion that Troy witnessed from his father was his anger when anything large or small did not go exactly according to plan. The man had never shed a tear as far as Troy knew. That kind of sentiment just did not exist in his father.

Troy once attended Portside Church regularly. Those were the days when David Lang was the pastor. David was the instrument that saw the modest gray, stone church increase from thirty members to three thousand. He retired two years ago. The associate ministers handled the chores with his assistance until a lengthy search produced one Alan Matthews. The search committee voted eight to one to offer the job to Alan. This astonished Troy. How could eight people have witnessed the pompous attitude of this man and not run from his mere presence? The one lady that chose not to vote yes felt so strongly about it that she left the church. Troy was certain that history would prove she was not only the lone female on the search committee, but the only one who possessed wisdom in the decision.

David had shared the pulpit with his associate pastors liberally. In fact, there were complaints from many in the congregation that he allowed them to speak too frequently. He was a popular speaker and he fielded requests to speak at seminars throughout the country. Still, he never lost sight that it was God who was to receive the glory, and he thought it this same God who desired that three fine young ministers be provided an opportunity to grow. He enjoyed being with each of them. They made him feel younger than a man in his early seventies had any right to feel. The associate ministers knew the preference of the members was to hear David speak at every service and they were always grateful that the lead minister insisted they be allowed to grow in what God had called them to do.

Alan, upon his arrival, put a halt to the sharing of the pulpit for all practical purposes. He preached nearly every service and when he was away, curiously, he more times than not brought in a guest speaker. Much to the dismay of practically every member, Alan refused to invite David to speak despite the numerous requests for him to do so.

Troy referred to the church now as the Alan Matthew's show. Initially, he tried to continue attending the middle service each Sunday morning with some sort of frequency, if for no other reason than to please a mother whom he adored. But each week brought more of the same long-winded intellectual speeches. He tried to gather one or two good things from the sermons but in time even that proved futile. He had not attended a service in nearly three months and right now he was dreadfully sorry that he was present today. Many times he was on the verge of rising and walking out, and each time his mother seemed to know this, and he would feel the soft touch of her hand on top of his.

He stretched as much as possible in the crowded pew trying to ease the tension in his body. Tension brought on by too little sleep and a fool with a microphone.

The entire sermon was ridiculous. He understood that it was the church's way to abstain from sex before marriage. But two statements by the Rev. Idiot struck a raw nerve. The first was when he stated, "If you ever sleep with someone and marry another, you will never completely belong to your spouse."

The second was, "Ladies, if the man gets you to cheat with him before marriage, he will cheat on you after marriage."

Troy was flooded with memories of a young woman he once loved long ago. Truthfully, she was the only woman he had ever loved. She was a good woman who could never find absolution from a promiscuous period that occurred during her teenage years. This discourse would have brought torment to the wounds from which she could not escape. At least for this one day it was good that she was not present.

Alan's message had run past the scheduled time as had become customary. It was ten minutes to eleven. The next service would begin at eleven. Services may run well past their allotted time, but they never begin late. It created quite a logjam at the entrances each week. Hundreds of members attempting to enter while an equal amount were trying to escape. All of this brought on because a service that was scheduled to end at ten-thirty never did.

The saying 'Less is more,' came to mind. Troy speculated as to why ministers never could quite comprehend one of his favorite sayings. Saturate someone to the point where all they can think about is "will you ever stop" and "you have lost them." Why not a briefer message that leaves them wanting more? He knew of one minister that understood this scenario.

There was only one thing left for Alan to do. He scrapped the closing 'prayer for healing.' At this point Troy was just glad to know that an exit was forthcoming. Still, he knew this was yet another choice that David Lang would have never made. He recalled David often saying, "Each Sunday there is at least one person present who is broken-hearted and in all likelihood one sitting on each pew."

The 'prayer for healing,' occurred at the conclusion of service. Ministers and elders would gather in front of the pulpit area and those who needed special prayer would walk to them as soft praise songs played.

The concluding hymn was one verse of "Amazing Grace." Alan walked down the aisle to the front door of the church. The hymn ended and the service was mercifully concluded. He shook hands with each person who filed through, soaking up any praise passed his way. There was a gap in the line briefly and then an immense man approached him with purpose. He was tall, probably 6'5", and very solid looking. Alan gauged him to be at least two hundred and thirty pounds. He was dressed in blue jeans and a black denim shirt that he had made no attempt to tuck in. A little too casual for church attire, Alan thought. His brown hair touched down onto broad shoulders. There was slight graying around his temples. His face seemed angry and his cheeks were red. But it was his eyes that unnerved Alan. They were slate blue and bore through him with an intensity that quite frankly frightened him.

Alan extended his hand. Troy paused briefly and looked into his eyes. He started to speak, but stopped. He walked away leaving the misguided Reverend clutching at the air.

The nine-year-old Buick was cranked and ready to roar out of the parking lot. Tom Dawkins looked toward his bride seated beside him, as he still referred to her after nearly six decades of marriage. Her hand was still on the partially open door.

"I didn't think that man would ever shut up," he groused.

She was lost in thought as she watched Troy walk across the lawn. She was aware that Tom had spoken but she had no idea what he was griping about. She loved him dearly, but she had long ago learned to tune out his childlike ranting.

"Close the door, Honey, and let's go," he said, his agitation growing. Tom loved Ruth dearly. But his unquestionable love for her did not mean that she could escape his legendary impatience. "Close the door," he repeated, his voice biting.

"Just a minute, Honey," she said, patting his leg briefly, before moving quickly from the car and onto the lawn in pursuit of her son. Tom sat disgustedly behind the wheel, pouting. He was now being delayed from his next stop. There was an old sea green recliner that rested in front of his new wide screen television. The television was a recent Christmas gift from his children and it took just a scant amount of time before he disparaged his present. Criticism came easy to him, especially when it came to his children. He was also not happy with any change in his routine and he thought nothing of telling all of them how he preferred his older, smaller television. He told this at every opportunity that he deemed appropriate, which, in essence was each time the thought crossed his mind. Now that his old television set had been taken away he decided there was nothing wrong with the picture. His short term memory now amnesic about how he had constantly griped about the top six inches of the screen being several shades lighter than the rest. This well thought out decision arose when he spent five extensive minutes attempting to store the cable numbers into memory without success.

He watched the cars depart onto the main road. Frustrated, he smacked the steering wheel, cursing under his breath.

Ruth called to Troy, as she walked quickly attempting to catch him. "Troy," she called once again. This time he heard her and turned, searching the cluster of people to locate her. She moved from behind a group of patrons and continued toward him.

She caught him and put a hand on his arm, pausing to catch her breath. He looked down into her eyes. They were a mixture of gray and hazel, magnified by snow-white hair. And they were always warm with kindness. "Come home and eat lunch with us. We'll boil shrimp and you and I can talk afterward."

"Talk about what, Mom?" he replied gently.

"I know the preacher upset you. You were thinking of Alana, and if she would have been here today, and how much his words would have hurt her."

"Why do you care, Mom? You never approved of Alana," he replied, sharper than he intended.

"She belonged to another, son."

"She belonged with me and she would have been if not . . ."

They stood silently on the freshly mowed lawn under the towering pine trees. The sky was deep blue and Troy felt the warmth from the bright fall sun on his back. He was about to tell her that he had worked late and was tired. All he wanted was to go home and rest before his next work shift.

"Let's buy some shrimp. Help an old lady out. I feel bad."

He looked at her with a slight smile. She knew that she would get her way with him, and she knew that he knew this as well.

"There is nothing for you to feel bad about, Mom. You did nothing wrong."

"I pressured you to come to church today."

He hugged her tenderly. "It's not your fault the church hired a moron for a preacher."

A man passing by paused as he overheard Troy's words. "Did you just say?"

"Yes, as a matter of fact, I did."

The man looked at him uncertain of what to say to such boldness. "You shouldn't . . ."

Troy interrupted him. "Be honest, here at the church of all places? I should lie? Is that what you are saying?"

"Uh, no." The man now regretted stopping. He looked toward the parking lot. "My wife is waiting for me in the car." He smartly began to walk away.

"No. She is not. She is just coming out the church."

He stopped, caught in his deceit, and wondered why this man he did not know would know who his wife was. He glanced toward the door and saw his wife walking toward him. He turned back to him as his wife drew close to him.

"I work as a bouncer and that means to be good at it, I observe."

The man grabbed his wife's hand and briskly led her away.

"That was mean." His mom admonished.

"No. That was honest."

She studied her son and wished that at times he was not quite so forthcoming with his honesty.

"Would you have preferred I say liar, liar, pants on fire?"

Ruth stifled a chuckle and slightly shook her head. "Never mind that. What about the shrimp?"

He met her pleading eyes and nodded his answer.

She smiled. "Let me tell your dad. I'll ride with you and we will stop at the seafood house on the way."

He watched her walk away. "She always wins," he said quietly. But he was smiling as he said it.

*

TROY STOOD OVER THE OLD silver stock pot that like most of the kitchen items had been in the kitchen for as long as he could recall. They were frugal about the smallest of expenditures. Regardless of any economic forecasts they were keenly aware that the next great depression might well be on the horizon and they would be prepared. Troy's favorite kitchen relic was the butcher knife. The wood handle was deteriorating and the blade was so thin that by now it more resembled an ice pick than a knife. There was one thing in the knife's favor. There would be no worries about one of his elderly parents having a mishap and cutting themselves. If it wouldn't slice butter, and it would not unless the butter was melted, they were safe.

Satisfied that the correct amount of water was in the pot he opened a can of Busch beer and emptied the contents into the pot. He cracked open another and poured half of it into the pot and then drank the remainder. He did this all under the watchful eye of Tom Dawkins.

He braced for what he knew would be a suggestion on how to do it differently. It would come at some point regardless of which method he chose. It had always been that way. Little that he ever did was right in his father's eyes. But in fairness his father was that way with everyone. He loved to be right and have people heed his counsel. Troy suspected that many people listened and either ignored him, or went along with his opinion to prevent the imminent argument that would certainly take place if his viewpoint was not readily accepted as correct.

His older siblings, Wanda, Diane, and his brother, Tommy, were much the same way. They would argue endlessly over nothing that mattered just so they could be declared the victor. If it were not for his mother, he could dissolve himself fully from the lot of them. Fortunately, they all lived several hundred miles away so their paths rarely crossed.

He turned the stove on high and dumped in three pounds of shrimp. The late season shrimp from the ocean always seem to be the most flavorful.

The unwelcome help as always came. "Cut the heat off," Tom stated firmly.

"A few more seconds," he replied. "Go help Mom, with the hush puppies," he said, as he cut the burner off.

Satisfied that he was indeed still in charge in his house, Tom left to assist Ruth, who was cooking the hush puppies on a gas burner in the detached garage.

Troy turned the burner back on. Ninety seconds later he cut it off, leaving the shrimp remaining on the burner. He smiled at the thought of the old man not getting his way and wondered briefly if he was being equally as childish.

As he waited for the shrimp to finish cooking he glanced at the knotted pine walls that surrounded him. The wall to his left was crowded with pictures of the close family that his mom pretended they were but deep inside knew they were not. She was like that about everything. Always pretending that things were better than they actually were.

The house was over fifty years old. The kitchen opened into the living room and down the hall were three bedrooms and one bathroom. There was a half bathroom for the master bedroom.

The limited bathrooms were as poorly planned as the order in which the children were born. His sisters, Wanda and Diane, were born less than eighteen months apart. There was a six-year break and then Tommy was born. Six years later Troy arrived into the world.

The girls shared one bedroom. Troy shared one with his brother.

His sisters were always tolerant of their dad, though they had a point where they would not back off. Tommy was different. He would do anything to gain his father's approval. Troy had given up on his father's allusive support as early as Little League Baseball.

His eyes fell on a picture of him in his baseball uniform. He was ten years old. The happiest times of his childhood were spent playing baseball away from the critical eye of his father.

The back door to the kitchen swung open interrupting his warm and fuzzy reflection of his family. "Let's eat on the porch," his mom said.

He nodded in agreement.

She reached into the cabinet and pulled down a huge glass bowl and set it beside the stove. She touched the back of his broad back and patted him lightly. Then she gave him a playful smack. "Stop lifting those weights. You're too big."

He smiled as he moved to the sink with the pot of shrimp. She had been telling him this same thing now for over twenty years. He poured the contents into a metal colander that rivaled the silver pot in age. He allowed time for the water to drain and then emptied the shrimp into the bowl.

"Your dad says you don't listen to him about cooking shrimp, and he's been doing it for nearly seventy years."

"Well, by God, if it is his way then it must be the right way."

"Let's eat," she said quietly, ending the conversation.

They ate quietly on the large screened in porch. Troy recalled a girlfriend once saying how peaceful she found the sound of a screen door closing.

He had no such fond memories. He briefly looked over at the screen door. The association with the door that came to mind for him was the many times as a child when he excitedly took off to go play ball. The door slamming behind him.

His father would scream at him. "Do you have to take the damn door to Oleander Drive to close it?"

Oleander Drive was the highway through the woods, hundreds of yards away. As Troy, grew into his teenage years, and became less afraid of his dad, he sometimes slammed the door on purpose just to get a rise out of him.

As soon as Tom had polished off his meal, he rose, belched as if he were performing at Carnegie Hall, and retreated to his recliner to watch golf.

Troy and his mom remained on the porch. The steady hum of the ceiling fan made Troy drowsy. He had worked late and slept little. His thoughts drifted to his daughter Heidi, who lived in Hawaii. He smiled as he thought about her and was sad at the same time because of how far away she lived. He had never married and Heidi was the result of the one night that he and his best friend Carla crossed the lines of their friendship. Even though they immediately recognized that this was not the path for them to take they certainly never considered Heidi a mistake. She was always viewed as a delightful addition to their life. Troy was not prepared for all he felt that first time he held her. He thought of how he would shelter her from any harm but later he realized that in his darker times it was his daughter who protected him.

"Alan blew it pretty badly today, didn't he?"

Startled back to consciousness, he looked at her and saw the resolute look in her eyes. The conversation would have to take place. He breathed deeply. "I won't be in attendance as long as he is there. It is pointless when you leave church feeling worse than when you entered. I am pretty sure it is not designed to be that way."

It was still again. The wind rustled slightly through the trees. Oak leaves gave off a slight crunching sound as they moved across the deep green lawn. They heard a bird thrashing in the water in the nearby birdbath.

The answer did not please her. She wanted him in church beside her.

"Mom, you didn't agree with what he said, did you? I've heard you say that dad had his wanderings before you. Does that mean that he is still not completely your husband?"

She shook her head. "No, I think that was silly too."

"And if you slept together before marriage do you think that dad would have strayed after?"

"No, he didn't," she answered, before quickly adding, "he wouldn't."

He tried not to smile but he couldn't help it. Ruth had slipped up. His virgin mother was not that when the vows were exchanged.

"Before you let that rebellious mind of yours race off too far, I have never been with anyone but your father."

He held his hands up in defense. "Okay, okay, enough of the subject."

"Maybe you could talk to Alan, or write him. Tell him how you feel."

"Why?"

"So it won't eat at you longer than need be."

"What makes you think that it will eat at me?"

She shook her head slightly. There was sadness etched on her face. "Because . . ."

"Everything does," he said, finishing her answer. "It won't help. People with all the answers don't change."

She rose from her chair and kissed him on the head. "Lie down and take a nap. You have to be at work in a little while. I'll peel some shrimp for you to take home."

"Shrimp omelet for breakfast. That sounds good, Mom," he said, as he settled into the soft patio couch. "Wake me by three, okay?"

"I will," she said, as she bent down and kissed him again.

"Still tucking your little boy in?"

"Not so little anymore," she answered as she smiled down at him. The warmth of her smile remained with him as he dozed off moments later.

2

TROY FIDGETED IN HIS FADED gray beach chair, basking in the heat of the sun that beamed down from a faultless sky. He wished that his thoughts were as clear as the late October rich sky that was such a deep blue that it bordered on being purple. His mind kept revisiting the ludicrous sermon from the previous day.

It was mid-morning and the beach was nearly desolate. It was the way he preferred it. The solitude of the beach was one of the few places that he could experience fleeting moments of tranquility.

He felt fatigued, but that was the normal feeling for him in the morning. Most nights he struggled to find sleep until the wee hours of the morning and then it was at best a restless nap. Most days as was the case today he woke early enough to view the sun emanate from the Atlantic waters. Later, in the early afternoon he would take a lengthy nap.

The peculiar sleeping pattern was born from his job, and a restless mind. He was the head bouncer at *Mabry's* a local nightspot at Carolina Beach, a small beach town near Wilmington, North Carolina.

A retired couple, Nate and Mabry Wood, owned *Mabry's*. Troy first met Mabry over twenty years ago when he was a baseball player and a disinterested student at East Carolina University in Greenville, North Carolina, where she was a professor. During his freshman year he was encouraged by the upper classmen on the baseball team to enroll in her Creative Writing class. They assured him that it would be an easy class. After one week of her class he was without doubt that he had been duped by his more experienced teammates. He approached Professor Wood and informed her that he would be dropping the class. It wasn't like it was a big deal. Students dropped classes all the time, especially early in the semester.

The surprise came when he discovered it was for some reason a major concern for this professor. She in no uncertain terms vowed that she would make it very rough on him with her good friend, the baseball coach, if he insisted on dropping her class.

Troy didn't take her threat seriously. Several students had already dropped the class. He was confident that his coach would intervene on his behalf.

He blew her class off the following morning with no intention of returning. That afternoon he walked into the fitness facility to lift weights only to be met by his coach, Ed Wilson.

"Put your cleats on and meet me at the ball field," Coach Wilson, said evenly.

"I was going to lift, Coach."

He stared into Troy's eyes without speaking.

"Going now, Coach," Troy finally had the good sense to respond.

Coach Wilson met him at the field. "Five laps around the field to loosen up and then sprints."

One hour later in which time neither man spoke an exhausted Troy was down on his knees in the outfield. "Coach, I can't move."

Coach Wilson smiled ever so slightly. "Do you think when Friday morning comes around you can move your behind to Professor Wood's class?"

Startled, Troy looked up. This was what his punishment was about? He started to tell him of his plans to drop the class and add another. But there was no room for debate on the face of the man that loomed over him. "Yes, Coach. I'll be there."

"Dawkins, you will be at least ten minutes early. That should give you plenty of time to apologize."

"I got you, Coach."

"You better." He turned and walked away. "Don't forget to lift," he said, his words trailing behind him.

Nate Wood always teased his wife about how she often had a feeling about things, particularly people. Still, he knew that it went with the territory of being married to a creative, bright woman. And he would change nothing about her because he simply adored her.

There was something about Troy Dawkins that Mabry Wood could not put her finger on, and for that reason she simply would not allow him to leave her class.

It took very little time for her to see creativity in him that he failed to acknowledge, and preferred to hide, especially from his teammates. More importantly she saw someone who needed a life that reached beyond pitching a baseball and attending keg parties.

Each day Troy attended the Witch's class. His coach instructed him that he expected no less than a B in her class and he would prefer an A. There was one thing in life that Troy took very seriously, and that was baseball. He was a member of the team as a walk on and the approval of his coach was the most essential part of his college experience.

By the end of the semester, Creative Writing was his favorite class. He was quite proud to inform his coach that he had indeed made an A in Professor Wood's class, though by the conclusion of the semester it was not Professor Wood, or the Witch, but Mabry. In addition, he had become a regular dinner attendee at the home she shared with Nate, and their two sons, Todd and Kevin.

Mabry and Nate had been retired for ten years. The club provided them with a nice income that they didn't need. Her pension was adequate and Nate had done quite well with the architectural firm that he had founded in Greenville. He still owned a third of the business but the daily grind was now left to their sons.

They purchased the beach property that sat just off the southern end of the boardwalk eight years earlier. The land came with a three-story decaying hotel that was constructed shortly after World War II. It was in dire need of work, or in the opinion of the surrounding business owners, demolition.

Nate had no intention of razing the decaying wooden structure. No longer was he tied to a desk with all his plans limited to blueprints. Now, he could convey a plan from the beginning to completion. At times, he felt like an artist attempting to paint the consummate picture as the aged hotel took on new life. On a hot summer day, he stood in front of his newly concluded project. He glowed at the success of it much like a proud father gushes over a newborn baby. His critics that thought he was nuts not to demolish it initially now admired his vision. He was less enthusiastic about the project his wife wanted accomplished next.

Mabry insisted on purchasing the land behind the hotel for the construction of a nightclub. Nate argued that the noise would drive away the people from the hotel. Her sharp rebuttal was, "Good, because she didn't want a bunch of old farts staying there anyway." The truth was that she wanted to stay close to the young college students that she no longer taught. Many of her fellow professors had complained of disrespect and apathy in their students but what she saw was freshness and creativity. She had not wanted to retire but she did want to live on the coast with Nate. He had lived in Greenville, but for decades he longed to live with sand under his feet. She gave in because Nate had granted her everything she ever desired and it was her time to give back.

She won the nightclub argument and Nate constructed it to her specifications. Upon completion, he sarcastically asked if it would be all right now if he built them a home to live in, unless she was planning on living in a one-bedroom condo forever. She told him that would be fine but she expected to have the kitchen, dining, living, bedrooms, and bathrooms done the way she desired. "Well, that is everything, isn't it?" he asked.

"No." She smiled. "That is for the inside. I want cedar shake shingles on the exterior. Also, I want a long wraparound porch with white railings."

"No, to the cedar shake shingles. I will do vinyl shake shingles."

She smiled, before responding. "Okay, as long as my other directions are followed."

"Thank you so much," he sarcastically responded.

"Oh, Nate. You can do the garage anyway you like," she stated, walking away.

He shook his head in dismay and then he smiled broadly. "I will expect some romance tonight young lady."

She turned back to him and smiled slightly. "We will see, Nate. We will see." She turned and walked away. Not allowing her smile to break out until her back was completely to him.

Nate and Mabry first visited Carolina Beach on a short vacation soon after they were married. It took Mabry a few days to fall in love with the island, but Nate fell hard the first time he followed highway 421 South to the point where he peered out atop a high-rise bridge, known as Snows Cut Bridge. Under the expanse of metal and concrete was Snows Cut Inlet. To the right lay the vastness of the Cape Fear River and to the left you could see the Atlantic Ocean.

Once the bridge ended you were in Carolina Beach and for Nate it was as if he were leaving a part of life less pleasant behind. A sign upon entry proclaimed, *Welcome to Pleasure Island*. Pleasure Island was the name for an island that consisted of the towns of Carolina Beach and Kure Beach. The southernmost end of the island contained historical Fort Fisher, where battles of the Civil War were once waged.

Nate and Mabry became frequent visitors to the area. Years later they purchased a small ocean front condo on the north end of the Island, near the Carolina Beach fishing pier, for a weekend getaway. They made many weekend trips from Greenville to the coast, as well as a lengthy summer vacation when class was out. Mabry knew in time that trips would not be enough for Nate. It was his dream to retire and build a home in the area and he wanted to do it sooner, rather than later.

The north end, as the locals referred to it, began appropriately enough on the street that bordered the boardwalk on the north side. The north end was chiefly made up of two streets that were a little over one mile and a half long. *Carolina Beach Avenue North* ran parallel to the ocean and *Canal Street* ran along the canal. The street along the ocean began with several mom and pop hotels, while the beginning of *Canal Street* housed the Carolina Beach Marina. The marina was home to several charter fishing and large party boats that derived their living from taking tourists out to sea, and hosting company parties.

*

THE SUN DISAPPEARED BEHIND the edge of the large gray clouds that moved in suddenly from the ocean. "Let's roll, Max," Troy said to his constant companion. The yellow lab was a Christmas present from three years past. He pulled Max into his leg and rubbed him behind his ears, his favorite spot. His mind drifted to the day Max arrived at his door.

It was early December and he was sitting in his home when the doorbell rang. He opened the door to find no one there. He started to close the door when he noticed a cardboard box resting on the small porch. The box was wrapped with a large red ribbon. He heard a soft whimper come from inside the box. He opened the box and the frightened eyes of a trembling seven-week-old puppy greeted him. Delicately he picked the little fellow up and cradled him in his massive arms. The puppy looked at him again. He nestled against

Troy's chest and stopped shaking. It was love at first sight for each of them. There was a Christmas card taped on the box.

We thought you both could use the company.

Merry Christmas,

Mabry and Nate

He stopped petting Max and they walked together to the small, cream-colored wooden cottage that they shared. It was typical of the old cottages in the area. It was quaint at best, but the view, especially at sunrise was priceless.

The ocean front cottage, purchased by Nate and Mabry a few years back, was conveniently located a few blocks north of the club. It was yet another perk of his job with Nate and Mabry. He realized that it was ridiculous for a man over forty to be earning his wage as a bouncer. Still, for now he had no desire to move on. Of course, Mabry was constantly encouraging him to do just that and to stop wasting his God-given talents, whatever they might be, he deliberated.

He wasn't getting rich, but he was okay. During his college years he worked frequently as a bouncer, so he was familiar with the business. He was good at what he did and he took pride in that. The bar security was tight. The police bent over backward to accommodate almost any request he made simply because *Mabry's* was a welcomed relief from the more troublesome bars along the boardwalk.

Mabry's opened each year in March, the week after spring break, and closed for the season the second week of December. Bands played mostly alternative rock. It was music that Troy could barely tolerate and though he was just a child during the decade of the Seventies--it remained the era of music he most preferred.

The club was open Wednesday through Saturday night. Sunday the band of choice began playing in the late afternoon and finished around nine p.m.

He was paid four hundred dollars weekly even during the weeks the club was closed. It was not a bad gig for any employee, especially when you threw in the free rent. But he was much more to the Wood's than an employee. He was family. He didn't feel fortunate about much that life had cast his way, but he did know that he was richly blessed for their presence in his life.

He opened the front door to the cottage. Max impolitely charged in ahead of him. He would need to move on eventually, but to what? He had surrendered the dreams he once envisioned. The desire to battle, or to hope for anything better lay dormant now for several years.

He removed the orange juice from the fridge and poured it into a tall glass. He drank from it briefly and then turned to the old wooden bar that separated the kitchen from the small living room. He placed the glass on the bar. He heard Max shoving his empty food bowl across the kitchen floor.

He filled the bowl with dog food. Max ate furiously, giving only a slight wag of his tail as Troy patted his rump.

He sat in the black recliner in the tiny living room that did not even contain a television. He also might be the last person on the Island not to own a cell phone. The important people knew where to find him and as for the rest . . .

He lived a simple lifestyle that did not require much in the way of exterior trappings. He had just wanted someone to come home to at the end of the day. Someone special to share dreams with--little children that would grow up with ample love and unquestioned security.

During the darkest of times he railed at God for the injustices he suffered but these days he no longer cared to wage war with God. The conflicts only left him bare afterward. Besides, he found God's hearing to be selective.

Thoughts of God brought him right back to the sermon that had gnawed at him now for one full day, and one restless night. Once again, his mother proved right. Was she ever wrong? He decided to heed her advice.

"Let's roll, Max," he called. Together they walked the few blocks to the club. He turned his key in the lock of the front door, before realizing that it was already open. They walked inside.

Off to the right corner was a small, slightly elevated stage for the band. The walls were made of lightly stained pine boards. The floors were concrete-stained dark gray. The club held five hundred people at maximum capacity. There was a ledge attached to the wall everywhere but the bar area, which was on the back wall straight in front of him. Bar stools were tucked neatly under the ledge.

The office door behind the bar opened and Mabry emerged. She was tall, lean, and strikingly attractive. Each day rain or shine she walked five fast miles on the beach. The short brown hair that she had when Troy first met her had long turned to a shining gray. Her eyes were a vivid shade of green and they were perpetually vibrant with energy.

"It's Monday, young man. What are you doing here?" she asked, as she petted Max, who had nuzzled up to her.

"I wanted to use the computer to write a letter. I can come back."

"Nate and I were doing some paperwork. We are finished."

She turned back to the office. "Nate, don't shut the computer off."

Moments later, Nate walked out. "Troy, are you taking good care of my Jeep?"

Nate's weathered face often carried a look of slight amusement. It was as if under his curly, salt and pepper hair were secrets that no one else was privy too.

Troy realized long ago that Nate was so intelligent that he bordered on genius, but what Troy admired the most about him was his down to earth demeanor. Regardless of his superior intellect he never made anyone feel less intelligent. Considering that probably ninety-nine percent of the human race fell into that category, Troy thought that might just be the most remarkable trait about Nate Wood.

The question about the Jeep was part of their routine, Nate's anyway. Troy drove a vintage '79 Scout Jeep. It was dark green with a white top and it had less than one hundred thousand miles on it. The previous original owner was the small compact man standing in front of him.

Troy had drooled over the Jeep so long that Nate had agreed, quite reluctantly to sell it to him. He agreed because he was encouraged to do so by his wife. There was nothing that Nate would not do to please her.

As Troy watched them together he admired them as he often did and even more what they shared together. They were in their mid-sixties and had been married forty years, and they were still deeply in love. They respected each other and each day they tried to please each other, taking little if any of their good fortunes for granted. It had always been that way since the day he met them. He was sure that they had seen bad days together but right off hand he could not recall any.

"If you beat me you can have the Jeep back," Troy answered. "It was the same answer he gave each time."

Nate approached him confidently. His eyes were barely at the level of Troy's chest. "Maybe tomorrow, big boy. Maybe tomorrow," he repeated, as he took his wife's hand. "Besides, if I kick your tail you'll whine to my wife and I'll be cast to the doghouse."

"Don't be jealous. It's not becoming on you," Troy replied dryly.

"Let's go sailing, Honey, before I ruin this bouncer's reputation. If word gets out that I kicked his butt he'll never work in this area again."

Troy glared softly at him, trying to suppress a smile. "Sailing is so right for you. You remind me of Ted Knight, in *Caddyshack*. You probably even have a little white sailor cap you wear to enhance your being captain of the high seas."

Nate looked at him and shook his head in feigned dismay before turning back to Mabry. "Let's leave, Honey. The big ox has officially insulted me."

Troy watched them walk hand in hand to the door and was smiling as they disappeared out into the bright sunshine. He walked into the small, neatly kept office. There were pictures on the wall of students that Mabry taught. Hardly a week passed by that a former student did not show up at the club to visit their favorite teacher.

His eyes fell upon a photo that sat proudly on her desk beside pictures of her children. The young man in the picture with Mabry was attired in a baseball uniform. His smile stretched endlessly. His right arm securely held Mabry. He abruptly turned from the picture as if it was something physically real that could do him great harm. He stared into the computer screen and began to type.

Rev. Matthews;

I am writing concerning your sermon yesterday. It seems to me that church is the one place where we should be completely honest though it tends not to be that way. So I will be completely truthful with you.

Your message yesterday contained so little hope. I'm sure that there were people who with God's help had moved beyond their past. I thought of a girl I once loved long ago and I was grateful that she was not present for the harsh words you shared.

She carried many scars from a few promiscuous acts that occurred during her teenage years. Those unhealed scars eventually ended our chance together and much more.

I'm sure there were people with similar situations in attendance yesterday. Someone seated with their spouse that didn't need to hear about how they would never completely belong to each other. What happened to a God that completely forgives and forgets, eradicating our sin? In God's eyes isn't forgiveness absolute, and if so, shouldn't it be in our eyes, in your eyes as well? I struggle to find any benefit that could possibly be derived from such a message.

You also spoke of how if a man pressures the woman into cheating before marriage then he will cheat after marriage. Sex is not a man's idea alone and he is certainly not always the initiator. Surely you realize this and just used a poor choice of words. The girl I once loved so dearly would have never had to worry about me cheating on her if we would have been fortunate enough to marry and have a life together.

I was encouraged to write you for my sake, but really this letter is for all the people that you hurt without need yesterday with your harsh words.

Troy Dawkins

He folded the letter and inserted it into an envelope. The weariness derived from so little sleep came on him quickly as it often did. He moved to the long brown leather couch that occupied one side of the office. He could hear the sounds of construction nearby but he was so exhausted that it did not disturb him. He was asleep in seconds. Max snored peacefully on the floor beneath him.

3

IT WAS A FEW MINUTES SHY of noon the following Friday. Troy drove south on Highway 421. He was near the peak of the high-rise bridge that led to Carolina Beach. He looked to his right at the brackish waters of the Cape Fear River and then to his left at the Atlantic Ocean. He breathed in the scenery and thought of a lyric from an old Jackson Browne song, *Your Bright Baby Blues. Now I'm running home baby. Like a* river *to the* sea. The lyrics of the song flowed with life beneath him.

He stopped in the Food Lion on his right at the first traffic light in Carolina Beach to pick up a few staples. He exited the store and was stopped by an older gentleman. He was a small man and dressed for fishing. He was also good advertisement for Columbia Sportswear. He wore Columbia PFG mint green shorts and a long sleeve fishing shirt of the same brand and color. His hat was also the same make and the same mint green color. He reminded Troy of a double scoop of mint chocolate chip ice cream on top of a waffle cone. Maybe because his boat shoes were brown.

He noticed a man behind the gentleman taking up about a dozen parking spaces with his red Silverado 2500 pickup truck and what appeared to be about a twenty-two foot Pathfinder boat that he was pulling. It has to be his partner, Troy thought.

"Is there a place on the Island we can purchase some fishing supplies?" He paused before adding, "That is my buddy, Bryan in the red truck with the boat," he said as he pointed his thumb behind him without turning. Bryan waved. Troy did likewise.

"We have lived in the Morehead area now for several years. From up north. New Jersey originally."

Troy refrained from saying. Isn't everyone from up north these days?

"We have never been in this area and we were hoping for some helpful information." His face grew somewhat agitated as he added, "My wife is making me attend her baby sister's fifth wedding at Wrightsville Beach this coming weekend. I suggested we just wait for the next one but my humor was apparently lost on her. Anyway," he said, as he gestured with his hand as if he knew he was talking too much, "we are not that familiar with the area and . . ."

"Go back to the light," Troy instructed as he pointed. "Take a right and in less than a half a mile you will see Island True Value Tackle & Hardware on your right. You will drive through two traffic lights. At the second light you will see Bame Ace Hardware to your right. Good hardware store but for the fishing items you might be looking for, you will be better served at Island Tackle & Hardware."

"Thank you very much," he said as he extended his hand to shake. "My name is Jeff."

"Troy," he said as they shook hands.

Minutes later he parked in the dirt driveway in front of the cottage. Max lay on the porch where he had been commanded to stay two hours earlier. "Come on boy. Let's go get the mail." Troy purposely neglected to pick up the mail on the way in because Max enjoyed the trip to the Post Office way too much to be excluded.

Max ran eagerly to the passenger door. Troy leaned over and pushed the door open and Max scooted quickly to his place in the back seat.

Less than five minutes later Troy walked inside the Post Office toward the wall of small metal boxes. Max chose another direction, strolling past several customers before stopping obediently at the front counter. He sat and barked once, firmly but politely.

The postal clerk, Grace, smiled at the elderly gentleman that she was assisting. She gently patted the top of his hand. "Excuse me for one moment, dear."

She reached under the counter for the clear container of dog biscuits that she kept stocked. She pulled one out and leaned over the counter. "Here you go, Max."

Max lifted slightly and gingerly took his treat. He then retreated to Troy. Troy smiled at Grace and waved; they exited the building.

She smiled and returned to business. The routine was always the same and it mattered not how long the line was or whom it contained.

The mayor of Carolina Beach, Doug Alfred, had once complained about his and the taxpayers time being wasted for a dog. "A dog that should not be allowed in the building," he stated firmly with the voice of self-importance that comes from a power hungry small town politician.

Grace coolly eyed him and replied firmly. "First of all, I am not employed by the Town of Carolina Beach so what you think of my work matters not in the least to me. Secondly, and of even greater importance is the fact that the dog has better manners than you seem to possess. You come back tomorrow when and if you can behave better or you can drive to the Post Office in Wilmington. The choice is yours." She abruptly turned away and began to assist the next customer.

The mayor stood motionless. Surely, she wasn't serious about not allowing him to mail his packages. He heard someone snickering behind him and the gravity of his circumstances began to weigh fully upon him. Slowly and with as much dignity as he could muster, which was miniscule, he turned and walked away.

He went home and immediately called her boss to issue a complaint. He was told quickly that Grace had run the Post Office at Carolina Beach flawlessly for nearly twenty years, and if she wanted to give a dog a biscuit that was her business.

Realizing his local political power was of little value in the situation he returned the next day properly chastened. He arrived with an apology, flowers, and a box of dog biscuits. Grace accepted all three.

Rumors began to circulate soon afterward that Grace and the mayor, both widowers, began to see each other away from the post office.

Troy drove home and they walked around to the front porch and sat down. He discarded a couple of pieces of junk mail without opening them. The next letter was from Portside Church.

> *Dear Troy;*
>
> *Warmest greetings in the Lord! And thank you for your letter. In it I found the hurt of love gone amuck when we are intimate without the boundaries of marriage.*
>
> *In your letter, you accuse me of being harsh and unforgiving, but I encourage you to listen to my message again online. You will find that I speak freely of God's ability to forgive us.*
>
> *From the tone of your letter it is obvious that you are seeking to rationalize the sin in your life. I encourage you to be honest with yourself, and more importantly with God.*
>
> *My sermons are derived straight from the Bible and are inspired by the Holy Spirit. They are from the very heart of God.*

Perhaps I will meet you face to face one day. I pray you will grow strong in the Lord. Also, I encourage you to counsel with one of our associate pastors who are available to help you.

Sincerely,

Reverend Alan Matthews

Slowly Troy folded the letter and rose to his feet. He felt as if steam were rising from the top of his head. He knew the smart thing to do at the present was to let this go--at least until he calmed down. He also knew that was not going to happen. It took a lot to drive him to anger but one pompous pastor had just triggered that anger.

"Max, ride." Max, possessing clear knowledge of the word *ride* trotted enthusiastically toward the Jeep.

Minutes later he entered the parking lot of the church. He parked between a black Mercedes and a white Lincoln Town Car. He got out and looked back at his companion. "Stay," he ordered. Max slouched down disappointedly in the back seat.

Alan looked up at the intruder that had just barged through the closed door of the conference room. The three associate pastors sat with him around a large mahogany table. From the appearance of the table Troy thought that you could feed a needy family for half the year. Throw in the cost of the huge chairs and maybe the entire year was not out of the question.

Alan looked past Troy annoyingly at his secretary, Beth. "I'm sorry, Rev. Matthews, but he asked where you were and then he just charged past me."

Troy turned to her. "You did all you could ma'am. Now, please excuse us." He began closing the door slowly, and she stepped back into the hallway, praying that she still had a job.

Alan studied the man in front of him. He was dressed in khaki shorts and a snug black T-shirt. He was massive. It was only when he made eye contact that he remembered those same steely eyes that he encountered the previous Sunday.

The room filled with awkwardness. Finally, Alan stood up and extended his hand. "I'm sorry, but we are busy right now. Leave your phone number with Beth on your way out."

Troy ignored his gesture as he walked straight to him. Beads of sweat appeared quickly on Alan's forehead. His mouth quickly formed an acid taste. Man of God or not he was deathly afraid.

He felt the back of Troy's hand tap his chest and remain there. He stumbled back slightly from the impact. Noticing that Troy's hand remained planted against his chest he looked down. There was a piece of paper in the middle of his chest. He ascertained that he was expected to take this piece of paper and inspect it. Slowly and fearfully he gently took the paper.

"Not a very good reply," Troy stated. "So, I am here about that face to face meeting you mentioned in your letter."

Alan answered, "Maybe we could discuss this later." He sat down quickly because he did not trust his wobbly legs to support him.

Troy sat down across from him, ignoring the others seated at the table. "I think right now works for me. You certainly didn't grant me any consideration with that foolish letter of yours so I don't see where I owe you any courtesy."

"As head of this church I am your minister and you are expected to respect that fact," he stated as firmly as one can who is terrified.

"Don't flatter yourself. You are no minister of mine," Troy replied evenly, before adding, "and that is indeed a fact."

Alan looked briefly at the letter while wondering who this man was to question any message of his. He tried to sound strong, as an important man of God should but his voice was tiny, almost childlike, when he said, "I stand by my reply. You had no right to judge my sermon."

"But you have every right to judge me. Someone that you have never had a conversation with before this moment."

"You were just trying to hide from your sins," Alan replied, desperately trying to find his voice. His voice failed him again and it reminded him of a small girl.

"I don't hide anything from anyone, not God, and certainly not from an arrogant man like you." Troy paused, closing his eyes for a moment. "Now, Alan, I'm going to have my say and I will leave. If you don't want to hear what I have to say that's too bad. Try pretending you are one of the congregation and you are being forced to listen to a speaker as boring as yourself."

Out of the corner of his eye he was certain that he saw a slight smile emerge and quickly disappear from one of the associate pastors seated to the right of him. Apparently, he was not the only one who was tiring of the massive ego belonging to the man in front of him. An ego too large and too insecure to share the pulpit with the men seated at the table.

Alan decided to speak, but thought better of it. He leaned back in his chair. The others in the room were like a huge rock anchored in a mountain stream. Void of movement while the waters rushed all around it. Troy certainly had a captive audience.

He spoke evenly but with an undeniable edge to his voice. "There is one thing that is very clear about this situation. You read my letter and never once did you even ask yourself if there might be a possibility that you were wrong. Isn't there something in the good book about searching your own heart? You should try that sometime. It's a better solution than taking your high and mighty attitude, and saying how dare he question me, which is obviously what you did.

"You wrote that your sermons were from the heart of God. Maybe you should refrain from doing God such favors. You read two scriptures and then babble with your opinions for way too long and you want people to believe that is the heart of God? It's frightful when a man thinks that his words are God's words. What audacity.

"The heart of God I see is about mercy, love and tenderness. It is void of judgment and keeps no calendar.

"You failed to respond to the two main points of my letter. The cheating comment? What century did you drag that garbage from? And are you telling me that if your wife slept with another that she would not fully belong to you?"

"She would not have been my wife," he replied firmly, almost smugly.

"You would have walked away from love because of someone's past? That goes against all God is. He forgives. We forgive. He forgets. We forget. Isn't that the very root of all we believe?"

"I hardly need for you to teach me," Alan said as he smartly rolled his eyes. When his eyes returned to the man in front of him he was petrified by the even, emotionless look he saw. He felt the sour bile rise in his throat and he was glad that his sweaty hands were beneath the table in his lap so no one would become aware of how badly they were trembling.

"Hiding your hands under the table so that no one will see them shaking doesn't fool me, and I would venture that there is no one seated at this table who is duped by you. I bet about now you are wishing you would not have written such a foolish letter."

"I . . ."

"Shut up," Troy said sternly, pointing his finger at him as if he were admonishing a small child.

Alan did as he was told. He could feel the nervous sweat trickling from his armpits down his sides. He felt faint. His stomach felt loose, and he struggled to avoid further embarrassment.

Troy gave him a wry smile that was no smile at all before he continued--his voice flat. "Regardless of what you may think you do need someone to help you. One man that could do just that is *my minister*, David Lang, but you turn him away. He is often asked why he no longer speaks here and his reply is that he is not asked. The reason that he is not asked is because of the affection the congregation has for him. That threatens you. You quote writers of songs, books, and poems. You implement skits and plays but you shut the door on such a valuable resource."

"David is retired. The church needs to move forward," Alan interjected, finding his voice, and then wondering if he should have spoken.

"Retired, not dead," Troy stated. "The other resources that you use they are not threatening to you. All of that comes from you. It makes you look good, or so you think. Your knowledge, your intellect. That is really what this is about. The heart of God? I don't think so. More like the massive ego of Alan Matthews."

Troy looked directly at the other men in the room for the first time. He searched their eyes. "Is this what you believe? What he says?"

They avoided eye contact and remained quiet. There were mortgages, car payments, health insurance premiums, and children's college tuitions at stake.

He turned back to Alan. "You are a piece of work." Troy suddenly felt drained. His much needed nap before dealing with a night of drunks was beckoning to him. He rose from his chair.

Alan watched him rise and was desperate to regain an ounce of respect from his staff. "You say I judged you, well what is that you really know about me?"

Troy's reply was slow and deliberate. "The pulpit is the worse place for a large ego, which you obviously have. You say the Holy Spirit inspires your sermons. I say you have them outlined two years in advance and that they are what you think."

Alan's face wrinkled slightly as he recalled just completing his sermon plan for the second year out and had begun work on the third. Infuriated that this man could seemingly know so much, he rose quickly and started to reply.

Troy put his hand out. "Don't push it. I've had my say. It's best if you sit back down."

"Why, because you might beat me up in the house of God?" he stated mockingly.

He startled Alan even more with the calm manner he spoke. "I thought you at least knew the basics of your Bible, Alan. People are the church. God inhabits people, not buildings with fancy stain glass and cathedral ceilings." He paused to see if there was a reply. There was none. "I'll see myself out." He began walking toward the door.

He turned around at the door. "Do you really believe what you wrote?"

Alan remained seated as he answered. "Yes, I do. Great leaders are not always understood."

Troy shook his head slowly in disbelief and then amusement as he recalled a day on the beach with his daughter, Heidi, when she was nine years old.

They were seated in their chairs on a late season beach day. There were three high school kids in the water hoping for a ripple of a wave to ride on a day when the ocean was lake like. Nearly all the tourists were long departed and apart from a few walkers and joggers, the strand belonged exclusively to them. Their solitude was interrupted by a couple who with the entire available beach strand chose to plop a blanket down on the sand less than twenty feet from them. They appeared to be around thirty years of age. The man was rail thin and the bulk of his weight appeared to come from his eyeware of choice, which covered nearly half of his face. He had computer nerd written all over him. His wife was quiet, slightly overweight, and gazed at him as if he possessed all the pertinent information in the universe. He laid the blanket down, and she sat a large bag on top of it. He continued standing and seemed to be in deep thought about what was taking place in the water. Troy and Heidi could not hear their muted conversation and for that matter didn't care to. But there was no mistaking what they heard the man proclaim next. He had figured a great mystery out and exclaimed it loudly to his wife. "Oh, Honey, they aren't standing on the water. They are on surfboards."

Troy's statement to his daughter was one that lived to this very day. Many times, when they heard someone proclaim something really dumb they would revert back to the line offered that day.

As Troy looked at Alan with the words, great leaders are not always understood hanging in the air like a speech balloon in a comic book. He smiled and replied, "Being stupid is one thing, but being stupid out loud is another." There was a look of disbelief on Alan's face as Troy exited, closing the door easily behind him. He took one step to the right before colliding with a lady carrying an armload of books. The books flew from her hands, sliding across the freshly waxed floor.

"I'm sorry, ma'am. I wasn't paying attention," Troy said as he knelt down and began retrieving her books.

"It's okay," she said as she knelt to assist in gathering her books. "I'm going a mile a minute and obviously not paying attention to what I am doing."

They retrieved all the books from the floor and stood, looking awkwardly at each other.

She spoke first as she looked up at him. "I must really have been not paying attention to have missed someone as big as you." Right away she knew that a remark about his size was something that he had heard way too often by the bored expression that came over his face.

He looked at her forgetting for a moment his anger at the encounter a few feet away. Her eyes struck him first. They were big and brown, but so dark that they were a shade away from being black. There was strength in them, but at the same time there was pain. He had seen those eyes often, in the mirror. She was his age, maybe a year or two older. There were slight crow's feet beginning in the corners of her eyes. Her hair was black, straight, and short. Normally he disliked short hair on a woman but on her it was attractive. She was short, but basically everyone was to him. The baggy white blouse and loose fitting jeans did not hide the fact that she was in good shape and unlike most of the members of Portside, he was sure that she worked out on a regular basis. He was certain that she looked better now than in her school days. She was that special kind of woman that took a back seat to cheerleaders and prom queens in high school, but when the twenty-year reunion came had moved to the head of the class.

She tried again. "I'm sorry. You probably hear that remark as often as I hear I need a footstool to reach the light switch." Her eyes narrowed at the same moment mischief entered them. "I didn't hurt you, did I?"

Her attempt at humor to diffuse the awkward moment was met by a slight smile from the man in front of her.

Undeterred she continued, "I haven't seen you around here before."

"I came to try to straighten a situation out with a fool."

"Did you have any luck?"

He shrugged and answered, "No, I didn't. I should have known better than to try."

"And the fool? Who would that be?"

"The idiot minister the church mistakenly hired."

She smiled again and he was unsure of what to read in her smile. She moved the books to her left hand and extended her right hand. "It's nice to meet you. I'm Suzanne Matthews, the idiot's wife."

He met her handshake. "I'm Troy Dawkins."

She looked at him, surprised not to see even a hint of apology in his eyes. He gave her the rest of her books. "I'm sorry about the collision, ma'am." He walked past her in the direction of the side door.

She shook her head as she watched him walk away. Understanding people, reaching them was what she was good at. The man walking away had not angered her, even when he disparaged her husband. She watched him depart the building and instinctively placed the books on the floor and took off in pursuit.

He was nearing the parking lot when she made it outside. "Do you think maybe I could help?" she called out as she continued walking hurriedly toward him.

He turned back to her. His eyes narrowed. "Help me with what?"

"With your problem." She had caught up to him now, encouraged that she had gotten his feet to stop moving.

"I don't have a problem, and shouldn't you be the one asking for help?"

"How's that?"

"You're the one who has to live with him."

She chuckled slightly and arched her left eyebrow. "Do you always say exactly what you feel?"

"Pretty much."

"Good, I find that refreshing. You don't get that often in church, particularly if you are the wife of the preacher."

She waited for him to speak but he said nothing else. She glanced at the Jeep in the parking lot. "I bet that is your dog propped up in the front seat."

The hardness in his face softened slightly. Her persistence while annoying carried a slight charm to it. "I wouldn't think that the church would approve of psychics," he said admonishingly.

She put her finger to her lips. "They don't," she replied in a hushed voice. "Will you keep my little secret? Now, could I please see your dog?"

"Is it my dog you want to see, or are you one of those people who can't leave well enough alone?"

She smiled again, broader, warmer. "Troy, I really want to see your dog, and yes I am one of those annoying people who can't leave well enough alone."

His voice mixed with devoted love and sadness as he spoke. "My mom. She is like that. Always trying to fix things. Sometimes answers can't be found and it is best not to try."

"As in my husband?"

He paused before answering. "Those are your words," he said, as he turned and walked toward his Jeep.

He almost made it to the Jeep before she had caught him again. "Let me guess that remark about being stupid out loud was directed toward my husband?"

He turned to her again. "I thought you were walking down the hall, not eavesdropping."

"I was just walking down the hall," she quickly added. "That was all I heard. It was actually pretty funny, not very nice, but still funny."

"I wasn't worried about being nice."

This time there was nothing but hardness. "I think I could figure that out on my own." She paused, before adding, "Why don't you come back inside? I'm sure that we can work this out."

He opened the door and started the engine, effectively dismissing her. She was still standing in the same spot when the Jeep disappeared out of the parking lot on to the highway.

4

TOM AND RUTH SAT IN THE DEN that once served as the bedroom for their two daughters. Tom retired from the city fire department many years ago and one of his first tasks was claiming the old bedroom as his den. It was his room to watch television and take multiple naps each day in his worn recliner.

Tom was watching a golf show. Ruth was worrying and praying. The phone rang. Tom smiled at his bride. "You want me to answer that, Honey?"

"No. We both know what it is about."

He smiled warmly at her. "Maybe not this time," he said, as the phone rang for the fourth time.

"Hello," she answered.

"Yes, I know about it. Yes. No. I have not spoken with him. I realize you are an elder, Bill. Well, I don't think you have to worry about any discipline of Troy," she said, her voice rising slightly. "I doubt my son will ever want to return to church. At least, that is, under the current regime." She rolled her eyes at Tom, and shook her head in weary frustration.

Ruth rarely showed anger or even felt it for that matter but as Tom watched he knew her well enough to know she had just about been pushed to her limit. You did not mess with her baby boy but so long.

Whatever it was that Bill just said pressed her to that point. Her voice grew quite terse, and she said through clenched teeth, "You go right ahead and talk to Troy with your judgmental sanctimonious attitude. That is a great idea. He derives his living from his ability to fight. So, may God be with you," she exclaimed as she slammed the phone down.

Tom watched her and said nothing. He knew she would feel terrible later but truthfully, he was enjoying this. He always thought that leaders in any church tended to get a little too full of their perceived power.

The phone rang again. Tom grabbed it quickly as Ruth sat with her hands cradling her head as if she were trying to hold all the fragments together lest they disintegrate.

"Hello. Okay, sure. I will get her."

She raised her hand in a defiant "no" toward Tom without looking.

Gently he said, "Honey, this one will be all right."

She let go of her head and raised it to look at her husband.

He nodded kindly at her.

She took the phone. "Hello."

Miles away at nearby Wrightsville Beach, David Lang stood in his beach cottage and looked south out over Banks Channel. The narrow channel opened and he saw the many creeks and marshlands he never grew tired of gazing at. He was so blessed to see this daily.

David was in his mid-seventies and still a very handsome man. His vivid blue eyes twinkled as if he knew something no one else did or maybe he just knew it better. He kept his weight down by walking briskly, six days a week. His near white hair was wavy and full.

He thought of Troy and what most people considered an unlikely friendship. The bouncer and the preacher, though Troy was not always a bouncer. Troy did several landscape jobs for him several years back and a special bond formed between the two men.

David sensed right away that there was deeply rooted pain in Troy that he prayed would be brought to the light of Christ and be dealt with once and for all. He never asked what the darkness was, and he never sensed that he should. One thing he enjoyed was that if he asked Troy a question he could count on the unbridled truth. Ministers often heard what people thought they were supposed to say as opposed to what was true. He knew he could always count on truth when Troy spoke. He smiled as he thought of something that the good church folks at Portside did not know. He could call anytime and Troy Dawkins would drop everything to help. Each time a hurricane threatened the area Troy was one of the first to call to see if anything was needed.

Several years back they evacuated the island ahead of an approaching hurricane. They drove to Charlotte to stay with their son. The inland areas flooded so badly that they could not return home for days. They could get no word on the old cottage that they bought many years ago at a fraction of today's cost.

He recalled his son David Jr. calling him to the phone late one evening.

"Hello," he answered.

"Your home is fine."

"Troy?"

"Yes, don't worry."

"But citizens can't get on the island."

Troy chuckled. "You have heard of a boat haven't you? You know those vessels Jesus went out in occasionally?"

David laughed with relief, and mouthed quietly to his wife, Toni, that their home was fine. "That sure is good news. Toni and I have been concerned. I know it is an old cottage but it is home and it contains a host of memories."

"I know."

"There has to be some damage."

"There were a few shingles that needed replacing. Some water blew in the front glass but not too much. No real damage. We dried everything and aired the house out. I caulked the windows with some good sealant. All is good."

"You said we."

"Mabry let me take one of the guys with me. It is not like the club was open."

"Didn't the club have damage? You were probably needed there."

"The way Nate builds things? It would take more than a hurricane to hurt that place."

"Please let me know what I owe you. Oh, and please forgive me for not asking before but what about your place, Troy?"

"Everything is fine. Have a little faith, Pastor."

David chuckled softly. "I still want to pay you."

"Fine, you can take me to lunch at South Beach Grill. I have not been there in a while."

"I mean really pay you."

"You know I love South Beach Grill, and I don't eat there as often as I would like. I will show up hungry and make certain it cost you a small fortune to feed me."

"That is not enough."

"Lunch and your friendship is payment enough. It is more than a man like me deserves."

"But Troy . . ."

"I need to go David. We will talk later. Bye."

The line went dead and David stood there for a moment and then he began to laugh. He shared the conversation with his wife and son.

"How did he get in our house without a key?" Toni asked. She was a sweet woman but also quite brisk at times.

He smiled at her and there was a sparkle in his eye that she cherished every single time she witnessed it. "You want that I would have him arrested?"

She shook her head gently.

He would discover later upon returning home that Troy had vastly understated the repairs that were performed. He tried once more to pay him and he saw pain in Troy's face when he replied. "I am your friend and you are one of the few people that ever gave me hope. Please don't tarnish that with the mention of money again."

He never mentioned money or what Troy did. He thought of Matthew 6:1 *"Take care! Don't do your good deeds publicly, to be admired, because then you will lose the reward from your Father in heaven.* He also knew if there was a way that Troy could have done the entire repair in secret he would have. He called only to save his friend's worry.

David could hear the strain in Ruth's voice as she described the phone calls.

"Ruth, don't worry. It will all be okay."

"I almost cussed at an elder," she said, sounding like a small child caught in a bad act.

He chuckled softly. "God forgave you before you did it."

He heard her cry softly and he knew it was about more than losing her temper. She was a mom who spent countless hours praying and worrying over her son.

"Do you think if you called Troy he would come see you?"

"It doesn't matter. I am leaving now to find him. I will call you back later. Now, stop judging yourself so harshly. Bill gets a little too full of his so called elder authority. He has not comprehended 1Peter

5:3 about not lording over the flock but being an example. Now, before I go I am going to pray for you."

After the prayer Ruth placed the phone gently back in its place. She looked at Tom. "David is going to find him. He is on his way," she said.

"That is good," he replied as he turned back to his golf show.

She watched him view the television and a familiar sadness came over her. Why did her husband and the father of their children not even think about driving to Carolina Beach to see if he could help? He was a good man but from day one he followed the path of his father and most of the men of his generation. The dad provided and played the bad guy to the kids when needed. The parenting was left to the mom. Truthfully, she enjoyed being the confidant of the children, especially Troy, who deep down she knew she loved just a little bit more than her other children. Maybe he just needed her more. Still, at times like this she hoped her husband would at least think about leaving his comfortable recliner to talk to his son, and more importantly listen. It had never been that way. She accepted that short of a miracle it would remain so. Still, she hoped and prayed for that miracle.

It was not that Tom did not help his children. He did. If there was painting to be done, or an electrical job, he would gather his tools and work till the task was complete. She thought this was as close to being able to say I love you as he could manage.

She silently admonished herself for these thoughts. She should just be grateful for David and his love of their son. God always provided, maybe not just in the exact manner she would have preferred.

She rose from the couch and walked to the bedroom. The worn Bible lay on the nightstand. Beside her Bible lie pens and pads to write down prayer requests that were called in on a daily basis. Many of the calls were from the unofficial lady's prayer group she had been part of for years. Early this morning, the first phone call of the day, when the news leaked out about Troy's encounter was from one of those ladies, Catherine Grohman, who was like a sister to her. Catherine loved her dearly but she loved Troy as well and she called his name before the Lord every day.

Troy often referred to the group as the 'Little Ole Ladies Prayer Group.' Ruth tried to correct him that those ladies might not like that term but Catherine told her. "Troy means no disrespect Ruth. In fact, quite the opposite is true."

Ruth smiled again at her dear friend calling early this morning not to judge Troy as so many likely would but to offer comfort, hope, and prayer.

Some called her a prayer warrior, while others referred to her as an intercessor. She never viewed herself as either. Praying was just what she did. Many mornings she was awake before the sun rose and she would pray for each family member by name. Next, she prayed for her neighbors, followed by members of the church, and after that anyone else that might come to mind. She knelt beside the bed, resting her arms on the white comforter with huge pink flowers. She chuckled as she thought about her so called tough husband who never balked at her love for pink. It was because the one person he could really show love to was her. She took comfort in that and she knew her children did as well. She began to pray for Troy. The tears flowed easily as often the case was.

*

TROY HEARD MAX BARK FROM his position on the front porch. He was better than a doorbell. Max never strayed from the porch unless instructed to by Troy. His bark had different tones to it as well. If it were someone who was not welcome, his bark was more of a low muffled growl. Someone he was not familiar with but did not sense trouble he gave a couple of quick warning barks. Neither of these barks was in play. This bark came with a soft whine that meant it was someone that he knew.

Troy opened the screen door as David Lang approached. "Go ahead, Max."

Max joyfully bounded off the porch and went to David. He nuzzled him with his wide snout. Troy smiled as his friend bent down on one knee to rub Max's face while talking softly to him.

David was a lover of dogs. He once told Troy that sitting in his easy chair and petting his Chihuahuas was his favorite thing to do.

He rose and walked to Troy.

"The church sending out the big guns?"

David shook his head softly.

"Mom must have called."

"No."

They stood there looking at each other comfortable with the silence. "I thought we could take a walk," David said.

"Give me just one minute," Troy answered as he stepped inside. He emerged quickly and the three of them walked to the beach. David stopped and smelled the ocean air. "Jesus loved the water," he said softly.

Troy just nodded. He had heard his old friend say this countless times.

"Something so soothing about it I find it hard to put into words."

"You going to get to it, Pastor?"

David turned slowly and though his face was soft his eyes looked sternly to the man that loomed over him. "I don't require a title, especially among friends. David has sufficed this long and I would prefer we continue in that vein."

Troy nodded and looked away before returning his eyes to David. "I'm sorry, David."

David grasped the huge right arm of the gentle giant in front of him. He winked at him and smiled warmly.

"I guess you want to know what drives a man to threaten a so-called minister in the church."

"Yes, I would. I already heard enough versions from Alan and people that were not even present. Sadly, no gossip seems to spread like church gossip. Do you mind if we walk along the ocean?"

"Time with you is always good time, my friend."

"You as well, son. Now, share with me what transpired please."

"And you will believe my version when there was a room full of ministers?"

David walked slowly and kept his eyes on the ocean. "I know you see yourself as this flawed person but I would stack your honesty against any member in the church. You have never been less than truthful with me."

Troy filled him in on the events from the message to the letters, and eventually the confrontation.

They walked in silence as David meditated on what had transpired. Troy interrupted his thoughts. "One thing I forgot to mention was that on the way out I ran into his wife. She followed me to my Jeep even after I called her husband an idiot." He paused before adding, "She might just be the real deal."

"Toni and I went to dinner with them when they first moved here. I believe you are right. She seems to be a breath of fresh air not unlike you."

"David, with all due respect I am not anyone's breath of fresh air."

David placed his hand on Troy's arm pausing their walk. "Look at me."

Troy turned and looked down at the eyes that looked up at him. The warmth that he saw in those eyes never wavered, regardless of his tone of voice.

"I want to tell you something and I want you to listen."

"I always hear you. I realize I don't act on it the way that you would hope I would but I always hear you." He paused before adding, "My respect for you is without measure."

They began to walk again. "I realize something tragic occurred in your life at one time. You don't feel comfortable telling anyone--not even me. Whatever it is, you have to find a way to let it go."

He stopped walking and grasped Troy's arm bringing him to a halt once again. He looked him in the eyes and said firmly. "The way you may view yourself is not the way our Father views you. You may speak harshly about someone like Alan but the person you judge the harshest is yourself. That is not good. Nothing worthy derives from it. Your honesty is indeed a breath of fresh air. Do you know how many people would have told me the events of yesterday in a way to gain my favor? I heard Alan's version of the event. He told me what happened in a manner that might make him look more favorable. I know that you did not do that."

Troy started to speak and the one man on this earth that could shush him like a small child did just that. He held his wrinkled hand up in a stop motion. "I know you did not do that because I know you." He placed his palm over Troy's heart. He nodded his head and said, "Right?"

"I told you the truth." Standing on the beach strand the two men embraced and Max leaned his head in touching both their legs with his face.

"I would like to see those letters."

"I have them in my back pocket."

David smiled and said, "That is why you stepped back inside before we began our walk."

"Got time for a cup of coffee?"

"I do."

"There is a new coffee place. Crush & Grind on the very north end of the boardwalk. The coffee is much better than mine."

They walked in silence until they were inside. Dominic, the owner took their order. Troy had dropped in back in the spring when the Crush & Grind first opened their doors. Industrial concrete tables along with the rustic elements of natural wood walls seem to be a perfect blend of eclectic harmony. He had made it a habit to drop in a couple of times a week and have a cup of coffee and enjoy conversation with Dominic.

Troy made introductions and just as he knew David would prefer he introduced him as his friend. No minister. No titles.

They sat in the corner and David began reading the letters. A young married couple walked in with a beautiful little girl and a baby girl in the stroller. They ordered coffee and sat in the adjacent corner. Moments later the man took the baby into the restroom. His wife smiled as he took his turn to change her diaper.

David folded the letters back and sat them on the table. "I wish you would have come to me first."

"He won't even allow you to speak for the most part. Truth is he resents you and how people feel about you. I would even say he is jealous. Why is it that some of the biggest egos end up in the one place they should never be? Standing in front of a congregation on Sunday morning?"

"I don't know, Troy. It does seem that way though." He paused before adding, "I notice he offered the associate pastors the chance to counsel you. He dumps nearly everything off on them."

"He views himself as a great preacher."

They were quiet and David's eyes drifted to the cooler that contained craft beers. There were bottles of wine at the end of the curved bar.

"More than coffee served here," he said sternly.

Troy laughed and said, "Nice try, Padre. You don't have a judgmental bone in your body and lest you not forget what it is I do for a living."

David smiled amiably and said, "That is where you earn your wages now. I believe change is on the horizon." He rose slowly. "I need to depart. Toni made plans with the grandkids this afternoon. If something like this in the future occurs you will visit me first. Our door is always open."

Troy stood and replied, "I am not sure your wife always understands our friendship."

David never hesitated. "She questioned it initially but she has a lot of confidence in my ability not only as a minster but as her husband. I pray that you will find a woman, a spiritual woman that you will share a love like we have. And to walk in faith each day. That makes the hard days manageable, the marginal days good, and the good days great."

Troy started to speak and the wise man stopped him with a gentle shake of his head. "You would be great for someone. Don't tell me different. I won't hear of it."

Troy waved at Dominic as they exited. David began speaking very deliberately. "I was not there Sunday. It does appear that there are churches who desire me to speak. I did listen to the message online. He was out of line Troy and that remains here with us."

Troy nodded.

They walked to the street side of Troy's cottage. They said goodbye and David began walking to his car. He turned abruptly and looked back at Troy. He raised his hand and Troy could see the crooked finger that was injured from an automobile accident pointing in his general direction. His eyes were focused like lasers as he said, "Troy, it is a very special friendship we share."

Troy tapped his heart lightly as he felt tears well up. "Me too. Me too," he gently repeated. Troy and Max watched as the saintly man drove away in his modest, silver Honda Accord.

5

ALAN AND SUZANNE MATTHEWS entered the Oceanic, an upscale restaurant that protruded out into the sea at Wrightsville Beach. On certain nights, God provided a show of his majesty. Tonight, he was an absolute showoff. The stars sparkled over the ocean and the orange moon was nearing its peak. The illumination presented by the moon met the lights of the pier that extended out from the building that housed the three-story restaurant.

It was Saturday night. Long ago, they promised each other that this would be their date night. It did not matter if babysitters had to be hired, or if church business reared its ugly head. This night would always be sacred and as it was with most promises made by young married couples their pact was eventually abandoned.

They were long past the days of requiring the services of a babysitter. Their twin sons, Graham and Wesley were away at college. They had desired more children but the pregnancy and delivery was so hard that it took all the strength Suzanne could gather to deliver two healthy boys into the world on the last night of June, twenty years earlier.

The hostess greeted them and led them to a table. Alan eyed his wife as she walked. She was forty-five and looked even better than when they had first met as seniors in college. The midnight blue dress she wore was simple, yet glamorous. He thought it too short for a preacher's wife, but tonight he was feeling too good to balk at a dress a couple of inches above the knee. Besides, he didn't want to argue. The arguments had increased since the boys no longer lived at home. She was probably just experiencing the empty nest syndrome, he thought, comforting himself.

His new job as senior pastor had taken much of his time. It was supposed to have taken more of her time as well but that had not proven to be the case. It was an unwritten rule that the church hired the wife as well as the pastor--only she didn't draw a salary.

Her decided lack of involvement puzzled him. She was a brilliant counselor in her own way. He marveled at her ability to draw things out of people who were determined to keep their problems silent. She was gifted. There was no mistaking that.

She was one project away from completing her master's degree in Psychology. The move here had interrupted her pursuit of that. He had envisioned that one day she would hang out her own shingle as a Christian Psychologist. Lord knows he could send work her way. Of course, he would guide her on the spiritual side of things.

They were seated at a table at the corner of the room. The side facing the ocean was exclusively glass.

The waitress, a cute, perky, petite blonde, approached their table. "Hi, I'm Samantha," she said, as she passed out the large black menus. "Could I get you something from the bar?"

Alan seemed offended that his spiritual aura had not been noted. He answered quickly, "No, iced tea will be fine." His demeaning tone made Suzanne visibly cringe.

"Sweet or unsweetened, sir?" Samantha asked, her tone still kind and gracious.

"Sweet," he answered.

"What about you, ma'am?"

She looked at her husband. His sanctimonious behavior was becoming increasingly boorish. She didn't know why it bothered her so much of late because he had been on this particular path for a long time. Promotion had not worn well with him. They were happier at their first church. It was a small white church nestled in the Blue Ridge Mountains, in Woolwine, Virginia. The church on its most populated day didn't seat fifty people. He was a good pastor then. He was kind, caring, less judgmental, and fun to be married to.

"Will it be tea for you, ma'am?" Samantha asked again, interrupting her thoughts.

"No. I'll have a glass of red wine. Whatever you think is appropriate will be fine," she said smiling at the young lady. Samantha returned her smile graciously and walked away.

Alan studied his wife carefully. She was different lately. Almost like a defiant child. "Suppose a church member comes in and see you drinking wine? It would give off the wrong impression."

For so many years she tolerated all the refuse that came with being a preacher's wife. She disagreed often but most of the time she avoided confrontation. She did not practice what she had counseled others to do. Talk things out. Don't hide them inside. Don't allow today's minor problems to become next year's mountaintop to climb.

Now the mountaintop was such a difficult climb that she didn't know if it could be scaled. She also was not certain she cared to try any longer.

Her comfort had been in her boys. Sons that grew into young men and left home. Life was empty without them. All the years spent with young children, loving them, but at the same time looking forward to the day you could return to your spouse. She had counseled many that had made it to that stage of life, only to discover the magic had been set aside for far too long. Now, as she lived out the scenario that she had tried to assist others with she realized how inept her solutions had been.

She recalled the years when she longed for date night. The love, the passion, and the laughter shared with her best friend.

Samantha startled her from her thoughts. "Your wine, ma'am. Would you like to try it now? I can take it back if you don't approve."

She lifted the glass to her lips and drank briefly. She wished that she knew something to say appropriate about how one samples wine. "It's very good. You made an excellent choice," was all that she could marshal.

Samantha smiled again and walked away.

Silence hung over the table for several minutes. She drank her wine, which tasted better with each sip. Samantha returned to inquire if they cared for appetizers. They ordered one bowl of She-Crab Soup to split, though Suzanne knew that Alan would eat most of it.

They ordered dinner. She chose the Chef's Salmon--consisting of grilled salmon, garden rice, and roasted vegetables. Alan ordered shrimp and grits. He eyed his wife as they waited for their food. "Are you ever going to answer my question?"

Though she knew exactly what question he eluded, she feigned ignorance. "What question was that?"

Alan breathed deeply as if the air pained him. "What if a member of the church should see you drinking wine?"

She paused, as his agitation grew. Finally, she spoke, "So am I to assume that it would be perfectly moral to drink this glass of wine as long as no one sees me? Maybe I should sneak into the lady's room and chug it down."

"You know what I mean," he said with exasperated voice. "Whether I think that it is all right or not gives way to the fact that we should not do anything to offend someone's belief."

"I wonder, Alan, do you think Jesus hid to drink wine, or do you now believe it was Welch's juice? Now, before you answer I want to let you in on a little something. Welch's was a few centuries away from being a viable business." She sipped her wine and smiled curtly at him.

His face turned red with anger. He started to speak but refrained.

The meal was eaten in complete silence. The fun Saturday night was anything but. The drive to their home in Wilmington was completed without one word.

At home after stewing downstairs for a few minutes Alan relented and went upstairs to try and make amends, and to obtain what he had planned for on date night.

She was standing in front of the mirror removing her silver necklace. She reached for the zipper on the back of her dress.

"I'll get that," he said as he walked across the bedroom to her. "Couldn't we try and salvage tonight?" He kissed her softly on the neck and unzipped her dress.

He felt her tighten at his touch. "Don't be mad. Remember how we used to long for date night?"

She turned to him and forced an insincere smile. "Not tonight, okay?"

Quickly he drew back. "You are not in the mood? Since when have you ever not been in the mood?" he asked sarcastically.

"Maybe since the only sex we ever have is when the physical urge builds for you. I believe that is about once every three to four weeks now."

"You know how it is with new churches, especially this one."

"Don't blame it on new churches. It has been this way for a long time."

He was perplexed as he studied her face. Regardless of any circumstances she was always the eager and willing participant. He could always count on that, until now.

"You've never said no to me before. I can't believe it is over some silly disagreement at the restaurant. What is it really?"

"Everything is on your terms. Your church, your life, your timetable, even with sex. It's always about you."

Her words stung him and he sat on the edge of the bed. He relented, "I know that I have neglected you. What can I do to make it right?"

She studied him and his pitiful look and speculated as to the sincerity of it. Was he being the pouting poor boy just hoping to get his physical needs met? She decided to answer his question with total honesty. "Be the man I married because he has been lost for a long time."

The sorrowful feeling left abruptly. "I am the same man. I matured more in the Lord than you, that's all."

The anger she had successfully stifled until now roared from her. "Don't you use the Lord as an excuse and don't you dare pass judgment on me.

"You want the truth Alan? I'll give it to you. You were once passionate, loving and caring. You took me to bed as if I was a princess. You caressed every inch of my body. You made me feel so loved, so desired, but now it is only about your relief. Now, you are no longer interested enough to be good for anyone but yourself."

Her words stung--wounding his pride. "You are trying to impair me because I don't have sex with you enough?"

"Hurting you? I thought I was being honest with you. Somewhere along the line you became so holy that you only want sex when you are about to explode. I don't know what I could have done differently to keep you interested. I take care of myself. I've always responded to you but sex isn't fun anymore. It's like you feel too guilty about it, or something else, to enjoy it for what it is."

He sighed heavily and narrowed his eyes. "Don't attempt to analyze me. You won't get involved in church with people who need help, but you want to help me. Get busy with them."

She smiled and narrowed her eyes in return. "In other words, you don't need help. Here's a news flash for you. You are human just like the rest of us," she said with a shake of her head.

He stood glaring at her. He said no more as he undressed and got in bed.

She opened the chest drawer and fumbled through it until she found an old pair of yellow gym shorts and an oversized green sweatshirt. "You selfish pitiful man," she said, closing the bedroom door harshly. She took two steps and turned abruptly back to the door. She stood outside telling herself not to say anything else. She opened the door. "I was wrong about the last statement," she said, and then gave an eloquent pause. "Selfish, pitiful, child is more accurate." She smirked at the shocked look on his face and shut the door gently. Softly she said, "Get used to being alone."

She walked downstairs to the kitchen. She opened the fridge hoping to find more wine. Occasionally there was some white wine around for cooking purposes. She searched diligently but found none. Her eyes settled on the container of milk. She decided on hot chocolate.

She sat on the couch, huddling the steaming drink with both hands. She breathed in the aroma and tasted it. The warm liquid soothed her, and her mind drifted to another time, as it did each time.

The fondest memory of her childhood centered on a kitchen table and hot chocolate. Whenever she had a problem for as far back as she could recall, her father would make hot chocolate and they would talk like grownups, even when she was a very small child. The thought of her being a little tot sitting and discussing her problems like an adult warmed her. There was never a time that her father didn't make everything better. She longed for one more chat seated at the old weathered kitchen table. One more time for her father to repair all that was broken in her life. He was her hero. He never once raised his voice to her, but then he didn't need to. She had always sought to make him proud of her.

He had been gone now for five years come Thanksgiving. The bone cancer that consumed his body accomplished what nothing else was able to. It reduced her father to a mere man, a mortal.

She held onto him for as long as possible. She left Alan and her boys for the last three months of his life, returning home to Athens, Georgia, her hometown. She helped her mother care for him and more to squeeze every tender moment that was left with her daddy.

He left the hospital in early October and vowed that he would not return. It was the Monday before Thanksgiving when her father garnered the strength, the courage for one last kitchen table discussion. The hot chocolate was exceptionally pleasing to the palate that afternoon. Her father's request was not.

She watched as he drank slowly from the scratched mug that stated boldly, 'World's Greatest Dad.' The cup was created with her dad in mind and was a Christmas gift from her when she was nine years old.

He sat the cup gingerly down on the table. The effort required apparent by the wince in his face. His once short, powerful body had been ravaged. "Sus," the only name he ever used for her. "It's time for you to go home and get back to your life with Alan and the boys. They need you."

She tried without success to stave off the tears as she said, "I don't want to leave Daddy. Don't make me."

He grasped her hand tenderly. His hand reduced to little more than bone and loose skin. He touched her tears with his other hand. Smiling at her, he asked, "Have I ever made you do anything?"

He was quiet as he watched her try so diligently not to weep. "You realize that you're keeping me here, don't you Sus?"

"I don't understand, Daddy."

"It's simple really. You pray all the time for me to get well when we both know that it isn't going to happen. God knows that you are not ready to let go of me. He knows how scared you are to face life without me."

"I am, Daddy," she sobbed.

"Sus, all I ever did was love you and you made that so easy. You've always been a good girl, a strong girl. You can do this also."

She rose from the chair and moved to him, kneeling on the floor. She rested her head in his lap and he gently stroked her hair as she soaked his faded red pajamas with her tears.

"Explain it to me, Daddy. Tell me how I'm keeping you here and how I'm supposed to let you go."

He spoke deliberately, his voice weak. "Look at me, Sus."

She gazed up into his gray eyes that time had faded. They still held light in them despite the pain that engulfed them. She saw his eyes begin to tear.

"Sometimes, I think we view God as so big that he is indifferent to our problems. We forget that somehow in the midst of a world with billions of people that he makes time for us one on one. He's here in this room and the closer that death comes to my door I can feel him all the more. I'm unafraid to walk through the next door because I know the light of God will show me to my final home. A light that will instantly rid my body of this horrid disease and return me to the young strong man I once was. He's listening to your each and every word. Close your eyes and picture what I'm telling you." She rested her head in his lap and closed her eyes.

"I want you to picture God, not in the sky sitting on some huge throne, but sitting at the third chair at this table. He wants to take me home with him, but he is torn because of your pain and your love for me. So he waits for you to be ready and he cries with you because he is the only person that has ever loved you more than me. You must never forget that."

Two nights later Suzanne was on her knees beside the bed in her old room praying. Her mom tapped lightly on the door and entered. "Oh, I'm sorry, Honey." She started to leave.

"It's okay, Mom. Stay."

They loved each other but never with the profundity that she shared with her father. It was a fact that had caused obvious resentment from her mother. Suzanne and her dad never intended to hurt anyone. It was just the way things were.

"Mom, do you want him to go?"

Her mom sat on the edge of the bed and touched her face lightly. "No. I want to keep him forever, but it is selfish of me to feel that way. He's suffering and I don't want that. There is no hope, no miracle that will bring him back. I love him too much not to want him free from this horrible cancer."

"Are you scared, Mom?"

"You bet I am, but I try not to let him see that."

There was silence as her mother searched for the right words. "Suzanne, I want to apologize."

Suzanne rose from her knees, joining her on the side of the bed. "For what?"

"God help me I was so jealous of the two of you. I always thought that a daughter would cling to her mother more, the way I did with mine. But I knew from the beginning that I had no chance. From the time you were old enough to walk you seemed to spend most of the day waiting for him to come home. In the summer, you would stare out through the screen door until his truck pulled up. When it was cold you would stand on the couch looking out the window. I should have enjoyed that. May God forgive me I was resentful.

"When you were three I moved the couch away from the window. I told myself I was tired of the same old look in the living room, but I think I just wanted you to stop looking for him out that window."

"But Mom, I always remember the couch being by the window."

Her mom chuckled as she took her hand. "That's because it only stayed that way for one day. You dragged a chair to the window while I was in the bathroom. You tried to stand on it and you fell and hit your head. You cried for twenty minutes and do you know when you stopped crying?"

"When?"

"When I moved the couch back to where it was." She chuckled again before adding, "I guess the couch was too heavy for you to move."

They embraced each other with laughter and tears, and a love that swelled beyond all they had ever felt for one another.

It was past midnight. Suzanne lay in the bed, praying, meditating, and longing for sleep. She rose and walked down the hall. She bent down over him. His breathing was labored as he struggled for oxygen.

"Daddy," she whispered.

He awoke quickly. "Sus, what is it?"

"I love you, Daddy. I want one more thing from you."

"You name it, kiddo."

She kissed him on top of his bald spotted head. He once had thick wavy black hair but it had long ago yielded to chemo treatments. "Go home, Daddy. Go home. I'll be all right."

He smiled at her and fell back asleep. The next morning, he was gone.

The memories of her father's death brought a chill that numbed her skin like a northeast wind from a fast moving cold front. She pulled her knees up to her chest--keeping the mug in her hands. Tears trickled down her cheeks. Her mother died one year later of a heart attack.

She looked at the stairs. She could go and make up with Alan. No. She decided that would just be another temporary fix that would heal nothing.

She drank the remainder of the hot chocolate and placed the mug on the coffee table in front of her. She walked to the linen closet and removed a blanket and pillow. Tonight she would sleep on the couch. It was another promise broken that was once made by a young married couple.

6

THE FAINT RADIANCE OF THE false sunrise filtered its way into Troy's bedroom. He stirred in his bed yearning for extended sleep. He tried in vain to fall back asleep for several minutes before surrendering to the beginning of his day.

He rose from bed and walked to the window and tugged on the blind that had proven negligent in blocking the morning light. Peering out the window at the luminosity that hovered over the gray Atlantic sea, he watched for several minutes. The sun began to rise partially over the water. It always seemed as if this huge orange ball was immersed in the depth of the ocean, before slowly rising out of the water, shaking the last remaining droplets prior to bringing forth another day.

He moved from the window to the kitchen where he stopped to pour a cup of coffee from the automatic coffee maker. Max was waiting at the front door. Troy opened the door and watched Max take off with purpose. He sat down in the rocker on the porch and gazed at the sun.

Beneath the sun the horizon was clear. Just above the sun the sky offered glimpses of blue, overshadowed by the ominous gray clouds that were poised to govern the sky.

The weather prediction of near eighty degrees and clear skies for the day appeared to be slightly off target. It was fruitless to get upset with the weather forecasters. Living near the coast meant the only constant in the weather was how swiftly it changed.

He watched Max chase a flock of seagulls. The weather predictions were not totally off base. The temperature for this late October day was unseasonably warm. The humidity felt as sticky as a June morning.

The wind blew from the south, bringing with it additional warmth. He watched Max run joyfully through the trails but as he had been taught, he stayed clear of the dunes and the precious vegetation that held them together. The sea oats gave off a peaceful sound as the breeze moved them.

He once worked for one year planting sea oats and American Beach Grass on the shores of eastern North Carolina. The work was hard and the days long but he enjoyed the simplicity of the work.

The business was pretty much a family business and at times Troy felt like an outsider. They were good, hardworking, no-nonsense people. The family once worked in farming but as with many small farms they sought other opportunities. They constructed greenhouses and through trial and error learned to grow healthy sea oats.

The greenhouse was located in Bolivia, North Carolina. Working in the greenhouse was one part of the job Troy did not care for. Especially, when the sea oats needed trimming in the summer and the temps could easily reach one hundred and twenty degrees.

Troy worked most of the time with Ralph, who he had worked with previously on another job. Ralph was a good country boy who worked as hard and as long as anyone Troy could recall. On a good day, he could match Ralph for the first part of the day, but as the hours stretched on, and the heat rose, he would slow down and Ralph would still be working at the same pace, and at the end of the day several hundred holes ahead of him.

The dune closest to the cottage was almost bare of vegetation at one time. The owner of the business, Steve, saw it once and walked to his truck and gave Troy several hundred plants and said, "Why don't you plant that?"

Now that one dune was thicker with sea oats than any of the ones surrounding it. Troy smiled as he thought about Steve and Ralph. He hoped they were doing well. Maybe before the year was gone he would drive to the greenhouse and visit.

Troy watched the sun surrender into the blanket of clouds. The rays through the clouds lent an array of colors. The dominant shade was aqua but there were streaks of red, orange, pink, purple, and other colors.

When he was a little boy he would notice the different colors in the sky and ask his mother for an explanation of why on certain days the sky contained so many colors. His mom replied that God was painting the sky. He found her answer most satisfactory. After that day when the sky glowed with colors he pictured this large robed figure, suspended in the clouds with a pail of paint and armed with at least a four-inch paintbrush.

He watched as Max stopped and looked at him eagerly not understanding how his master could just sit when they could be chasing the most annoying birds in the universe together. At least there were no tourists who thought it fun to feed them and then would wonder why they wouldn't leave when the meal was finished being served. "Rodents with wings," he mumbled softly.

It was near the last gasp of beach season. Fall was here and winter to follow. The club would close in a few weeks and he would depart the beach for a log cabin in southern Virginia, which was owned by Rich Busby. Rich was his catcher at ECU during a time when life seemed promising.

Troy thought about that day when his arm died. He stood on the mound, surrounded by his coach, trainer, and teammates. Rich stood in front of him and when Troy looked at the smaller man and he saw tears streaming unashamedly on to Rich's perpetual three day beard and though the diagnosis would come later that day, Rich and he both knew already that his career was over. The relief pitcher, Mike Brown, entered from the bullpen and Coach Wilson gave him the ball. As Troy walked off the mound, the fans and players from both teams stood and clapped slowly and steady for five minutes. He never knew that behind him Coach Wilson's eyes were a little watery as he put his arm around Rich and said to him softly, "Put your mask on, Son, and let's go back to work. If this is the last game Troy pitches I want it to be a win. Mike will need your help."

Rich pulled his mask down over his face. "I got it, Coach. Leave the boys to me." Coach Wilson nodded his head ever so gently and walked back to the dugout.

The tough little catcher looked at the infield first and then to Mike. "This one is for Troy. No excuses accepted. Mike you will throw the pitches I call for and you will hit the location where I signal. There will be no debate. Are we clear?"

Mike had been known to think he could call the game better than his catcher but today he knew this was a line he could not cross. "You call it and I will hit the target."

He did just that.

Troy received the news later of the torn labrum in his right shoulder and when he returned to his apartment, his catcher was sitting on the steps. Rich rose and said evenly, "It has been my honor to catch you. Thank you. I don't know if you will make it back or not but regardless of the outcome I am your friend for life. If you ever need anything ..." he walked away, his word trailing behind him.

Rich graduated that year and went on to own and operate several lucrative businesses. He would leave his own family and during the time Troy resided at his cabin he would show up unannounced and spend a couple of days with his pitcher. They never spoke of that day Troy's dream died and in a way, Rich's dream died as well. He knew he would never play in the big leagues but he thought when Troy made it a little part of him would be in the majors as well.

Departing for the mountains was Troy's way to avoid the holidays and his birthday that followed three days after Christmas. Sometimes he thought it was his way of waging war with God for the injustice of life. *Look at me God. Here I am, all alone. The breaks of life continually going against me and you never stepped in to make anything right. Not once.*

He shook his head and realized how foolish it was to think that any argument with God could be won. It was equally irrational, he decided, to think that because of hard times you were owed some degree of fairness.

He had watched three unwelcome incidents rob him of any chance at a decent life. Eventually, he fought back and found the strength to rekindle hopes and dreams after the first two strikes. After the third deadly blow, he chose to hope no more. It was easier.

He sat his cup down on the weathered rail and looked again at the sky. Softly, he mumbled, "Hey God, while you are up there painting such a pretty picture." He did not finish his request. He was certain that the grand painter of skies would choose not to respond. Minutes later the bleak sky touched the grayness of the Atlantic water, forming one solid mass of gray.

*

SHE SAT AT THE DESK in Alan's church office. He was delivering his third message of the day. Suzanne attended the middle service. It had been implied by the elders of the church that she should be at both the middle and the last service as they were each filled to capacity. She refused. One sermon a day was enough regardless of who occupied the pulpit.

There were no additional words between Alan and her about the events of the preceding night. She slept fitfully on the couch and her first look in the mirror nearly convinced her to remain home. She wore more makeup than customary, attempting to conceal the dark circles under her eyes.

She stood and fumbled in her purse for her keys, dropping them in the process on top of the desk.

They landed on a stack of papers. She was retrieving them when a letter caught her eye. *Dear Troy,* it began. She inadvertently read a couple of lines before she realized that it was linked to the man in the parking lot that she had attempted to converse with. She asked Alan about his encounter with Troy and he had filled her in on the events, painting Troy as quite the villain. "He is just a thug that really does not fit in here," was Alan's final remark on the subject.

She sat back down in the huge leather chair that dwarfed her. Troy's letter was beneath the paper that had caught her eye. She began reading the letter. She sat it down when she finished and began to read Alan's response. She read it carefully. There were tears in her eyes when she finished. She stared at the ceiling and softly whispered, "No. Alan. No."

She took the letters to the copy machine and made a copy of each. She folded them in half and slipped them into her purse and walked away.

Minutes later after a stop at home for running gear she was at a local park. She ran five miles Monday, Wednesday, and Friday mornings. Today she would add an additional run in her routine to see if it might somehow help her sort through her troubles. That was her favorite part of running. The way it helped to clear her mind.

The fitness benefits were important also and she surely didn't think it a sin to care about her appearance. Her legs remained lean and strong, though the size of her hips bothered her at times. They were firm also but slightly too big for her body and she had never been able to trim them down.

Her body was far from perfect but that didn't mean that keeping in shape didn't draw comments from certain members of the congregation who were mostly unfit and overweight. Those same people were often full of harsh judgments on the sins of others. They would rail against abortion while ignoring the sin in their life. She could not recall where she once read it but it was something she never forgot.

People don't like it when others sin in a way different than their own.

Alan used to take care of his body, long ago. Now, he joined in with most of the congregation with their excuses of not having the time to exercise. Well, she thought it was a shortcoming on their part to not take care of their body. It seemed obvious to her that the better physical shape you were in would lead to more energy to carry out the tasks God might want you to do.

The main attraction of Greenfield Park was a large lake. It was built during the great depression. The construction of the lake was one of the many projects constructed by the Worker's Progress Administration that was created to help men put food on the table. Gigantic Cypress trees were scattered throughout the lake. There was an asphalt trail that wound around the lake that was bordered by thousands of azaleas. During the spring when they were in full bloom the place was breathtaking.

She stretched for a few minutes and then slowly began to run. The humidity was so high that she was grateful for the cloud cover. She was sweating profusely before the first mile. Her body ached, probably from the lack of sleep the night before but somewhere before the three-mile mark her body loosened and she hit her stride. She wasn't a fast runner but she wasn't bad either. She finished the four-mile loop in less than thirty-five minutes.

The clouds loosened their grip on the sun momentarily as she sat in an area of fresh rye grass and stretched. Her mind wandered as she watched a squirrel race up and down a huge oak tree.

She didn't know if the run had freed up her mind, but she had come to at least one conclusion. Alan was leaving soon for the Holy Land. It was a trip planned with part of the congregation. She decided somewhere around mile three that she would remain home.

*

ALAN'S MESSAGE CONCLUDED at 12:35 bringing his forty-eight minute-oration on how the authority of this particular church should be carried out to a close.

He did not see his wife seated in her customary place and for once he was glad. She would not approve of what he was about to do next.

The prayer for wholeness was being carried out when he made contact with his right hand man, Bill. He nodded ever so succinctly to him and Bill returned the gesture. He would faithfully carry out his mission that was discussed prior to the beginning of the service.

The service had scarcely ended when Bill approached Ruth Dawkins. He was relieved to see her husband was not with her. "Hi, Ruth. How are you?"

Ruth looked at Bill and speculated as to just what he was up to. She had a feeling that she was not going to like it. She wished Tom was with her but he woke feeling poorly this morning and she insisted he stay home. She knew he really did not mind. He attended church mainly for her.

"What can I do for you, Bill?"

"Alan would like to speak with you in his chambers."

Did he really just say chambers?

"What's this about?" she asked, though she knew exactly what the relevance was of the meeting.

"He just wants to make sure that we all have peace about everything moving forward." Bill was also the treasurer of the church and he was sure to be gentle with Ruth. He did not think she would leave the church because of her son's belligerent behavior, but she was one of those who faithfully tithed ten percent and above. You could never have too many of those in a church family. "Please, let's walk to his office."

So it is an office now. Chambers was probably closer to the truth. Still, she was never one to stir up trouble or take part in it. Troy often said she swept the family troubles under a rug while hanging the Norman Rockwell painting on the wall. She sighed. Troy was right, as bad as she hated admitting it.

David Lang and his wife were standing in the corner of the balcony. The balcony was small, seating maybe thirty people. He and Toni sat in the top right hand corner to not be so visible. He was not the senior pastor any longer and he did not want to detract from the leaders of the church by garnishing the attention of the members. He appreciated that he was thought of fondly and people longed for the old days when he was in charge, though he never viewed it that way. He took his role as Shepherd of the flock quite seriously, but the flock belonged to God, not to him.

"David, what is wrong?" Toni asked as she placed her hand on his arm.

He continued to watch the scene below.

"Something or someone sure has your attention."

She gazed down at the people filing out of church. Her eyes caught the door to her right at the front of the church. Bill was leading Ruth through that door.

"Oh," she said. "That can't be good." She paused and looked back to her husband. "You don't want to get involved do you? Let's go home."

"I am not sure that is the correct course of action."

"It was the daily things such as this that you had your fill of long ago. That is why you stepped aside."

"You might be missing something."

"And what would that be dear?"

"Friendship and loyalty."

"To whom?"

David looked at her with clear, firm eyes.

She smiled at him. "You mean your other son? The one I did not give birth to. I won't say I always understand this friendship you share with Troy but I have always trusted you. You do what you feel needs to be done. I will be waiting for you."

"Toni, do you recall how church leaders reacted to us returning to Wilmington and accepting the call here? Particularly, that one meeting and how a fellow minister spoke about me and this message of the Baptism of the Holy Spirit he feared would be harmful."

She gritted her teeth and said tersely, "I wanted to rip his head off."

He smiled warmly. "I know you did and while I told you that was not the way we would handle it I was also touched by your fierce loyalty. The way you have always felt the need to protect me. And now I think someone can use my protection, and possibly safeguard someone else."

"Someone else?"

"Alan and Bill."

She looked at him with a puzzled expression and then her face cleared with understanding. "You mean what could happen to them if Troy gets wind of them pushing his mom around."

David took hold of both of her arms, gently but firmly all the same. She knew he was about to be very serious with her.

"Thank you for trying to understand my friendship with Troy. I know you don't really see in him what I do. But I am going to tell you something and I want you to never forget it."

She nodded to him gently and waited.

"Our sons live out of town and I want you to know that if we were ever in serious trouble and needed help that Troy would be my first call. He would let nothing deter him from getting to us. So, he is not the good Christian that people here think that he should be. But here is what they and you are missing. He is the most loyal man I have ever known. You, his mom, and others see how fortunate it is that Troy has a friend like me but I view it another way. I am the one favored by God to have a friend like Troy."

Tears rolled gently down her cheeks and she knew she would never question this friendship with her husband the minister and his friend the bouncer again. "Go now, dear," she said, as she touched his face. "Go now."

David tapped lightly on the door of the office and then walked in. The first thing he noticed that ripped at his heart were the tears flowing easily down Ruth's face.

Alan looked up and said, "With all due respect this is private."

David looked at him sternly. "With all due respect to Bill and you, I am going to take Ruth with me now and I hope both of you gain a sliver of wisdom in how to deal with your members that you are supposed to protect."

"You are not in charge any longer," Alan stated.

It was very rare that David ever got angry. It was a gift that aided him immensely in dealing with church issues that rose frequently throughout his career. He was about to blow his cool when suddenly he had an idea. It was an idea that produced a silly childlike grin.

Bill and Alan looked at him with perplexed expressions. "Are you okay, David?" Bill asked.

"I am a lot better than the two of you will be if her son ever gets wind of this foolhardy idea of yours," he said, looking at Alan with a sly smile.

"She won't tell him because she knows what he might do. Still, bullying his mom is not in either of your best interests."

Alan raised his eyes and shook his head slightly. "It is kind of hard to understand a minister having such a friend."

David smiled in such a way that it shook Alan. "Maybe I choose to look past outward appearances and look on the heart. I am certain that is what our Lord does. 1 Samuel 16:7 seems to state that rather clearly."

"We are not through talking with Ruth yet. Please feel free to leave," Alan said, and looked away.

David walked to the far end of the table and picked up the telephone. "First, I think I will make a call."

Alan looked at him fearfully as it dawned on him just what David had in mind. "Who are you calling?"

"Troy."

"You wouldn't."

"I would, and I will."

Alan stammered as David began to press numbers. "Wait. Stop. I think we are through anyway." He patted Ruth's arm gently. "This is church business. No need to repeat it."

She snatched her arm away from him and stood. "Maybe I should tell Troy."

David walked toward her and escorted her out the door.

Bill looked at Alan. "I told you this might not be a good idea."

"Shut up, Bill," Alan replied.

7

SUZANNE SAT ON THE COLOSSAL mauve couch in their living room. She surveyed the too expansive house that was yet to feel like a home as she sipped her coffee. It was ironic that after years of cramped living that they now had their dream home. It was nearly three thousand square feet and with her boys gone most of it was wasted. Alan had insisted on purchasing it. She continued looking around as if she expected the furnishings to speak and explain how it was that she arrived at this place and she was debating more than a house that was far too big.

So, this is it, the big house, the right job, and no more financial struggles. Oh, the boy's college expenses added up but they had planned well for it and long ago purchased mutual funds were taking care of nearly all the expenses.

Thoughts of her sons brought sorrow. They chose to remain at the University of Tennessee when Alan took the job. Both had met girls during their freshman year and became serious with them. She didn't blame her sons for not wanting to follow them on yet another move. It was time for the boys to make their way in life. She hoped they would succeed where Alan and she had failed.

She heard footsteps coming down the stairs as her husband made his way to the kitchen. Their limited conversation had been strained yesterday. She had not yet informed him of the decision made during her run yesterday.

He entered the living room and smiled forcibly. He was dressed in a far too expensive dark gray suit to be going to the office on a Monday. His tastes had left those of the simple country boy he once was and were now decidedly upscale. She was grateful that they did not struggle financially any longer but her tastes were simple, as they had always been. This big house and all the furnishings meant little to her and Alan spent far more on clothes than she did.

He sat down on the opposite end of the couch. He waited for her to speak and when she didn't he did. "Suzanne, the trip to Israel is right around the corner. I was thinking that maybe the time away will do us good. I mean, I realize that I will have to spend much of my time with the others, still I'm quite sure that we will be able to carve out time just for the two of us."

She sat her coffee cup down on the glass table in front of her. She looked in his direction as if he were not in the same room with her. Her voice was strong and unflinching when she replied. "I won't be going on this trip. Maybe a break will serve us even better."

He sighed audibly, but he was determined not to let this evolve into yet another heated quarrel. His first thought was about how her decision would reflect with the members of the trip and of course the ruling board of elders. He was aware of the numerous comments concerning her lack of participation in the church. "Let's don't be mad any longer. I need your support on this trip. I need you with me."

She looked away from him with complete indifference. The pause made him squirm in his seat. Slowly, she turned back to him. "I'm not mad at you Alan, disappointed in you, but not mad. And be honest, you are more worried about how my not going will be viewed by the congregation than any other reasons you may have."

He started to speak but she cut him off. Her voice was low but without room for debate. "Let me make this perfectly clear for you. Under no circumstances will I be going."

"Suzanne . . ."

She interrupted. "And I don't care what any of the church members think about my decision."

Alan searched for the right words to sooth his belligerent wife. "Are you jealous of the church, Suzanne?" His tone was like a therapist who upon hearing a patient's remark would lean in and ask, "And how did that make you feel when your daddy wet you with the garden hose when you were five years old?"

She chuckled slightly at his preposterous notion. "No. This is your church not mine. I never wanted to come here. You knew that and you chose to take the position anyway."

"It was where God wanted us to be."

"It was where the money was better," she replied coolly.

There was silence once again. He felt the anger inside of him growing but he refrained from allowing it to escape. His voice was low as he pleaded with her. "Suzanne, I need your support. It is important to me."

"I'll support you where I can but not at the expense of being dishonest with you or even more so with myself. I told you that I did not want to leave Knoxville and my children but you charged ahead anyway. So here we are and you want me to pretend all is well when it obviously is not."

"I thought in time you would choose to be involved."

"You can't make decisions for both of us and expect me to fall in line. You once cared what I wanted. What I thought. But now you have gotten so full of your own perceived greatness that you decide everything. New church, let's go. Trip to Israel, put us both down."

"I'm head of the church and this family," he answered firmly.

She shook her head as she rose from the couch. She looked down on him. "Don't give me that stuff. Men have used that for their own personal gain for a few too many centuries now."

"So now you don't believe in the word of God?"

"Word of God, yes. Men that use those few scriptures to control their house? No. I absolutely do not believe in that. Maybe they should read further where it states that the man should love his wife as Christ loved the church."

He started to speak but she cut him off.

"Before you speak let me be very frank in stating that in no way do you love me as Jesus loved the church.

"Lately, you seem to think all that emerges out of your mouth on Sunday morning is inspired from God."

He shook his head smugly. She felt like slapping the condescending look off of his face.

"I guess that you believe everything that you speak from that pulpit is accurate and what God wants?"

"I'd like to think so."

"Well, do yourself a huge favor, don't. That sermon on sex was ridiculous. It was harsh and it was cruel. There was a time that you would have thought about the effect your words might have on people. You would have thought about the lingering pain it may cause. Somewhere along the way you lost the reason you started down this path. You used to be a caring and compassionate man but your ego has grown to dangerous proportions. You were a far better minister, a far better man when you were humble. Remember how you were at that first little church in the mountains?"

"That was a long time ago. I moved on, maybe you should."

"Pride goes before the fall, Alan."

"I have no intention of falling."

"How many foolish men have made that statement? None of them ever see it coming. You won't either."

She nodded her head slightly and wondered just what had become of the man she married. Sighing softly, she walked across the room to the small table that sat in the foyer and removed two folded pieces of paper. She walked back to him and tossed the papers in his lap.

"What is this?"

"One of those letters is from the man that wrote you concerning your sermon on sex. The other is your reply. Remember you told me that he was upset with the truthfulness of your sermon? Well, I read the letter yesterday, along with your reply. In fact, I have read it several times. He had every right to be angry with you."

"You were snooping through my papers."

"No. I came across it by accident but if you were so right you have nothing to hide. Trouble is you were not right. You owe the man an apology."

"I do not."

She fought to retain her composure. Her voice was low but there was no mistaking the edge to it. "The man wrote you a sincere heartfelt letter. He was obviously speaking from pain and he reached out to you for some understanding. You gave him none. You have been wrong before but I can't ever remember you blowing it so badly. What you should do is seek him out and apologize and while you are at it express regret to the entire congregation for those thoughtless remarks."

He was wringing his hands together as he spoke. "I will not. Sex is just an uneasy subject for some. There were things in that sermon that needed to be said."

"Oh, all of it wasn't bad. If you want to warn young girls and boys about the dangers of premarital sex that is fine. Just don't say things that people can't do anything about because it's in the past. What good can come from saying that someone never will completely belong to his or her spouse because of past sexual partners? And that comment about the man getting you to cheat? I can't believe you said that. Troy wrote a good letter and he had two very vital points that you never responded to. He was right. There is nothing in the Bible to back up what you said."

He started to speak but she interrupted. She leaned forward and grabbed the Bible on the end table. She thrust it toward him. "Show me, Alan. Show me where it says that if you are with another and marry someone else that you will never completely belong to them. While you are at it show me the part that says if you sleep together before marriage the man will cheat once you are married."

He stood silently, making no attempt to take the Bible from her. His reason was simple. He knew there was no such passage in it to support his claims. Weakly, he offered, "I believe that what I said was right in God's eyes."

She shook her head in dismay.

"I need you with me on this trip and I expect you to go," he said, in a firm but strained voice.

She looked softly at him and felt a twinge of pity. Did he really think that he could command her to follow orders? "I tell you what Alan, you go to that man and grant him the heartfelt apology that he deserves and I will consider going to Israel with you."

He looked at her blankly and said nothing. "Have fun in Israel," she said, as she turned and walked up the stairs leaving him with the realization that he was not the king of the empire that he perceived himself to be.

He shook his head at the events of the morning and was surprised that they had not turned to his favor. He rose quickly and walked to the garage. He started the engine of the BMW X6 and drove away to work.

She watched from the upstairs window as his car backed out the drive and drove away. She walked back downstairs. The letters were left on the couch. She picked them up and read the address. "Well, Troy Dawkins, someone in this family is going to offer you an apology. Even, if you don't like it," she stated resolutely.

She walked back upstairs and dressed for her morning run. Light gray running shorts over white spandex tights and a dark blue T-shirt over a jog bra.

Minutes later she was in her red Mazda CX-5 SUV driving toward Carolina Beach. The last remnants of gray clouds surrendered, leaving a flawless, cobalt sky. She opened the sunroof and soaked in the beauty of the day.

She crossed a bridge so high that looking down at the water beneath it made her stomach quiver. She had no idea where Troy's house or anything else on the island was located and the letter contained no phone number.

Recalling her only encounter and how much he wanted to get away from her she wouldn't have wanted to give him any type of warning anyway. She saw a shopping complex off to her right with a Food Lion grocery in its center with several smaller stores flanking it. She kept driving and then she spotted a sign ahead of her. Post Office, with an arrow pointing to the right.

The Post Office was empty with the exception of the short lady with neat silver hair standing behind the counter. "Could I help you, hon?" she asked with a pleasant smile.

"Yes. I wanted to know how to get to this address," she said, handing her the scrap of paper that she had jotted the address on.

The smile rapidly departed from the lady's face and was replaced with a very stern expression. "What do you want with Troy?"

"I just want to talk with him," she answered hurriedly, almost feeling as if she were up to something devious. "Do you know everyone's address right off the top of your head?"

"Just the regulars," she answered, her eyes drawing closer together.

Suzanne stammered, before saying, "I'm sorry, my name is Suzanne Matthews," she said, extending her hand.

"Grace," the lady in front of her replied as she deliberately stretched out her hand.

The older lady gripped her hand firmly and held it for several moments as she stared intently into Suzanne's eyes.

Finally, when she retained property of her hand she asked determinedly, "Well, Grace, are you going to tell me or am I going to have to walk the streets?" She was on a mission and not even the intimidating postal worker with the death grip handshake was going to deter her from what she had set out to accomplish.

Grace refused to budge. Her eyes were gray and slightly unnerving. Suzanne looked at her and smiled barely. "Grace, I promise you that I am not here to make trouble. My husband is the pastor of the church that Troy attends or probably did attend. Alan, my husband upset him and he is too pigheaded to admit that he was wrong. What I want is to offer the apology that my husband refuses to grant. I promise you, Grace. That's all I want."

Grace smiled and her eyes softened. "Get back on the main road and turn right at the light. Go to the third light and take a left. Follow the street numbers from there. It's a cream-colored cottage right on the ocean."

"Thank you," Suzanne answered, as she turned toward the door.

"If he is not at home walk south a few hundred feet and you'll see a nightclub, *Mabry's*. He works there. It's not open but he may be there anyway. He's a big handsome man."

She was halfway out the door when she looked back. "I know. I've met him."

Grace's face turned stern once again. "You better be nice to that boy, you hear me?"

She smiled back at her and gave a mock salute from the other side of the glass door. The expression on Grace's face clearly spelled out that she was the only one that thought her gesture to be witty.

According to the instructions, Troy lived on the north side of the boardwalk. She was sitting at the third light when she decided to drive past the boardwalk and park on the other side. She felt nervous and thought that maybe the stroll would give her time to calm her nerves. She parked her car in a space that had a huge pipe on the sidewalk beside it but no parking meter. She got her running belt, stuffed the letters, her keys, and some cash in it.

The boardwalk was sparse with people. A few locals milled about. Two men dressed in tattered clothes sat on a bench passing a brown bottle partially concealed in a paper bag. The buildings were weathered looking and most were boarded shut for the season.

She walked through the boardwalk and soon she was on the street that Grace had described. She scanned the numbers on the houses and condos as she walked. Before she recognized the house number she spotted the same Jeep that she had watched him drive away in that day. It was parked to the right of a cream-colored cottage. There was a picket fence with a gate beside his Jeep. She paused outside the gate. She whispered to herself. "You've come too far now to chicken out."

The hinges squealed as she opened the gate, startling her. She attempted to close the gate quietly but the noise seemed even louder. There were steps made of stone that led to a small stoop.

She breathed deeply as she stood in front of the door. She knocked firmly. Hope he is not a murderer or anything terrible, she thought wistfully. No one came to the door so she knocked again. She got the same result.

She walked around to the ocean side. There were empty rocking chairs swaying in the ocean breeze. She decided to walk to the nightclub.

Minutes later she tapped on a large, dark brown door. An attractive older lady opened the door. "It's a little early."

"I know. That's not why I'm here."

"I figured that."

"I'm looking for Troy Dawkins."

"Come in. I'm Mabry," she said, walking away.

Suzanne followed her to the bar.

"I was having some coffee. Join me. You do drink coffee, don't you?"

"No. I mean yes, I do, but I don't care for any."

She walked behind the bar. "Cream or sugar," she said as she poured the coffee into a cup.

Suzanne was startled by the business-like manner of the woman. "I said I didn't care for any."

"And I said, cream or sugar?" Mabry said evenly.

Suzanne felt uneasy as the woman stared at her waiting on an answer. "Grace called me from the Post Office. Now, what will it be?"

"Both," Suzanne replied wearily. She pulled out a barstool and sat down. Mabry sat the cup down on the bar and remained standing.

Suzanne pursed her lips together and sighed. "I just want to talk to him, not light him on fire and cast demons out of him. I guess it is safe to assume that Grace didn't leave out any details," she said smartly.

"You watch that tone of voice when you speak of Grace, young lady and tell me just why this is so important to you?"

"How about because it is the right thing to do? How about he has pain in his eyes and maybe I think I can help?"

She looked back at her for a few seconds as if she was privy to information that Suzanne did not know. "Who's helping the pain in your eyes?"

There was silence as Suzanne looked away from the penetrating gaze of Mabry and into the large mirror found behind the bar. She studied her reflection attempting to see the pain that was spoken of. What she saw was weariness, and as bad as she hated to admit it, pain.

She turned back and met Mabry's eyes. "I didn't come here as some sanctimonious Christian with all the answers. I'm here simply because it is the right thing to do. Now, can I ask a question?"

"Bring your cup into my office." She followed her into the office. Mabry gestured toward the couch with her hand and rolled the swivel chair from behind her desk and sat across from her. "Ask."

"Does everyone protect him?"

"Those that care about him do."

"You're not his mother, are you?"

She saw a smile cross her face as if the question had more meaning to it than Suzanne could ever know.

"No."

"Does everyone who cares about him feel such a need to protect him? He's a big boy. He looks like he could take care of just about anything."

"It's not the outside that is troubling. It is what he carries around inside of him that worries all of us." She sipped her coffee and then returned her eyes to Suzanne. They were softer now as she spoke. "He's had some hard knocks in life."

"Haven't we all?" she responded callously.

The look returned to her informed Suzanne that she was at fault once again. She had minimized the hard knocks, whatever they were, and had rendered them generic.

"He is a dreamer, or at least he was." Her voice was lower now and her eyes drifted to another time. "When I say hard knocks don't categorize it as what we all go through. He's seen things that would have stifled the life out of all of us. Trilogy of tragedy," she said, barely audible.

Suzanne listened to the pain in her voice and wished for the right words to say, but it was a time like this when silence was a better answer. She rose from the couch and looked at the pictures on the wall. Her eyes drifted to a picture of a baseball player with his arm around an attractive lady close to her own age. She drank from her cup. "So, he works for you but obviously he is much more than that."

Mabry looked at the picture that was taken by Nate a lifetime ago.

Suzanne studied the picture and read the inscription.

To the best teacher in the whole world

From your future major leaguer,

Love,

Troy

"You were his teacher," she said with a nod. "Did he make the major leagues?"

"No." She paused, before adding, "that was only the beginning."

Suzanne observed the distant look in Mabry's face. She waited patiently for her to explain.

Mabry's eyes refocused on her. "There are certain things better left alone. If you want to apologize for your husband, fine, but if you have some kind of plan to counsel him, I fear you'll do far more harm than good. It's past eleven o'clock now so he is either home or out on the beach. If you are so determined to see him, go now." Mabry rolled her chair back behind the desk and proceeded to work as if she were the only one present.

8

SUZANNE, DISCONCERTED BY the proceedings of the morning, walked outside into the effulgent sunshine. She sat on a bench outside the club, debating her next course of action. Maybe it would be best to pack it in and forget her plan for this day. Trouble was she was not one to stop once she had set her mind to do something. It was true that she wanted to offer the apology she firmly believed he deserved. Still, there was a story behind the pain in his eyes and for some odd reason she had to know why it existed, and maybe even offer a little help. As unwelcome as that help may be.

Why was she so intrigued by his story, when as Alan had so succinctly pointed out, she wouldn't get involved in the church at Portside? Her thoughts led also to Mabry's remark about the pain in her eyes. It was a blunt suggestion that maybe she clear up her problems first.

She rose and began walking in the direction of the boardwalk. She strolled through the mostly closed stores along the worn, uneven boardwalk. There was an old man seated on a wooden bench that had weathered to a dull gray. His shirt was faded denim with the sleeves cut out of it. Perched on top of his head was a NASCAR cap with a huge gaudy 3 on it. He was eating peanuts from a brown bag and tossing the empty shells onto the wooden floor beneath him. Behind him, between two buildings, there was a walkway to the beach. She heard the sound of the waves in the distance. She offered him a smile as she walked past.

The sunlight shimmered on top of the water like shards of dismembered glass. She had never lived close to the coast before. As she walked along the shoreline and took in the vastness of it all she began to understand why so many would sacrifice so much to call this wonderful place home.

The tide was low and the sand along the tidemark firm. She tightened the running belt around her waist. She stretched and double tied her shoes. She checked her watch and began to run.

Her body responded to the invigoration of her first run on the beach. The muscles in her legs loosened quickly and inside of ten minutes she was running south at a nice easy pace.

There were walkers of all ages strolling easily along the shoreline. She passed several people surf fishing. She ran under a tattered pier and continued on for another ten minutes before turning back.

She ran back to where she had begun and stopped. She checked her watch. She had run for just over forty minutes. Running once again had cleared her mind and she was filled with resolve. She had come to Carolina Beach this morning for a reason.

She walked back to the boardwalk. The old man, still seated, and eating peanuts methodically. Minutes later she was in front of the small cottage again.

She knocked on the door once again to no response. She walked around to the ocean side where the large man she had met in the church hallway sat in a wood rocker on the porch with his yellow lab beside his feet.

Max spotted her first and came to greet her. "Hey, boy," she said, stopping to pet him.

She was standing on the sand in front of the two steps that led up to the porch where Troy sat. He looked through her as if she were just another part of the landscape. "May I come up?"

The silence proved deafening. "Do you remember me? Suzanne, from the church parking lot?" she added, nervously. She silently admonished herself. From the church parking lot. What a dope I am to say something so stupid.

He nodded in silence.

She stood there awkwardly. The sweat dripping off her body. She wiped it from her eyes and wished that she could see his eyes that were hidden by dark aviator glasses. She felt a little light headed and wondered if it was dehydration from the run or the precarious position she had placed herself in. Probably the latter, she thought.

"Could I please have some water? I just finished running and I . . ."

He rose from the chair without a word. He was wearing black swim trunks and no shirt. The middle of his back had a deep indentation that ran from the middle of his shoulders down toward his lower back. The muscle on each side of the line reminded her of two sides of beef hanging in a butcher's shop. He returned with a bottle of water and a dark blue towel.

She took both. "Thank you." She drank hurriedly from the bottle and set it down on the rail and dried herself with the towel. "May I come up, please?"

"Why?" His eyes shifted annoyingly at Max who was sitting obediently by her left side not understanding why this nice lady had not been invited on the porch to sit.

"I want to talk with you, and I would like to do so sitting down."

He seemed larger standing two steps above her, nearly engulfing the frame way of the porch. His upper body appeared as hard and rigid as a bowling ball. His stomach was flat and his arms were thick and strong. There was a pronounced scar on his right shoulder that began near his armpit and ran toward the center of his shoulder. She wondered if it were a knife wound.

Her eyes moved to his face and he was looking at her with a hint of amusement. "It is not a knife wound," she heard him say. He moved his chair to the side and pulled a white wicker chair out for her. He gestured with his hand.

She unzipped her running jacket and pulled out the folded white paper. She sat down and unfolded the letter.

"I heard that you were looking for me. I saw you out there," he said, gesturing toward the sea with his hand. "You were trying to decide what to do when you went for your run."

"Damn," she muttered. "I think that it would have probably been easier to see the governor than to slide past your defense shield."

"Preacher's wives cuss, huh?"

She noticed his mouth did not move but there was a glimmer of a smile in his eyes that held a hint of sarcasm. "Preacher's wives are human," she answered curtly.

He nodded slightly, amused at her quick retort. She finished her water and without a word he rose and brought another.

"Thank you," she said. She opened the letters. "Look, I know that you or no one else wants me on this island so I'll make this quick. I think that my husband's response to your letter was completely inadequate and I want to apologize."

He chuckled ever so slightly. "I hope that you didn't overtax your brain arriving at that conclusion." He paused before adding, "Now you didn't write the letter, or preach the sermon. So why are you the one apologizing?"

"Because he is too stubborn to admit how wrong he is. I think it took a lot for you to write that letter and his reply was woefully lacking in grace."

"Does he know that you are here?"

"No."

"You just came out here all alone to talk to a rough, mean bouncer that you don't know?"

He was trying to intimidate her and it was working. She blurted out, "But I do know you. I met you in the parking lot."

Quickly she realized again how moronic her reply was. What gift did this man possess that made her converse like such an idiotic fool? She took a deep breath and spoke calmly and with more conviction than she felt at the moment. "If you were so dangerous those ladies would not be so protective over you."

His eyes narrowed as he turned his head slightly to the side. "That's great. It is even worse. You probably want to help and maybe even save my soul. You're probably one of the church counselors or worse someone who thinks they are a psyche major."

"Actually, I am very close to a master's degree in psychology."

Dryly he asked, "Is that supposed to impress me?"

She shook her head and breathed deeply. "So, you don't like counselors or psychologists?"

"I think far too many people place their lives in the hands of counselors or psychologists. People who may have their own demons they have not overcome."

"Maybe they need their help."

"And maybe those therapists are just getting rich from other people's misfortune."

She studied him and wondered if he sincerely meant his words or if he were speaking for effect. Maybe it was both. Maybe it was his way of preventing her from getting near him. Stop analyzing so much Suzanne, she lectured herself. One thing seemed evident. No one wanted her here.

She rose quickly. "I'm sorry that I bothered you. You were right about your letter and I wanted to try to make things right even if my husband refuses." She turned and began to walk away.

Max rose and watched her disappear around the corner. A perplexed look covered his face as he looked back to his master.

"Don't you even think about following her," he stated firmly.

Max continued to stare at him.

"And don't look at me like I've been rude or something."

Max cocked his head to the side and then looked back at his master, sighing loudly, followed by a slight growl.

"No," he said sternly.

Max replied with a loud bark and walked over to Troy and with his stout nose nudged him to move.

"No, Max."

Max replied with a low growl and another nudge.

He shook his head at man's so called best friend, but then he relented. "Okay, okay," he said as he threw up his hands. "I'll go get her. Thief stole my towel anyway."

He moved hastily off the porch as Max joined him. "I don't suppose you would consider staying on the porch, would you?"

Max bounced playfully and shook his head from side to side as if he were indeed answering the question.

As he walked around to the front of the house, he said disgustedly, "I can't believe you would allow a woman to come between us."

Max nudged him in the back of his legs and barked. Troy reached the boardwalk but he didn't see her.

Max sat by his side and looked up at him. He was shivering with anticipation not unlike when he waited for a ball to be thrown into the ocean.

Softly and with a hint of exasperation, Troy said, "Go. Find."

Max was running the moment the command was issued. Troy watched him race down the boardwalk before turning back a few feet, and then he disappeared around the corner.

Troy stood there wondering just what had possessed his dog. Moments later he was forced to suppress a grin when he saw Max with one end of the blue towel in his mouth and Suzanne holding on to the other.

Max led her and the towel to Troy. She gazed up at Troy and started to speak. He saw the pain and disappointment in her eyes.

"Preacher's wives steal people's towels?"

She handed him his towel and said, "Thanks for the towel and the water." She turned and began walking away. Her shoulders slumped in defeat.

He watched as she walked away. "Max, she has really nice legs," he said quietly. "Oh boy, I just said a preacher's wife has nice legs. It's no pearly gates for me Max."

Max looked up at him trying to comprehend what pearly gates meant.

Max watched her walk away as he sat obediently by Troy's side. He gazed up at Troy expecting action from his master, who had been a little slow on the draw this morning.

Troy rolled his eyes at Max. "Go."

Suzanne had made it about seventy feet. Troy watched in amusement as Max ran past her slightly before turning to face her, impeding her progress. Each time she began to move, he moved toward her barking viscously. This went on for several minutes as Troy watched with a huge smile.

Suzanne turned back to him. He wondered if she knew what he knew. That she was in absolutely no danger of being attacked.

"Do you want to call your dog off me?"

"Well, now technically he is not on you."

"Please," she said. "It's been a long eventful morning at wonderful Carolina Beach and I just want to go home," she said, her voice filling with frustration.

She turned and took a step and Max immediately gave his most menacing growl. "I know he is not going to bite me, Troy," she called out loudly.

Troy decided the fun had gone on long enough and just when he decided to call Max back the good times turned abruptly. Troy enjoyed a good relationship with nearly every police officer on the beach apart from one. And that one, Sean McGill had just appeared from around the corner. He was running briskly, with his pistol drawn and was pointing it in the direction of Max, who was still playfully growling and barking at Suzanne.

Troy moved toward Suzanne and Max. "He's playing you moron. Put that gun away," he demanded.

Max hearing the tone from his master quickly realized that the game had changed. He stopped barking and turned toward the officer who kept moving toward him with his gun still aimed.

Max growled in a tone that was in no way playful as Troy kept moving steadily toward the situation. "He was playing with her you idiot. Now, put that gun up before I feed it to you."

Suzanne watched all of this and felt helpless, unsure of what to do. And then to her surprise, she suddenly knew just what to do. She could prove what she knew all along that she was in no danger if Max would listen to her.

"Max. Heel," she commanded firmly.

Max looked toward her and then at the officer and growled savagely once again.

Firmer, louder, she stated once again, "Heel, Max," and pointed at her side. Silently, she prayed, "Please God. Please help."

Max walked behind her and circled to her left and sat down, training his eyes once again on the officer, and then Officer McGill did a very strange thing. He moved his gun in the direction of Troy. He waited for the big man that he detested to flinch. He was disappointed.

"Go ahead," Troy stated dryly.

Suzanne's heart raced as she could not believe what was happening. She watched the officer and for a moment his finger on the trigger moved slightly and then he lowered his gun.

Troy's voice rose slightly above a whisper. "You're an idiot, McGill. You point a gun at my dog, me, and around a woman. I suggest that you put it away."

Troy wasn't sure what registered in the peanut size brain of Sean McGill. Maybe he came to his senses, what little there was of that. Slowly, he holstered his pistol.

By now Troy had a firm grip on Max's collar, who was growling softly. Troy moved in front of him and engulfed his mouth with his hand. He wanted eye contact with Max before he issued an important command. He grasped his mouth firmly and shook it slightly to get his full attention. Max looked intently into his eyes. Troy smiled at him. "Go home, Max. Go home, now," he said, gently. Max looked in the caring eyes of his master for several seconds and then he turned and ran home as commanded.

Troy relaxed as he watched him and then knowing what would ensue, he turned to the officer. "Do not open your mouth."

Officer McGill was caught with his mouth half-open. He was set to holler at Max.

"I'll need to impound that dog."

Troy stared intently at him. It seemed to Suzanne that minutes of unspoken tension eased by before she heard Troy speak. "McGill, I don't think that you will be taking my dog today."

"Well, you are not the law around here."

"And neither are you, Wyatt Earp." Before he could reply, Troy said, evenly, "If you got a problem with this take it up with Billy C . . ."

"Billy C. is a sergeant, not the chief," Sean answered defiantly.

Troy looked at the officer as silence hung heavy over them. Sean was 5'8", and almost that wide from lifting weights and more so from injecting steroids. His hair was red and receding rapidly for someone that was yet to see the age of twenty-five. His face was occupied by a plethora of freckles. He was, in Troy's opinion, the worst officer on the island and not just because he hated Troy. Every time a young lady at the club complained about harassment from an officer, Troy would describe Sean McGill to the lady before she could finish her story. As is typical in a small town the only reason that

Sean McGill kept his job was because his daddy was a big supporter of one of the Town Council members.

Suzanne broke the silence. "Max was playing. I was in no danger."

Sean nodded, and said, "I received a 911 call that a woman was being attacked. I had no choice but to draw my gun."

Troy took two steps toward him. "Prove it. You bring me the dispatcher's log of that call and maybe I'll bring Max in."

Troy knew from the look in the officer's face that he was caught in a lie. There was no call. It was a weekday and off-season. The sparsely populated boardwalk contained a few locals and they all knew Max. He was a friend of the community. Something this little over abundance of testosterone would never be.

"I'm going to get you one day, Dawkins. Count on it." He turned and walked away.

Troy started to reply but then he felt Suzanne's firm grip on his hand. He sighed and watched him walk away.

He looked at Suzanne. "Friend of the family," he said dryly.

"Yeah, boy," she replied with a slight whistle.

"That was good thinking to get Max to heel."

"I guess I brought a lot of problems you didn't want today."

Troy remembered how much Max had wanted to go after Suzanne and said, "Actually, all of this is Max's fault."

"Care to explain?" she asked, as her face narrowed.

"No," he stated. "Now, there is a place about two blocks from here that serves a great grilled chicken sandwich. Walk with me to my house so I can grab a shirt and we will get some lunch."

She was shocked at the turn of events and barely managed to mutter, "Okay."

They walked back to the cottage and he slipped on a faded yellow ECU baseball shirt and invited Max to come along. She watched as he knelt on the porch, rubbing and talking to Max for several minutes. He looked up and noticed her smiling at the love he was giving to Max. "I was just telling him that this is what happens when you allow a woman to become a distraction."

She smiled warmly.

She sat at the table and watched as he stood in front of the L shaped counter. The place was rustic to say the least. There were a few empty tables equipped with bar stools. The walls were weathered so dark they were nearly black. Uneven frames containing pictures of men holding huge fish were scattered roughly throughout. Interior decorating was not a priority in this establishment.

He returned with two paper cups containing sweet tea and sat on the barstool across from her. "So, why did you suggest lunch?" she asked.

"It was time to eat."

She smiled softly at him. "Lots of excitement today."

He shrugged nonchalantly and she knew he didn't care to talk about the main event of the morning.

She decided for another subject. "I guess you won't be returning to church."

"That is a fact."

"So, you are going to hold a grudge?"

"Your husband hardly merits a grudge."

The man behind the counter called his name and he walked to the counter and returned with their food. Two grilled chicken sandwiches, two small garden salads, and one order of seasoned fries.

He watched her as she bit into the sandwich. Her eyes lit with surprise. "Wow, this is great," she said, as she hungrily bit into it again.

"Things are not always as they appear."

She watched him smiling at her. "What?" she asked, not aware that there was a sliver of mayo at the corner of her mouth.

"Nothing," he said, as he reached across and dabbed the mayo away.

Slightly embarrassed, she followed up wiping her entire face with her napkin.

"It's okay. It's gone."

"Thanks."

They chatted during the remainder of lunch about their families. She did most of the talking. Telling him about her twin boys and about the move from Knoxville to Wilmington. They finished eating and Troy paid the man at the counter and stuffed a few bills in the tip jar. They walked outside. Max had slept obediently under the glass window just outside the door. He rose slowly to follow.

Troy yawned noticeably. "Sorry, but it is past my nap time. I have a kind of strange sleeping schedule."

She waited for him to continue and when he didn't she prodded him. "Tell me."

"By the time I get home from the bar and unwind enough to sleep it's two or three in the morning. If I am lucky I might sleep four hours. Usually I go back to sleep around noon for a good long nap. Even on days like today when I don't work I can't break the routine."

"When do you have to be at work?"

"Eight o'clock. Except on Sundays when we open earlier and close earlier."

"When do you lift weights?"

"What makes you think I lift weights?" He deadpanned.

"I'm not as dumb as I may appear to be," she stated dryly.

"After I wake in the afternoon."

They left the diner and walked along the boardwalk toward her car. She slowed and pointed to a sign. "Britt's Donuts. One of my guilty pleasures is two Krispy Kreme glazed donuts."

"Never make the mistake of comparing any donut to Britts. Not on this Island anyway."

"Good?"

"Beyond good. They open on the weekends in late March and close soon after Labor Day. This past Spring when they opened it was rainy and nasty."

"So a slow first weekend?"

"No. They open at four on Friday. There were so many people in line that they opened an hour earlier. People drive from two hours away for that first weekend. During the summer when they are open seven days a week you should expect a line. On big weekends like Memorial Day people stand in line for over an hour."

"For a donut?"

"No, for Britt's donuts. And not for a donut but for several donuts."

They continued walking until they reached her car. She started to open the door but stopped. "Thanks for lunch and for not running me off."

"Had to deal with you sooner or later."

"Maybe I would have given up."

He shook his head no.

"How do you know?"

"It's in your eyes. You don't give up." She heard a hint of sadness rooted in his words. Did he mean don't give up like me?

She then asked a question she knew immediately was a mistake and whatever goodwill she had built was quickly destroyed. "What is this trilogy of tragedy?"

His eyes grew harsh and his body stiffened. "Goodbye, Suzanne," he said, turning abruptly and walking away.

"Way to go, moron," she whispered to herself as she watched him swiftly put distance between the two of them.

9

TROY WAS EXHAUSTED when he returned to the cottage. He checked Max's water bowl and filled the food bowl beside it. He walked into the small bedroom and fell onto the bed. Max curled up on the floor beside him. They were both asleep in seconds.

The bad dreams that beleaguered him with their unwelcome visits usually did not come with the light sleep of early morning. It was the afternoon nap that usually rendered Troy his deepest sleep, and the nightmares often arrived like an obnoxious intruder, showing up rudely at a party with no invitation.

The dreams varied in intensity from bad to just plain horrifying. They visited and departed in continuing cycles. Sometimes they would leave for weeks and he would cling to a hope that they had left for good. The moment he seemed to let his guard down they returned with an even greater fury. Sometimes the power of the dreams was so severe that he was apprehensive to go to sleep. As he lay down today he had a bad feeling that the nightmares would attack without mercy. Sadly, he was right.

The dream was a familiar one. It began as it often did. He was young and throwing a baseball with ease, power, and pinpoint accuracy. The batters standing before him had no more chance to make contact than if he were throwing a Ping-Pong ball that danced in the wind and they were armed with only a toothpick.

Then his features changed and he aged rapidly before his eyes. He was elderly and frail. Each pitch he threw was hit rudely back at him as violently as a bullet leaving a rifle.

That scene departed, only to be quickly replaced by another. He was standing in a room behind little children. He could hear their laughter and it soothed him. He walked to them and placed his hand gently on one little blonde haired girl's shoulder. His hand felt wet and warm. He was smiling as he lifted his hand to inspect it. Terror consumed him when he saw the blood that covered his hand. All the children turned simultaneously toward him and he was horrified at what he saw. Their clothes covered with blood. They began to float about the room as he begged them to depart. Alana walked into the room clothed in a blood soaked ragged robe. She walked to him and touched the side of his face lightly. He stood frozen unable to move. "Why, Troy? Why did you not come sooner, before we were all gone?"

The room and the dead it contained vanished and he was in a graveyard. It was pitch dark, save the tombstones that surrounded him. They were illuminated brightly as if a spotlight shown on each one. As he walked toward the tombstones he discovered they were all members of the people he loved. He tried to escape but he was held in the circle by an unexplainable force. He sat down amongst the dead, empty and alone. There was no one left that cared about him. He wept bitterly and longed to join those that were departed.

He heard a dog barking furiously. He looked throughout the graveyard but could not locate the source of the sound.

Max continued barking loudly trying to wake his master from whatever was prompting his cry of anguish. He plopped his heavy paws on top of his chest and barked loudly just inches from his face.

Troy woke abruptly. He tried to focus his eyes. His heart was racing and his mouth was dry as dust. He kissed Max on top of his stout nose. "Thanks boy," he said as he sat up. "That was the worst one yet." Max compassionately laid his head on Troy's lap. Troy rubbed him for a few moments. He rose and walked to the fridge and retrieved a bottle of water. He drained its contents without pausing. He looked around trying to get his bearings and was thankful as always that it was merely a dream. Through the window he could see that it was late afternoon. The sun lay low in the sky.

He thought of the nightmare. "I'm sorry, Alana. I tried. God help me, I tried." And once again he asked, "God, where were you that night?"

Troy arrived at the club at eight o'clock along with Max. Normally the club was closed on Monday, but tonight they were open for a special group. The singer of the group was Stacey Storm and she was the sole reason that the group was here. Mabry was her teacher at East Carolina and like Troy she became a part of Mabry and Nate's family.

Mabry was seated at the bar drinking coffee. She usually left by ten before the crowd arrived. Still, for some of the bands she occasionally remained until the first set was complete. Sometimes, she even danced with some of the regulars before returning home to Nate.

The club was virtually empty. There was one bartender working and no bouncers except Troy. All that would change shortly. Three college students sat at a table getting a jump on the night's buzz. By ten o'clock there would be five bartenders slinging drinks aided by cocktail waitresses walking through the crowd taking orders. There would be seven additional bouncers working. Mabry's caring touch also included one parking lot attendant on duty to stop anyone that was impaired from getting behind the wheel of a car. The attendant would call a local cab company and if the patrons lacked the money Mabry had a standing agreement with the company that she would settle the debt the next day.

Troy was still listless from his afternoon nap and the dream that remained within him. The weightlifting session had failed to improve his mental state as it so often did. He sat down beside Mabry and asked the bartender for a Diet Sun-Drop.

Mabry considered his distant eyes and saw the weariness mixed with pain. Tenderly and lovingly, she patted him on the back. "Bad day, buddy?"

He looked ahead and said nothing. She studied his face in the mirror behind the bar. Gently she rubbed his wide back in a circular motion. "I heard about that idiot, McGill."

"It's not that," he answered.

She smiled as she continued to rub his back. "Nightmares?"

He nodded lightly.

"Do you want to go home?"

"That is the last thing I want to do," he replied evenly.

"I guess I owe you for working an extra night."

His face strained tighter in slight insult. "No, what you pay me for this job is more than fair."

"Let's go into the office," she suggested as she began walking that way not wanting to give him a chance to say no.

He followed her into the office, where Max was already curled up in a corner snoring. Troy plopped wearily onto the couch.

He was always reluctant to talk about his nightmares or the tragedies that had consumed his life to the point where he was not living as much as merely existing one long day after another. Surprising her, he spoke first. "Do you think these nightmares will ever stop?"

Her heart went out to the boy she looked at as a son. And in truth maybe she loved him even more than her boys, though she tried not to think of it in those terms.

"I think so. Some day . . ."

"I'll get a break," he said.

She nodded and said, "But maybe you need to get back out there in life. You spend too much time by yourself."

"I work. I go to the gym."

"When is the last time you dated anyone?"

He shook his head and looked away.

"I think there is someone special and wise enough to appreciate a man like you."

"You mean a man who wakes in a cold sweat from the dreams that haunt him? A man who works as a bouncer at an age when most are securing their retirement plans."

She spoke sternly to him. "I mean a woman who would see a man with a big heart. A man who never intentionally hurt anyone. A man who always keeps his word."

But I did hurt someone intentionally. You just don't know about it, he thought. "I must have done something wrong to deserve all that has happened. Maybe God is punishing me for …"

"I don't believe that for one second," she interrupted angrily. "I don't know why some people have so much misfortune thrust upon their lives. I am, however, certain that you did nothing to deserve it. And if I thought for one moment that God had anything to do with hurting you I would say the heck with God." She paused before adding softly, "We both know he is not that kind of God."

"I feel like if I allow anyone in my life that they might get sucked into my misfortune."

"And maybe you are due a break. Overdue," she stated, correcting herself.

"You know the first two times life floored me I managed to get back up. It took a lot of time and effort but eventually I did. I found my way back to times where I was optimistic about life, about the future."

He did not speak for minutes and Mabry waited patiently for him to talk. He ran his hand through his hair. "You think that there might be a good break waiting for you around the corner but then another break came and someone else died. And maybe I was the reason."

"You were not," she responded tersely. "He suffered a brain aneurism."

"But we were working so far from the hospital. If I had left him in his old job maybe he would have lived. I should have never asked him to go into business with me."

"Why do you think that he would have lived?"

"The plant had medical emergency people on staff and he wouldn't have been but a few miles from the hospital. But he was with me doing a job out in the country."

"There was no guarantee that he would have lived."

"I wonder if my sister blames me. She never wanted him to leave his job at the factory and go into business with me."

"Kent was happy being outside and working with wood. He hated working at that plant. He told you that and he would never blame you for one second. You are not responsible for your brother-in-law's death."

"Why do you fight so hard for me, Mabry?" he asked with the softness of a small child.

She felt tears rise quickly. "I could love you no more if you would have come from my womb."

She saw tears in his eyes that he would not allow to fall. He smiled at her with appreciation. He ran his hand through his hair once again. His eyes drifted far away from her as he softly said, *"Spend all your time waiting for that second chance, for a break that would make it okay."*

She looked puzzled. "What's that son?"

"A lyric to a song from a movie I once rented."

The leggy woman with long blonde hair, soft blue eyes, thin lips and rosy high cheekbones had appeared unnoticed in the doorway. She was in her early thirties and was strikingly attractive. She wore blue jeans, black high heels, and a loose fitting long sleeve white shirt. Her voice was slightly throaty as she said, "The song is *Angel*. It is by Sarah McLachlan."

They both looked up startled. "Sorry, I didn't mean to intrude. I thought I walked into a rock and roll Jeopardy show and was expected to answer."

Her slight laugh and smile was engaging. Mabry rose quickly to meet her. "Stacey, how are you?"

"I'm great," she gushed. "God, it is so good to see a familiar face," she said as she hugged her warmly.

"This is . . ."

Stacey extended her hand to him. "Troy," she said, finishing Mabry's introduction. "I have heard so many good things about you."

Embarrassed slightly, Troy stood and shook her hand. Her grip was firm and strong.

When he failed to reply, she remarked, "Oh, the strong silent type."

He was even more embarrassed now and it showed in his red cheeks.

"I'm sorry. I didn't mean to make you uncomfortable." She turned back to Mabry and hugged her again. "I've been touring for so long and it's so good to see a friendly face, Teach. I have been looking forward to this. I've been counting the miles. Man, the road is a lonely place."

"Now, how can a girl surrounded by thousands be lonely?"

"People wanting a piece of you for all of the wrong reasons."

She looked back to Troy. "I think it is safe to say we have something in common."

"What's that?" he asked, finding his voice.

"We both love this woman," she said as she looked at Mabry warmly.

She spotted Max and knelt down on the floor to pet him. He murmured appreciatively.

"You'll get dog hairs all over you," Troy warned.

"Who cares?" she said, not looking up as she continued enthusiastically rubbing Max, who desiring the full effect was now lying on his back with his belly exposed.

"Can I get you something to drink?"

She turned back to him. "Some coffee, black, if you don't mind."

He left the room. She gazed up at Mabry. "He's good looking. Does he have a girlfriend?" she asked jokingly but a spark of interest registered in her eyes.

Sadness enveloped Mabry's face quickly as she replied, "No, he's a loner. Bad things have happened to him. I would love for you two to be friends but please be careful. Don't add any confusion to his life." The emotion of his pain and the warm feeling from seeing Stacey overwhelmed her and suddenly tears flowed gently down her cheeks.

Stacey hugged her tightly and then pulled far enough away to look into her eyes. "Hey Teach. I don't play with people. I'm still the same girl you raised through college. What you and Nate taught me stays with me every single day of my life."

"I'm sorry. I know that. He has been hurt so much and I try so hard to protect him. He's had a bad day. It's a long story and then seeing you. Well it's a lot on an old lady's emotions."

Stacey grabbed a tissue from off the desk and dabbed the corners of Mabry's eyes. "You are good at taking care of people, Teach. You always were. I was all alone and feeling sorry for myself. My parents were two drunks that didn't know I was alive. Even with the academic scholarship I could never have made it through school. You gave me a job and you took me into your home and even better, into your life. None of this happens without you."

Mabry's kind face was streaked in tears. "So how long have you been on the road?"

"The better part of two years. One hit song and they won't let you go home until you have played it everywhere. But I'm tired and this is it. In no uncertain terms, I have told them I am taking a break.

They wanted me to sign up for another six-month tour and I told them absolutely not."

"You didn't have to play here. I know it is far smaller than what you are accustomed to."

"Hey, Teach. This is where I want to play. For you and Nate. Is he coming?"

"He will. He's home napping so he can stay up late. He's old, you know," she added with a slight smile.

She rolled her eyes and said, "Sure, as if either of you will ever be old." She embraced her once again. "It's been too long."

"I've got rooms for the band in the hotel, but Nate said you wanted to stay with us."

"Yes, I do and I want your out of this world French toast in the morning," she said smiling broadly. "Teach, the band is going home tomorrow. I was thinking about hanging around for awhile, if I could." She knew the answer before she asked.

"I would love that."

"Thank you, and let's allow people to think I flew out with the band. It's not as if everyone recognizes me or I can't do my own shopping still." She paused, uncomfortable to think of herself as some kind of star. "I just want privacy," she added. "So what kind of weekly rate can I get at the hotel?" She winked knowing Mabry would not take one penny from her.

Mabry kissed her lightly on the cheek. "I think we can work something out but you know that you can stay at the house as long as you want."

"I know. I'll stay a couple of days and then move into the hotel. I would like to look at the ocean and unwind. Maybe write some songs. But Nate and you are going to see so much of me that you will get sick at the mere sight of me. You never did teach me to cook and I'll get fat if I eat out every night."

Mabry smiled warmly at her. "Good. It's slow during the off-season so no one should bother you. I'll get you a room on the end overlooking the water and the stairs are right beside it so you can come and go quickly."

"That sounds great." She paused, unsure about whether to ask her next question. "Now, forgive me for being nosy but I know that I walked in on a heavy-duty conversation. The pain in his face and in yours."

She nodded in agreement. "It's a long story and there are parts that I don't know about. I don't ask because I can't stand the grief that emerges."

Stacey waited to hear more.

But all Mabry mumbled was, "He has bad dreams." Her eyes were in another place as Troy walked in with fresh coffee for the two of them.

Mabry took her coffee and said, "Show her around Troy, while I make a phone call."

Troy nodded slightly. "Yes, ma'am." Stacey was almost out the door when she stopped and turned back to Mabry. "Teach, do you think that I could stay through the holidays?"

Mabry smiled as her eyes glistened. "I was hoping that you would. You should be with family for the holidays. Now, Troy, escort this young lady out of here before she makes me cry again."

Troy obliged and when the door shut Mabry dialed the number of his friend, and the mother of his child.

She heard the voice on the other end. "Carla, he's hurting. He had a nightmare today. He didn't say what it was but I know that it was really bad."

"I'll be there in the morning," Carla answered.

Mabry placed the phone back on the desk. "God," she whispered. "Please give my boy a break."

10

CARLA AND TROY HAD BEEN best friends since they were eight years old. That was when Carla's family moved next door to Troy's family in a small community known as Sea Gate. It helped that she was a tomboy and loved to participate in every sport the boys played, including football. Troy never shied away from their friendship despite the ribbing he constantly endured.

Both left Wilmington to attend East Carolina. He went because he was offered a chance to try out for the baseball team. She attended to pursue a degree in nursing. They roomed together in a small cramped apartment off campus.

They were both coming out of relationships shortly into their sophomore year. Carla's relationship ended when she found out her boyfriend was cheating on her and Troy's ceased when his jealous girlfriend insisted he change roommates. He merely shook his head at her request and walked away.

They stayed up late one night drinking beer on the tiny balcony that overlooked the city. It was three in the morning when they kissed each other intimately for the first time. The night ended with them together in the same bed.

Troy left early the next morning for class. They both avoided each other the following day. Each of them was thinking the same thing. They had made a huge mistake.

He returned home at midnight and she was waiting up for him. They talked things out and discovered with great relief that they both were feeling the same way about the one night their friendship crossed over. They elected to put the night behind them and not allow it to destroy a relationship that had stretched on now for over a decade. They continued their friendship and during the following weeks it was as if what took place on a night when each was filled with pain and loneliness never occurred.

But Carla began to wake to morning sickness and she knew that she was pregnant. She struggled with the option of abortion. Troy never tried to encourage her in either direction. He did what he always had done. Be her best friend.

She chose to have the baby and months later, a baby girl, Heidi, was born with ruffled blonde hair like her mother and eyes the shape and color of her dad.

At the end of the semester, Carla moved back home to her parents' house and continued her education at UNC-Wilmington. Her mom kept Heidi during the day, while Carla pursued her degree and worked a part time job at the PT's Grille, near the college.

Troy came home every weekend possible though he was never allowed inside her parents' home again. Carla refused to allow him to quit school because she wanted him to get his education and also she knew what baseball meant to him. He had made the team as a walk on during his freshman year and by his junior year he was on a partial scholarship. He worked as a bouncer when time from class and baseball allowed it. In the summer, after the baseball season was over, he moved back to Wilmington and worked with a landscape crew. He aided the financial care of his daughter as best he could, and he willingly and lovingly spent much of his time with her.

After they both graduated Carla went to work at a local hospital. Troy worked different jobs in Wilmington as he struggled to find his way but his daughter never went without love or his financial support.

Carla's parents relentlessly tried to drive a wedge between their daughter and Troy, but she never allowed it to take root. As soon as she began her nursing career she rented an apartment where she could have the freedom to raise her child as she saw fit. It was needed freedom that allowed the father of her child to be actively involved in his daughter's life without interference from intrusive parents.

Heidi was seven when Carla married Ryan. Their marriage was a strong one that grew better with each passing year. Ryan loved Heidi like she was his own child but he never failed to recognize and respect the place of her father.

Carla explained everything to him about Troy when they were falling in love with each other. As much as Carla loved him she told him that he would have to understand that her best friend, and her daughter's father was always going to be welcome in their life, and if he could not abide by that without issue there was no need for the two of them to go further.

Ryan struggled at first with the scenario, but he loved Carla dearly, and in time he viewed Troy as part of the family.

Ryan and Carla had a son, Ren, two years after they were married. The godparent was Troy.

Troy and Carla's friendship that began as small children never wavered. Not by a new husband and child, and not by her parents trying to shove Troy crudely from the picture.

There was never a child support or visitation schedule authorized by the courts. They worked it out together with love and respect and by what they deemed best for their daughter.

Carla's parents once sent her to an attorney, a friend of the family to draft a will. The will, however, was only part of their scheme. After discussing the will the attorney attempted to persuade her to drag Troy into court to pay the going rate for child support and to reduce his time spent with Heidi. These were all instructions from her meddling parents.

Carla was a strong woman who took little grief from anyone. She stood and politely told him to crawl back under the same rock from which he had derived.

Her next course of action was to drive to her parent's house. She told them in no uncertain terms that this was the last straw. They could accept the fact that two consenting adults had spent one night together that resulted in a beautiful child and that there was no one at fault. To think otherwise was to think that her daughter was a mistake and not a gift from God. That was misguided thinking that she would have no part of. Furthermore, this was their last unwelcome intervention in the matter if they wanted to see their grandchild, or her, in the future. They never warmed to Troy but they refrained from ever prying into the matter again. They believed that their strong confident daughter would indeed carry out her ultimatums.

*

IT WAS EARLY THE NEXT morning when Carla knocked on Troy's door. Age had done little to diminish her natural good looks. She still wore her blonde hair long. She was dressed in blue jeans and a long sleeve coral shirt from Hawaii, courtesy of their daughter.

Heidi was in her last year of college in Hawaii. Her passion for surfing and love for her boyfriend Mike were the reasons she moved to Hawaii three years ago.

Mike was from Hawaii-- had never lived elsewhere and had no intention to ever leave. They met at a surf meet in Florida and things blossomed between them from their initial introduction. One month later she visited him at his home. She fell in love with him and with the surroundings. She came home and immediately began planning how to go back and stay. By the next fall semester, she was a student attending the same college as Mike.

Troy opened the door and smiled. He welcomed Carla with a warm hug.

He fixed coffee for each of them and they sat on the porch in the rocking chairs and looked out at the vividly blue Atlantic. The day was clear and cool.

"Mabry called," Carla said softly.

He nodded and stared out at the sea.

"The dreams are back?"

He sighed deeply. "They never really go away."

"Same type as usual?"

"Yes, but more graphic. Don't tell Heidi," he added.

She shook her head. "I won't." She put her hand over his and clasped it tightly. "We did so well. We couldn't have asked for a better daughter."

He nodded his head softly in agreement.

"Not for one second have I ever wished that it would have been anyone other than you to share her with." She smiled and took his hand. "Not even, Ryan, and he is the man that makes my dreams a reality."

She let go of his hand and looked out at the sea. "I'm surprised she hasn't felt the vibes and called you. I remember the times when she would look at me and say, "Mommy, daddy needs me tonight. She was so young. Sometimes, you would have just brought her back home."

His eyes glistened as he stared out at the serene waters. The softest part of his heart was where he kept his daughter safely tucked away. Often the mere sound of her voice from thousands of miles away would bring immediate tears. "She always knew the nights I needed her most. I always tried to bluff my way through it. Pretend that I would be fine. That I wasn't really hurting."

He paused and his face saddened. "She is mad at me now. She wanted me to visit her for Christmas. I told her I was going to the cabin in the mountains. She hollered at me. I can't ever recall her doing that."

Carla rubbed his shoulder gently. "Maybe you should go. Might meet some nice Hawaiian lady," she added with a chuckle. "Besides she just wants to show you her life there. Let's face it we have lost her to the State and to her future husband."

"I know. At least he is a nice guy. It's funny the way things happen. If Mabry fails to talk me into taking the job at the club and living here then my daughter probably never becomes the surfer girl that she is and she might be here now with us."

"Is that what you wish?"

"No," he said softly. "Obviously, I miss her, but I like to think that something good came out of what drove me here." His eyes lit up as if he could see her riding a wave at that moment. "I never cared about surfing but I often sat here and watched her ride for hours, or I drove her down to the north end in front of the rocks, where the break was usually better. She took to it so easily. She really angered the boys because she was better than most of them almost from the beginning."

He laughed softly at a pleasant memory.

"Please share."

Troy smiled and said, "One day a bunch of boys her age ganged up to shut her out of each wave she tried to ride. She came in to shore and sat with me and was so frustrated. It was the one time she was almost ready to quit something, at least for that one day.

"A man with his surfboard approached us, Robbie Johnson. You could see the compassion in his eyes, and he asked Heidi gently, what the problem was.

"Heidi told him and his tender eyes grew hard. I will handle this right now, he responded. Heidi asked him to just let it go but he would have no part of that. He walked to the edge of the water and called those boys in. He gathered them all together and he gave them a lecture we could not hear. We could, however, see those young boys drop their heads.

"Next, we saw him point to us and then seven, very humbled boys, gingerly approached us and apologized to Heidi and asked her to join them back in the ocean."

Troy chuckled once again. "Not only did they allow her to join them but anytime any other young surfer thought he would close her out on a wave the first line of defense was those same boys that terrorized her in the ocean that day. In fact, one obnoxious visitor from Wrightsville Beach was especially rude to her."

He laughed softly again. "One of her now defenders told the visitor to hit the beach. They both paddled in and dropped their boards in the sand. The guy from Wrightsville Beach said something very off color about Heidi and the next thing he knew he was laying on his back along the tide line with the ocean trickling around him. He picked up his board and left, never to return. The boy that defended our daughter that day merely picked his board up and paddled back out beside Heidi. He told her, 'Let me know if he ever comes back and bothers you.' And then he took off on the next wave like it never occurred. All of that because Robbie saw something one day he did not like and he took care of it. I will always be grateful to him."

Carla grabbed his arm. "You never told me this story before. Why did Robbie do that?"

"Robbie has one child as well, a daughter. And those boys knew his daughter and they knew Robbie and respected him. He had coached most of them in a youth basketball league at one time.

"Robbie told me after the boys apologized that day that they were good boys, but like we all did at that age, got a little too cute for their own good at times. I asked him what he said to the boys that humbled them so quickly.

"He told me that they were all friends with his daughter and he asked what they would do if someone was messing with her. The kids said, "Coach, you know we would take care of that."

He smiled at the boys and said, I know that you would. Now, you are going to do the same for that young lady sitting on the beach with her dad."

"The boys shuffled their feet and said, 'Yes, sir.'"

"Do you see Robbie around?"

"Occasionally he pops into the club early before all the kids get there. He will have a couple of beers and talk with me. There has never been one time that I saw him at the club or bumped into him on the Island that he has failed to ask about Heidi. He is a good guy with a heart of gold."

Silence passed as they watched two joggers run easily along the shore. "So, why don't you visit Heidi?"

"You know I go to the mountains during the holidays."

"I know. But you are alone so much. And at that holiday maybe you should go."

He rubbed his hand through his uncombed hair. "I know and I hate her being mad at me."

"Oh, she isn't mad. She never could stay angry with you. Me, maybe, but not her precious daddy."

"Jealousy doesn't become you," he deadpanned.

And just as when they were eight years old she punched him in the arm.

There was silence except for the slight noise the small waves made as they rolled onto the beach. "The dreams are more frequent of late. I just told Mabry about the last one. I kept the others to myself." He paused before adding, "I'm scared to go to sleep."

Her heart went out to him and her eyes moistened. "You have got to find a way to let this go."

"It is the aura of death that won't release me. A lady from the church came by the other day. She is or was a counselor. For a moment, I thought maybe I could talk to her, but . . ."

"But if you tell her *everything*."

"I know. We both would be at risk. I promised you that I would never speak of all that occurred that night." He turned to her and said, "And have I ever broken a promise to you?"

She answered him with a smile. "That's why you are my best friend and you always will be."

Her smile dissipated and she looked away from him and stared intently at the ocean. "Maybe it was unfair of me to make you promise not to speak of that night but it seemed the only way. We had a child that needed both of us. There was so much at risk and what was done was done."

He nodded softly in agreement, but said nothing.

Max nudged the screen door open and made his way to in front of Carla. He sat stiffly waiting for attention. She obliged, rubbing him behind his ears.

Carla perked up. "Hey, I hear that there was a big night at the club last night."

He nodded and failed to respond.

"How was the music?"

"Stacey and the band were good. It was a welcome change from the alternative and techno stuff I have to hear."

"I have her music on my IPod."

"Why didn't you call me? You could have come."

"I wish that I could have, but I was helping my young man prep for a math test. Did you talk to her?"

"Yes."

"What is she like?"

"Believe it or not, pretty much like a real person. Stardom doesn't seem to have gone to her head. Yet," he added.

"It probably won't. She belongs to Mabry right? Just like you."

"How well did her record do?"

"You might know these things if you stayed a little more current."

His face winced mockingly as if she had hurt him.

"How well did her record do?"

"49."

He arched his eyebrows and pursed his lips. "I think that Mabry wants me to pal around with her while she is here."

"Go ahead."

He said nothing and pretended to see a spot on Max's leg that needed immediate attention.

"Nothing ventured, nothing gained."

"What?" he asked innocently.

She smacked his hand. "There is nothing on Max's leg so stop weaseling out of this conversation. You should be ashamed for using Max in a blatant attempt to deceive the mother of your child."

She was one of four women in this world that could see right through him. He should have known better than to be nonchalant with her.

"Now," she demanded. "Tell me. Were you attracted to this lady? And bear in mind I already know the answer."

Absentmindedly he bent down and started to reach for Max's leg.

"You touch that dog's leg and I will swat you into next week," she said bluntly.

He looked up and found her eyes frozen on him. They carried a look of exhausted patience.

He smiled but found no change in her look. "Don't look at me like that."

"It seems to me that you can take a chance or be alone the rest of your life."

He looked at her and then looked away. He knew that she was right. She was always right when it came to him. It was possibly the only thing about her that he did not care for.

Gently, he spoke as if he did not want the words to travel far. "I guess that I hold on to the tiniest hope that I could meet someone and have something special. But it's hard to find someone at this stage of the game. I've dated for the sake of dating or to keep from being lonely. I'd rather sit home with Max than go through the motions. Besides, it does not really help the loneliness. Why are we talking about this? Look at her world and look at mine."

"So you choose to doom something to failure when you don't even know if she would go out with you on one date."

"Yes. I do," he said, trying to sound more confident about the matter than he actually was.

She playfully tapped his arm. "Spill it, buddy."

His eyes grew mischievous and he spoke as if he were a child. "Teacher told me that she thinks I'm good looking."

They laughed together. She rose from the rocker. "I have to go. Both my men say, hi and to come eat dinner with us," she said as she kissed him on the cheek.

"Okay, I will."

She was almost around the corner and nearly out of sight when he called to her. "Carla."

She stopped and looked back at him. The sunlight seemed to sparkle on top of her vivid golden hair. "Did I ever tell you that you are the best friend that I could have ever hoped for?"

She answered with a smile and blew him a kiss. "That road travels both ways."

11

SUZANNE SAT AT THE KITCHEN TABLE, munching on a blueberry muffin, drinking her favorite blend of Port City Java coffee, and reading the newspaper. Alan left yesterday for the trip to Israel and would be gone for close to two weeks. She couldn't remember when she last felt so tranquil. She felt a moment of remorse but quickly dismissed it.

She gazed out the window. The birds were singing in flawless pitch about what a glorious day it was. She walked out on to the back deck and felt the warmth of the sun. The sky was a rich blue and there was not a cloud to be seen.

Troy came to mind again as he often had since her insertion of foot in mouth that day. Her mind drifted to a picture she saw in Mabry's office and then she had what she perceived to be a great idea to bridge the gap with this man that intrigued her so.

She was rummaging through old boxes in the garage when she found what she was looking for. Two worn baseball gloves and a baseball from when her boys had played in high school. She took them into the house and stuffed them into a small black duffelbag.

*

It was mid-morning and she was hoping that Troy would be sitting on the beach. She parked in his drive and walked past the house. He was sitting in his beach chair, reading *The Death of Santini* by Pat Conroy. Max sat by his side studying the ocean.

She walked around in front of Troy. "How are you? Great day, don't you think?"

He looked in her face and then his eyes moved to the bag she had in her right hand. He gazed back up at her.

She knelt and began fishing in the bag for the gloves and ball. She pulled the contents from the bag and smiled proudly at her idea. "I thought that we could play catch. And don't patronize me about being a woman. My boys got their athletic ability from me not their father."

His eyes were away from her now-- lost in the ocean. It was as if his face was now concealed behind smoked glass. She had hurt him as surely as if she had taken a baseball bat and struck him beside the head. But this pain was deeper than any inflicted externally. She knew that as certainly as she knew that the Atlantic Ocean rest behind her.

"Why is everything I do wrong when it comes to you? I just wanted to help or maybe I thought we could be friends? It's not as if I have any here."

He sat in silence his eyes still pealed on the ocean, refusing to acknowledge that she was still present. She wiped the tears of frustration from her eyes as she stuffed the gloves and ball back into the bag. She walked away dejectedly. He made no attempt to persuade her to stay and even Max sensed that it was out of his persuasive power to alter the events born from a bad idea.

*

IT WAS NEARING MIDNIGHT. Mabry's was slower tonight than usual. Troy stood against the wall surveying the area. He had a keen eye for spotting trouble before it happened. Rarely was a punch ever thrown in the club. Much of it was because of who was allowed in the door. Usually he worked near the door. That was the place to stop trouble the most effectively.

The club was private, which granted him much leeway with allowing non-members access. Those he didn't want to allow inside were given an application and told to fill it out and mail it to the club. The undesirables seldom went to that extreme and if they did their applications were politely denied. Technically what the club was doing skirted on the illegal side but the police looked the other way. This was one club that they seldom received a call to visit. It was one less headache for an overtaxed Carolina Beach police force to deal with.

Michael was working the door. He was Troy's best employee. He was near Troy's height but his body makeup was far different. He was slender and each muscle was hard and striated. His body fat was less than five percent and it showed in the deep indentions in his six-pack abs.

Troy liked Michael. He was dependable, honest, and always willing to learn. He was twenty-two and raising his two-year old daughter, Tomeika, aided with the help of his mother. There was no mother in the picture as far as Troy knew and he certainly was not one to ask.

Michael dropped out of college initially to support his daughter but now he attended on a part time basis working toward a business degree. He worked full time at the club and part time in construction. His schedule was taxing. He took care of his daughter, kept up with school well enough to keep his GPA in the 3.5 range, and worked. Troy never once had heard Michael complain about his circumstances.

There were two couples at the door. The guys were quiet, decent looking fellows but the two women with matching puffy blonde peroxide hair were intoxicated and loud. Drunken women who thought everything they said was cute was a quick way to trouble. One commented about how handsome Michael was.

Michael's features were smooth. His hair was cropped close in military style. His strong chin jutted out slightly.

But despite comments about how handsome he was they were turned away. The girls argued intensely for a few minutes but he refused to budge from his stand. "There are bars that way," he said, pointing in the direction of the boardwalk.

Michael looked across the club at Troy. Troy gave an ever so slight nod of approval.

Michael turned back to the door and watched the blondes and their companions disappear down the boardwalk. He was wondering if their hair was that big naturally or if they styled it that way. He chuckled softly at his next thought. Why would they want to? The attractive lady approaching him interrupted his thoughts. Lady was the term that came to his mind because she was older than the normal clientele. She was dressed in black jeans and a hunter green long sleeve shirt. It was from a 10K race that she had run in Knoxville.

He felt Troy's hand on his shoulder. "She looks like trouble. Should we allow her inside?"

"Your call, Boss."

She smiled at Michael nicely and walked inside. She stopped at Troy. She forced a sad smile and said, "I'm sorry, Troy. I couldn't leave things the way they were. I hurt you and I don't know why. But I didn't mean to."

He had felt bad about what happened ever since she left the beach, or more accurately that he had run her off. Maybe it was the pain in his life that made him feel guilty to be a source of hurt to anyone else. "I know you didn't. I owe you the apology. You were just trying. I started to go after you but I just didn't. Believe it or not I'm not as big a jerk as you may think."

She touched his arm. "I don't think that at all."

They moved away from the door and walked toward the bar. The band finished their last song and began to pack up.

They were at the bar now and Suzanne ordered a Corona with lime. She placed her money on the bar.

The bartender looked over her shoulder. Troy slightly moved his eyes. "This one is on me ma'am," the bartender said with a smile.

"Thank you," she said. She turned back to Troy. "Thanks."

He studied her a moment. "Isn't it kind of late for you to be out?"

"Alan is in Israel. I'm glad too. Isn't that bad?"

"No. Not if that is how you really feel."

They walked to a corner and sat on bar stools around a small table. "I bet you really do always say just what you think."

He shrugged his shoulders slightly. "Either that or I say nothing. I do that frequently also as you may have noticed."

She smiled back at him. "It certainly beats being dishonest." She drank from her beer. "Do the people usually leave right after the band stops?"

"It varies. When I am ready for them to leave earlier, like tonight I play tunes on the jukebox. Tunes that I specifically ordered."

"What type tunes?"

"Old stuff, like the Allman Brothers."

"As in really old when Duane was playing?"

"Yes."

"But I love that music."

"I do as well but this is an alternative crowd for the most part and they don't."

"Pretty slick. Why don't you try it, now? Do you have *Sweet Melissa*?"

She watched him walk toward the jukebox. He was dressed in khaki shorts and a black T-shirt with Mabry's on the back and staff in small letters across the front. As he walked back toward her the sounds of "Sweet Melissa" filled the air.

She watched the remaining twenty people. Their faces looked as if they had just stepped in dog poop. Four of them left but the remaining crowd stayed huddled near the bar.

"Doesn't always work." Troy laughed. "I only do it when it's just a few people. I would never do it if there was a lot of money still being spent. Mabry might get upset with me and for sure the bartenders would."

She smiled and replied, "I don't think that Mabry would get too upset with you over anything."

"Oh, you would be surprised. She is still the teacher."

Her beer was empty. "Do you want another?"

"It is a long drive. How about a bottle of water?" she said, as she reached in her purse.

His head shook slightly. "That's okay." He walked behind the bar and retrieved a bottle of water.

"Thanks."

"Are you hungry?"

She thought for a moment and remembered that her dinner had been one protein bar. "I could eat," she responded.

"There is a place on the boardwalk that opens right about now. They serve breakfast from one to noon. They catch the late bar crowd, the night owls who can't sleep, and the morning breakfast crowd."

Moments later they walked to the door, stopping at Michael. Troy made the proper introductions. "Would you mind closing down tonight, Michael?"

"No problem, Troy. Can I play "Freebird" and really clear this place out?"

"You may."

"Good, you know how I enjoy the looks I get when they see a black man playing a southern redneck song."

They stepped out into the cool night. "Have a good night, Boss."

"Good night, Michael. Bring Tomeika by. Mabry said she hasn't seen her in a long time."

"Sure thing."

The wooden planks thumped slightly as they walked. Suzanne rubbed her hair back in the breeze and drank in the salt air. The ocean roared in the distance.

"Are you worried about what your church might say about you being out in the night life this late?"

"No. I'm not. Besides I don't think that we will be running into any of them."

"Don't be so certain. Wilmington may have tripled in size since I was a boy but when it comes to who knows what about who, it is still a relatively small town."

They walked in silence for a few minutes. She placed her hand on his arm. "Troy, can I tell you something and you try to accept it?"

He nodded.

"Alan used to be a minister, a person that you would have liked. He just got lost somewhere along the way."

"Do you think that he will find his way back?"

"No. I don't believe that he will."

"Where does that leave you?"

"I don't know."

"You're lonely living here."

"Yes. Especially since the boys aren't here. Alan doesn't even know them anymore. He is so sure about everything. He doesn't even know that while his two sons do indeed live together, their girlfriends live with them. I would rather they not do that but it reaches a point when you allow your children to find their own way. If Alan knew he would react in a holier than thou manner that would only drive them further away. Love, encouragement, lending hope is what reaches people. It is certainly not a bunch of religious rhetoric and judgment."

It was silent again before he broke the quiet with a pertinent question. "How long have you been thinking of leaving him?"

She studied his eyes. The intensity they so often carried was gone. She saw compassion. Someone who far too well understood pain and did not want others to suffer it.

"Never seriously until shortly after we moved here."

"What will you do if you were to leave?"

"I don't know. Move back to the mountains maybe. Maybe be a psychologist," she said. Suddenly she shook her head as if she were having a private debate with herself. "No. I don't think that I even want to do that anymore. I like trying to help people and believe it or not some people find me easy to confide in. But being in a practice would be different than just trying to help people. Maybe I don't want to take money for other people's misfortunes. Maybe I should find a way to live a happy life myself before I try to help others." She forced a laugh. "Boy, am I babbling or what?"

They entered a small diner. The smell of hash browns cooking filtered through the air. The floor was bare concrete and the walls a dinghy white. They sat in a booth in the corner.

The waitress approached them to take their order. Her aged face was leathery from too much time in the sun. There were deep creases outside her eyes. Her hair was dyed jet black and worn in a dated beehive. The white apron she wore was spotted with coffee stains and grease. She smelt of cheap perfume, nicotine, and grease. She was probably younger than either of them but the weariness of life made her appear as if she was in her mid-fifties. Troy and Suzanne ordered link sausage, scrambled eggs with pepper jack cheese, hash browns and orange juice.

It was just past two when they walked toward her car. The boardwalk was nearly desolate as Troy told her about Heidi and Carla.

As they neared the club Michael was standing outside with Max. "I think Max was scared you had forgotten him."

Max bounded toward his master as if he had not seen him in days. Troy smiled at Max and rubbed his back firmly. "Thanks, Michael. You didn't have to wait with him. He would have been fine in the office until I got back."

"No problem. I was just going to let him out for a little while before I left. I'll see you tomorrow. Good night, ma'am." He walked away from them toward his car.

"He's nice, but I wish he would drop that ma'am stuff. It makes me feel old."

He chuckled softly. "It's not an age issue. It's being a southern gentleman. He was raised to treat women with respect and politeness. I feel sorry for women that are insulted by a man holding a door for them or calling them ma'am. They think it somehow is demeaning when it is just a case of being a southern boy, and in my case, being raised by a southern mother and grandmother."

She smiled at the somewhat lengthy dialogue coming from him. "I understand. I am from Georgia."

"Well, I had you pegged as a northerner. You don't speak southern all that fluently."

"I did grow up on the north side of the house. Maybe that is it."

They were at her car now. She sat on the hood. "Thank you, Troy. You made a bad night much better."

He said nothing. She studied him for a moment. "Do you think we could be friends if I don't attempt to analyze you?"

His eyes narrowed at the thought, and then his face lightened like a mischievous school boy. "Preacher's wives have mean bouncers for friends?"

"Not currently, but I would like to think that it might be a possibility."

There was silence and then Troy looked over her as if he were focusing on an object in space. His voice was low, expressionless, as he began to speak.

"I went to East Carolina because the coach, Ed Wilson, gave me a chance to walk on the baseball team. The offer came because my high school coach, Jack Humphrey, urged him to give me a shot. They once played on a minor league team together in the Braves organization. It didn't matter how I got a chance as long as I got one.

"I was always a smart pitcher but coming out of high school I lacked the power that colleges want. I made the team but for the first two years I never entered a game. Between my sophomore and junior year I had a late growth spurt. I grew two additional inches and put on fifteen pounds. Something happened to my arm, too. When baseball resumed that spring I was throwing harder than I ever had.

"The good thing was that for all those years I had to get by with being a smart pitcher. I won by outthinking the hitter. I knew how to mix my pitches and I could place the ball where I wanted to on a consistent basis. So I had those tools and suddenly, I had power to go with it. I was clocked once during my junior year at 97 m.p.h. By the end of the season I was the ace of the staff. I finished with a 13-2 record. Scouts started to show up the latter part of the season. I was projected to be picked among the first thirty players in the Major League Draft that summer."

He paused as he thought about a decision that had cost him so much.

"What happened?" she asked eagerly.

"I decided to stay for my senior year. The coach, Ed Wilson, had stuck with me when no one thought I should be on the team. I didn't think it was right to walk away. I wanted to extend the same loyalty that he gave to me. He tried to talk me out of it but I refused to leave and take my big pay day."

She watched as the pain surfaced again in his eyes and without thinking she gave his arm a reassuring grasp.

"Everything was great the next year. I was pitching even better. I had lost once all year, a 1-0 game against Miami. Now, I was projected to be a top five pick. The Red Sox were picking fourth and they were very interested. It was a childhood dream because I love the Red Sox.

"It was late May and we were playing Old Dominion. It was a beautiful afternoon. The sky was a vivid bright blue and there was not a cloud in sight. Days that were created with baseball in mind.

"It was the eighth inning. I had given up one hit, a dribbler down the third base line that the leadoff batter legged out. The score was 3-0 and I never felt more in control of any situation in my entire life.

"Almost every pitch was exploding into the catcher's mitt exactly where I wanted it to. I had struck out seventeen batters. My catcher and I were so in sync that it felt to me as if there were only the two of us on the diamond. The hitters were mere annoyances that were scarcely noticed. The stands were full of scouts pointing radar guns at my pitches.

"I struck out the first hitter in the inning and had two strikes on the next. I was going right after him with the next pitch, high and inside with lots of smoke. But when I threw it the ball landed harmlessly on the ground twenty feet up the third base line. I don't remember any pain at that time but I think I heard a slight pop. I took a practice pitch and the ball landed halfway between the mound and the plate. It was as if my arm was no longer attached to my body. "The labrum in my shoulder had torn. I had surgery and I rehabbed for a year but I never threw hard again."

"And if you would have left the year before, you would have made a lot of money."

He nodded in agreement and said, "My daughter would have never wanted for anything. But . . ." He was silent again for a few moments. He shook his head and smiled sadly. "I found out later that the pitch I threw right before the one that took my arm was clocked at 101 m.p.h. I remember the hitter wanting to swing and not having the time to react. My catcher told me later that he muttered under his breath, how in the hell am I supposed to hit a lightning bolt?"

"What makes you think that Heidi ever did want for anything? I bet she has always had food, clothes, and most important a dad that loved her?"

"It doesn't hurt that she has the best mother in the world."

"Give yourself a break."

He ignored her and continued. "So, I turned from anything to do with baseball after that. Maybe it would have been different if I had a son."

"Were you disappointed that you had a girl?"

"No," he answered quickly. "I was just glad that she was healthy. But at the time I thought that one day I might meet someone and have more children. Maybe even a boy who would want to throw baseball with me."

"So that is why you have that scar on your shoulder."

"I know it is not as sexy as a knife wound," he said with a wry smile.

Suzanne knew not to press for any more answers. He had confided in her and though she had countless questions dancing in her head she refrained. She would not repeat her bonehead mistake.

"I'm sorry that I brought the gloves and ball."

"How could you have known? You better go home."

She nodded in agreement. "I think I'll sleep easy now." She rose from the hood and hugged him. "I had fun tonight."

"Be careful getting home."

She got into her car. She put the window down. "So, can we?"

"Can we what?"

"Be friends."

She waited for an answer and when he was about to reply she interrupted. "I know. You can't get past that whole preacher's wife thing. You're right. After all, what would the congregation think?" She pursed her lips and her eyes narrowed. "Who cares?"

He feigned being shocked, clutching at his heart. He waved and walked away. Max, obediently heeling by his side.

12

THE EXTENDED INDIAN SUMMER that had basked the area with warm, comfortable temperatures departed hastily the day before Thanksgiving. It was late morning as Stacey sat on the couch in flannel boxers, a heavy dark blue sweatshirt, and gray wool socks that nearly rose to her knees. She perused her outfit and decided it was not exactly fashion statement material. She chuckled softly in her attempt to be warm. She gazed out the window at the block of grayness. It was a day when you could feel the cold outside even from the comfort of a warm room. She shuddered slightly looking at the dreary day. The wind outside howled vigorously and the building seemed to vibrate with each gust.

She was spending each day doing practically nothing and loving each minute of it. The last two years proved rewarding but exhausting as well. Still, she was grateful for her big break. Finally, after playing in countless bands she hit the proper mix at the right time.

She knew the day that she wrote *Watch Me* that she had something special. It was a song detailing the abuse she had suffered as a young girl and it was her not so subtle reply to her parents.

Parents, who had reminded her daily that she would never amount to much.

But here she was, thirty-four years old, and while she was not Alicia Keys by any stretch, she was doing okay. She wasn't rich but she had been smart with the money she had made. The public was fickle and she did not assume that they would stand in line to buy her next record. It helped her as well that the vices that ran unrestrained through the industry did not touch her. She drank a couple of glasses of wine occasionally but she had never touched drugs and she never would. She also did not sleep around or have multiple relationships on her resume. She sighed heavily as she recalled just how long it had been since she had a man in her life.

Her thoughts drifted to Troy and produced a smile. The smile departed as quickly as it came when she thought of the great lengths he seemed to go to avoid her. It was as if he was afraid of her. As crazy as it seemed she had been attracted to him long before she ever met him. She would sometimes stare dreamily at the pictures of him in Nate and Mabry's home when she was a college girl.

Nate and Mabry, kept her on a proper path from the time Mabry rescued her. She was where she was primarily because of them, and she would never do anything to disrespect or disappoint them. As far as she was concerned they were her true parents, and for that she would always be grateful to God.

Much of her time on the road was spent alone in hotel suites but it was different in this small hotel room. She was relaxed. There was no concert tonight or planes to catch. No people to meet.

The solitude in this room did not produce the loneliness of being on the road. She spent time with Mabry during the days and joined Nate and her for dinner nearly every night. She was the daughter they never had. Their love and support had more than balanced out what she failed to receive from her birth parents.

The last she heard from her parents was when her mom ran off with yet another man. This time to California, several years back. Her dad died shortly after that during one of his alcoholic binges. She had no idea where her mother was today, or if she was even alive.

She grew up an only child in Princeton, North Carolina. Her parents were alcoholics as long as she could recall. Mom would get drunk and think every man was charming. She was known affectionately as the town whore and she did little to dispute her title.

Dad was the type of mean drunk that no one wanted to associate with when he was drinking. Trouble was no one could recall a time when he wasn't drinking. Subconsciously, she rubbed her jaw as if she could feel the sting of one of his many backhanded slaps. It was better when they expended their energy fighting with each other as they customarily did. That way she avoided being the brunt of their brutality.

She bent and picked up the guitar from the floor. She strummed it and thought about the struggle to escape her parents.

She was accepted at East Carolina on a partial scholarship. She left her hometown on a bus with three hundred dollars that she saved working at a local diner during high school. All her belongings packed in one oversized travel bag.

She worked the late shift at Krispy Kreme to pay her way. Often, she worked all night and then went home to her tiny roach infested apartment to shower and dress for school. She slept in the late afternoon and early evening. One good thing about the night shift was when it got slow, as it did in the dead of night, the manager allowed her to study.

It was near the end of her first semester when God sent her a sorely needed angel. Mabry was the one that rescued her, but she always believed that God orchestrated the deal.

Mabry was one of her professors that semester. On a night when Mabry was troubled about an incident that occurred that day in school with a fellow professor, she did something she never did in the middle of the night. She went for a drive to try and sort through her day.

It was two in the morning when she decided to stop for a doughnut and a cup of coffee. She was surprised to see Stacey working when she knew that she had an eight a.m. class. She knew because it was her class.

Stacey was shy and kept to herself but she was a bright student. She sat up front each day and paid strict attention. Mabry liked her.

The Krispy Kreme was empty except for the night manager and Stacey. She sat at a booth and ordered a chocolate doughnut and a cup of decaf coffee. She asked Stacey to sit and talk.

It took a while but gradually she got Stacey to open up and explain why she had to work all night to make ends meet. Stacey had tears in her eyes but undeniable grit in her voice when she stated, "Professor Wood, I can't go back home. I have to make it. I don't care if I have to live on stale doughnuts, so help me God I won't return home."

Mabry reached across the table and touched her arm and held it firmly. "You won't have to. Now young lady let's tell your boss that you are quitting."

"What? I can't do that."

"Yes, you can. And you will. You are going home with me, right now. My husband, Nate has an architectural firm. He needs someone to help in the afternoons. You can work for him. And you can live with us. We have an extra room." She had created this new position with Nate at that very moment.

The tears rolled down Stacey's face. Mabry smiled at her and said, "Today you can skip my class and all your other morning classes. I want you to sleep in and get some rest. I don't want to see you in my class again with dark circles under your eyes. You call me this afternoon after you are fully rested and Nate and my two sons will pick you up and get you moved."

The memory of that night brought tears to Stacey now just as it had then and every time she reflected upon it. "Thank you, God," she whispered, wiping the wetness from her cheeks.

She lived with them for the next three and a half years. They became her friends and in time the parents she never had. Todd and Kevin referred to her as their little sister. She never returned to Princeton again.

She strummed the guitar and began singing.

Jesus loves me.

This I know.

For the Bible tells me so.

Little ones to Him belong.

They are weak but He is strong.

Outside the door Troy paused from knocking and leaned closer to the door to hear. It reminded him of his mom and being a little boy. It was a time when God painted the skies, baseball cards were a simple pleasure, and life was free from night terrors.

When she stopped he knocked on the door.

"Who is it?"

"Troy."

"Can you wait a minute?"

"Sure, but all I need to do is to tell you about dinner tomorrow. Mabry asked me to come by."

Almost silently, Stacey said, "Why didn't she just call?"

"She wants you to come by at four. That's all I needed to tell you. I'm going to go."

"No. Wait. Okay?"

He stood awkwardly in front of the door. His hands shoved into his pockets. Finally, he relented. "Okay."

She rushed to the bedroom and grabbed her jeans off the floor and shimmied into them. Quickly she moved to the bathroom and brushed her unruly hair. Next, she wiped the wetness from her cheeks. She was running across the floor when she tripped over her guitar and crashed to the floor just short of the door.

"Hey! Are you okay?" He pounded on the door.

She rose to her knees and opened the door, looking up at Troy's puzzled expression. She surprised him by singing, "Do you want to see me crawl across the floor?"

Looking down on her with a smirk, he dryly stated, "Eric Clapton, 'Bellbottom Blues.' You are not the only one who can answer Rock and Roll Jeopardy questions. Well, that is as long as the questions are old," he clarified. He reached out his hand and helped her up.

"Are you always this graceful?"

She straightened up slowly, checking to make sure all her parts remained in order. She cast an annoying look in response to his question. He was dressed in black shorts and a long sleeve deep blue T-shirt. "It's what, forty degrees outside and you are dressed in shorts? Are you nuts?"

"That is a subject of great debate in various circles," he answered curtly.

"I think I liked you better when you didn't talk."

He stood in the doorway as she walked toward the couch, sat and observed him. He was yet to move in any direction. "Come in and close the door."

"It's okay. I am just delivering a message."

"Are you scared of me?" she asked with slight agitation in her voice.

"No."

"Then come in. I do not bite." He stood frozen. "I promise," she added.

He closed the door and entered. She gestured toward the couch for him to sit. She turned to face him pulling her legs up on the couch and sitting on her feet.

"Tell me about Thanksgiving dinner, please."

"Mabry said we would eat at four but she would like it if you would come earlier and help her. Actually, I think she would like it just fine if you would move in and never leave."

"Is Mabry's adopted son jealous of her adopted daughter?" Her expression flashing a hint of rascality in her smile.

"How did you guess?" he asked dryly, avoiding eye contact with her.

"Who will be there?"

"Knowing Mabry, who knows?"

"She is a saint, isn't she?"

"Well let's just say that if she doesn't get rubber stamped through the Holy Gates then I know where my future lies."

"Who do you think will be at dinner for sure?"

"Michael, one of my bouncers, his daughter, Tomeika and his mother for sure, and you."

"What about you?"

"I will eat lunch with my family. Lots of fun to be had there," he added sarcastically. "But I drop by Mabry's later."

"What about her sons, Todd and Kevin?"

"They are going to be with their wife's families this year."

They sat uneasily as silence filled the room.

"I heard you singing. I mean when I was outside the door."

"Surprised?"

"By what?"

"My choice of song."

"No, not really."

She stared intently at him. "I don't think that I believe you. I think that despite what you hear that you think I am a lot different than you. Big star, big ego, lots of men. Hung up on fame and fortune. You know all the labels."

He sat there stiffly in silence, before replying, "I don't know you. I don't think badly of you."

She noticed his head drop slightly and his eyes seem to find something interesting on the floor. Softly but firmly she asked, "Troy, please look at me."

He lifted his head but his eyes remained distant.

She touched the side of his face lightly. "No, please really look at me. I have enough people who think they know me but they don't listen to me."

His eyes found hers.

She smiled softly at him as she removed her hand from his face. "That's just it, Troy. You do know me. We slept in the same room during college. I was a student just like you, struggling to make it through difficult times. Mabry saw something in us that others could not see. Maybe that even we could not see in ourselves. And she wanted to help us overcome the obstacles that were impeding us.

"With me it was coming from an abusive family with no money and trying so hard not to return to that. I wanted to make it. At the time, I didn't know it would turn out to be music. I didn't even know that I had any talent at the time because I never sang except when I was alone."

Troy squinted for a moment. "And with me it was someone she wanted to look beyond baseball and keg parties."

"She told me about what happened with baseball."

He said nothing.

"Back when I was in college. I saw pictures of you and I asked who you were. Naturally, I was interested because you were also someone that they adopted into their family. I guess I always felt a certain connection with you, because of our similar paths."

He was quiet as she looked in his sparkling blue eyes and wondered what was behind them. "Troy, if I tell you something do you think you could please believe it? Believe me?"

He saw the earnestness in her eyes. "You don't have to convince me of anything," he answered delicately.

She smiled at him and said, "Yes, but I do." She waited for him to speak but he did not. "Troy, I do not think of myself as a star. This could be over in a year."

"And if it was?"

"I'd be fine. I'll always sing and write music and I hope that people want to listen. But if it comes down to sharing a song with a few friends in a coffee shop that will be okay."

Troy nodded his belief and rose from the couch. "I'm going home. I'll see you tomorrow."

She rose to walk him to the door. "Are you going to work out today?"

"Yes."

"What time?"

"Probably around four."

"May I go with you?"

He hesitated.

"I know my way around a gym. You won't have to babysit me. In case you haven't noticed I am in pretty decent shape."

"I noticed."

"Well, I'll be."

"I'll be here at quarter to four," he said, as he walked out the door.

"Troy," she called out.

He turned back to her.

"Thank you."

"I don't mind you going to the gym, really."

"Not for that."

He looked at her and waited.

"For believing me."

He nodded his head ever so slightly with understanding. "It was important to you. Sometimes people just really need someone to listen and believe in what they say, and who they are."

Her eyes opened slightly as the words reached her.

He looked away and then looked back at her quickly "I am sorry if I ever led you to think I thought anything bad about you. It was not intentional and my actions have far more to do with me than anything or anyone. Don't take it personal. Don't take me personally," he added.

He turned and walked away. She watched him disappear behind the door to the stairs. "That might prove rather difficult," she said in a hushed whisper.

*

AT EXACTLY FIFTEEN MINUTES till four he returned. She met him at the door in long black Lycra pants and a long sleeve white T-shirt. She wore a black baseball hat and her long ponytail hung through the hole in the back. She grabbed a teal and black hoodie off the couch. North Face was written in large white letters across the front. "Thanks for allowing me to tag along."

He nodded his response.

They were at the gym ten minutes later. She went straight to a stair stepper and was sweating furiously within minutes. He went toward the free weight area and began bench pressing.

After thirty minutes on the stepper she began working out with a combination of free weights and machines. He observed her form and routine. She obviously knew what she was doing.

After forty-five minutes of working his chest, shoulders, and triceps he began riding the recumbent bike. A few minutes later she joined him on the one next to him.

They stared out in silence at the scant few people that were present the afternoon before a major holiday.

She motioned toward a guy who was talking with a woman who had arms the size of a muscular man. He was wearing long black and yellow jungle pants and a green bodybuilder shirt with an image of a big man squatting heavy weight. The shirt had an oversized opening around the neck. Maybe it was to get his inflated head through.

"Why don't you dress like that?"

"I think not."

"Do you know him?"

"Yes. He is usually part of a group that lifts together. They dress the part and scream critical stuff at each other like 'big chest.' 'You the man.' They've asked me to join them but I respectfully decline."

"You don't go for that I take it."

"No. I lift weights quietly and alone. I focus on what I am doing and I don't want my concentration spoiled by some idiot that thinks I need to be shouted at to be motivated."

She watched the girl strut across the room to the water fountain. She was wearing black spandex shorts that were so small that the bottom of her behind spilled rudely out of them. Her top was multicolored and struggled to corral her 38 double D implants. She covered her chest with a light Gold's Gym jacket, which she strategically unzipped down to the bottom of her cleavage.

"Do you know her?"

"Not really. She won the state bodybuilding championship a couple of years ago and that was not enough so she really started in with the juice. She won a national contest out west this past summer. Now she struts around the gym like everyone is in her way."

"Did you ever do steroids?"

She could tell by his expression that he had been asked that often. "No. I got big from hard work and six meals a day."

"I didn't mean to insult you. You are just so big. When did you start lifting weights?"

"I began in high school and then more seriously in college, especially when I was rehabbing my injury. My body responded quickly to the weights. Too bad my shoulder didn't."

There was silence for several moments as she thought of what was the right thing to say. Maybe it was to say nothing, but she was not as adept at being still like he was.

"That was a hard blow. I'm sorry that it happened to you. You paid a hard price for being loyal, but I think you should be proud of being the type person who believes in things like that. The type of honor that often seems outdated in this day and time."

He looked at her and wondered if Mabry had left out any details about his life. He looked away when the haunting memory of the night Alana died suddenly came to him. That was one story that even Mabry didn't know the details of.

They pedaled five more minutes in silence and departed for the beach. He dropped her off behind the hotel, though the place was so deserted that she felt certain no one would know that she was a minor celebrity.

She was about to close the door to the Jeep when she asked hurriedly, "Would you like to come back for pizza later?"

Without giving it much thought he nodded. "Do you want me to bring some beer?"

"That would be great. Eight o'clock."

"I'll be here." He started to walk away and stopped. "What kind of beer?"

"How about Red Stripe?"

"My second favorite beer," he replied.

"What is your favorite?"

"Pacifico."

"I like that, too. You can bring that."

"No. I haven't had Red Stripe in a while."

She closed the door and then quickly opened it. "Bring Max, okay?"

He nodded in agreement and nearly smiled. She closed the door and watched him drive away.

13

IT WAS THE MORNING AFTER Thanksgiving. The false dawn glowed outside. The sun's radiance leaked into the bedroom. The previous day had proven long and trying and had rendered Troy utterly fatigued. Max arrived at his side and cocked his head at an angle as if he were trying to hear the thoughts that were dominating his master's mind.

"Hey, Max." He knelt and stroked his neck with both hands. Max pressed his wide snout into Troy's face.

"Let's go, boy." Troy dressed in jeans and a long sleeve white UCLA T-shirt. He grabbed a worn, saddle colored LL Bean barn coat from the closet.

They stepped outside into the wintry air. He gathered a chair from the porch and they walked out to the strand.

Troy sat in the chair and Max sat facing him, resting his head on Troy's leg. Troy looked at the ocean, while rubbing Max's head tenderly. The sun's entrance was nearly absolute as it rested on top of the water. He thought about the lengthy previous day. His thoughts were interrupted by a protracted yawn. "Why can't I sleep like normal people? Because I'm not normal, right boy?"

Max answered with a slight grunt and a thumping of his tail in the sand.

He thought about his family and their time together the previous day. As customary, his brother, Tommy, listened to every narrative that their dad offered, asking questions as if the stories were never previously uttered. It was pathetic really. His brother was nearing fifty and yet still trying so desperately to gain the elusive approval of his father. Troy wondered why he never needed his Dad's approval like so many other children, but he had not cared about it for as long as he could remember.

Still, Tommy was manageable, however, his oldest sister, Wanda, was not. After a couple glasses of wine, she thought it would be cute to take a couple of cheap shots at the bouncer in the family. Wanda and her husband, Stephen, had the big house on the hill, plenty of money in the bank, and they made certain that you were aware of their success.

His sister Diane was wise enough to stay home in Asheville where her children and grandchildren lived. She had moved there after her husband died.

Troy left right after the main course, before dessert was served and was grateful that none of his siblings would venture home for Christmas. He drove home, took a short nap, and walked with Max along the beach to Mabry's. That feast was far more enjoyable. Stacey was present, along with Michael, and his mother and daughter. It was a nice relaxing evening.

Mabry caught his eye at one point. She turned her head slightly as if there were a question that she had been asked but was not conscious of. He smiled at her and then felt guilty about a thought that surfaced concerning his two moms. The one seated at the table would have never allowed anyone to speak despairingly of him. He loved his mom dearly, but he wished that she would have stood up for him a long time ago but that was not in her genetic makeup. She was a great spiritual lady, but she grew up with an alcoholic father and she learned at an early age to keep quiet and avoid all things unpleasant.

He and Max walked Stacey back to the hotel after dinner. The boardwalk was desolate and they walked without words. All the buildings were closed save one tiny bar on the corner that was always open. There were three customers inside, drinking beer, smoking, and playing pool. The only intrusion in the stillness of the night was the sound of their feet against the wooden planks and the muffled roar of the ocean waves greeting the seashore.

His thoughts drifted back to the night when they ate pizza in her hotel room. She appeared to be so down to earth. A simple girl that you would never know was a star in the music world. He enjoyed the night so much more than he wanted to admit.

There was a part of him, as they walked, that wanted to reach out to her. To take her hand and see if she would leave it entwined with his as they walked along the boardwalk in the ocean breeze. He thought of how good it would feel. His hand became damp with perspiration by the thought of it. But even if she was receptive, what right did he have to invite someone into his world? A world dominated by sadistic nightmares that lingered well after he woke.

As they reached the door to her hotel room, she kissed him lightly on the lips and then smiled up at him as if she knew a secret that he did not. She said good night and closed the door.

On the walk home his thoughts kept drifting back to how soft her lips felt, and her fragrance, which permeated from his clothing. He was almost home when he turned and walked with purpose to her door. He raised his hand to knock and then he stopped. He turned in defeat and walked home once again.

The sun had cleared the water now. The sky was unblemished. It was a cold, beautiful day. He thought about the bar closing soon. The day after his last work night he would be on the road to the cabin in the mountains of southern Virginia, in a little place called Dugspur. Right now, he could hardly wait to escape to his place of solitude.

His thoughts traveled to Heidi. She still had not called since he had refused to visit Hawaii for the holidays. He felt guilty for disappointing her, but he would steadfastly adhere to his plans. The holidays were best spent with a loyal dog and no people.

It was an hour later when he heard a light rap on the screen door. Max barked sharply once and then sat at attention eagerly awaiting the visitor. Troy peered through the glass part of the door and saw Suzanne. She was dressed in black jeans, a white sweater with a loose-fitting neck, and a black leather coat. He opened the door.

"I thought that this would be a good time to catch you. Do you mind?"

"No," he answered. "Have you had breakfast?"

"No, I haven't."

He took her coat and hung it in the small coat closet just inside the front door.

He moved to the kitchen and began to prepare breakfast. She observed how at ease he was in the kitchen as he whipped up a dish of scrambled eggs and cheese, along with grits and hash browns. He seemed to read her thoughts as he poured her coffee. "I've been alone a long time."

Without thinking she remarked, "Me too."

He continued cooking as if he had not heard her but he had.

She looked around and noticed something that was not present. "You don't have a television?"

He shook his head no.

She tried to think of what to say next. Never had she been in a house that there was not at least one television.

"Really strange that a lonely soul like me does not own a television to pass the time, right?"

She looked at him curiously but refrained from adding to the conversation.

"I read a lot. Fiction mostly, but I keep the Bible by the bed and believe it or not I read each day."

"I believe everything you say, Troy."

"I venture out to the movie theater on occasion. I like movies. I don't want to watch sports, or news, or try to keep up with television shows. It seems to add clutter to my mind that has quite enough going on," he said, and rapped on his head. He smiled wryly, but it was anything but a genuine smile.

The first plate he served contained a mixture of eggs and cheese. He set it down on the gray tile floor for Max, who had been sitting and observing since the cooking began. He wagged his tail in appreciation and began to eat.

Suzanne smiled at Troy.

"Keeps his coat shiny," Troy said.

He carried two plates to the small dining table. He returned with orange juice, utensils, and napkins. They sat down and began to eat.

He noticed her move her grits around but refuse to partake. "You really did grow up on the north side of the house, didn't you?"

She smiled and replied, "I guess so."

They finished breakfast, and he filled their coffee cups again. "Thank you for breakfast. It was great."

"No problem," he answered. He had asked while they were eating what she had done for Thanksgiving, but she deftly moved the conversation to his day. He decided to try again but in a different manner.

"You spent yesterday alone?"

"Don't tell me that you would lecture me about being alone."

"Living like me is not something that you should aspire to. What did you do yesterday?"

She looked up from her cup and tried to smile, but it faded before it could land. "I spent the day watching old movies. My boys called, and I told them that I was invited to a church member's house. What I didn't tell them was that I never intended to go. I guess I was less than honest."

"Why didn't they come here?"

"This isn't their home. It's not even my home. They wanted to be with their girlfriends. I didn't want them to come out of obligation or simply because I was alone."

"You could have eaten with us."

"With your family?"

"No," he corrected her quickly. "I actually like you enough not to subject you to that. I meant at Mabry's."

"She doesn't like me."

"She likes everyone on Thanksgiving that doesn't have a place to be. Besides, I explained to her that even though you are without a doubt an intrusive pain in the butt that you were somewhat okay."

She smiled genuinely this time. "Thanks for the ringing endorsement."

"Mabry is just a little protective over me."

She arched her eyebrows. "A little?" She paused before asking, "So tell me about dinner at Mabry's. Who was there?"

He filled her in on the events and the attendants.

"Tell me about Stacey."

He told her that she was a singer and was surprised that she had heard of her. It seemed everyone but he knew who she was before she arrived. He filled her in on the details of her college life and about Mabry taking her in and how because of that she felt a certain kinship with him.

Suzanne listened attentively and when he stopped she asked, "What kind of person is she?"

He shrugged his shoulders slightly.

"I can't hear your shoulders shrug."

"Pretty normal I guess."

There was silence for a few moments before she spoke again. "Do you ever tire of the noise from the ocean?"

He gazed out the window and replied softly, "No, I never do."

"It sounds so serene." She drank from her coffee mug. She set it down and looked at him. "Troy, do you ever feel really peaceful with your life?"

"Sometimes early in the morning when the beach is empty and the only sound are the waves breaking softly. I watch the sun come up with Max. I think it is times like that or when I'm in the mountains and you have one of those views that stretch on forever that I feel like God is in the neighborhood."

"Do you ever feel peaceful at church?"

He hesitated before answering. "The music is so unique at Portside. There are talented singers, guitarists, drummers, violinists, pianists, organists, trumpet players, you name it. Add in hundreds of people singing and it is as if they are all united with a singular powerful voice. I don't like to join in because I want to just listen and because I sing worse than Max. The last song ends and you have this contented feeling and then your husband opens his mouth and it all dissipates."

He thought she might be angry but she was not. She nodded in understanding and her eyes moved to another place.

"Do you think divorce is a sin?"

"I think that staying with someone that you don't love is hypocrisy and isn't that what Jesus turned the money tables over about?"

"I never looked at it that way," she answered. She became silent and her eyes seemed far away.

He watched her for several moments and then asked, "Okay, your turn. You tell me about a time when you feel peaceful?"

She studied his face for a time. "I guess sometimes when I'm running but I'm not thinking about the effort. It is like I'm not conscious of this world and in that stillness, I find this tiny voice in my heart."

"What does it say?"

"'I love you Suzanne', and I believe that it is God."

He nodded his head slightly. "I believe it is too. And maybe he is saying that he will love you regardless of the choices that you make."

"But I'm supposed to put everything in his hands. Listen for his voice."

He rose and retrieved the coffee and filled their cups again. He sat back down. "You know I struggle with these people that say, God told me this and that. To hear them tell it God talks more to them than he did to the Old Testament prophets."

He drank from his cup. The steam rose and disappeared into his face. "What I do believe is this. The most powerful gift that God grants us is our heart. If we can clear ourselves from all the things that trouble us and follow what we know is right in our hearts, we won't need a big booming voice to guide us. Don't let anyone else try to tell you what is in your heart, or how you should think or feel." He breathed deeply as if what he was about to share caused physical pain. "And finally don't close off parts of your heart because then you lose your ability to discern what is right and what is not."

She was startled by the candor and the wisdom contained in his words. She deliberated for a few moments before asking, "You mentioned God speaking to us. Sometimes I wonder what he would say if he came to church one Sunday morning and talked to us as a people."

"I think it would be safe to say that he would not be as long winded as your husband," he said, chuckling softly.

Her eyes squinted as she pretended to be angry. "You just can't have a serious conversation for more than two minutes, can you?"

He took another sip of his coffee and smiled.

"Well, what do you think he might say?"

He thought for a moment and said evenly, "I think that he would encourage us to simplify our lives. To not let things or unreasonable schedules run us. To remember that the best things in life truly are free. A beautiful sunrise. A dog that misses you when you've only been gone ten minutes." He paused before adding, "Finding a new friend."

She reached across the table and touched his arm. Tears welled up quickly. "Thank you," she said, wiping her eyes.

He walked to the living room and retrieved a box of Kleenex off the table. He returned to his chair and set them down in front of her.

She took one and dabbed beneath her eyes.

"I guess I am not a wise choice if you were looking to be cheered up."

She shook her head. "It's all right. These aren't sad tears. Grateful for a friend." She blew her nose loudly and he laughed softly. "All lady, aren't I?"

"Yes, you are," he responded.

She regained her composure as he looked down at Max, who was sleeping on the floor. "Do you feel that you live that way Troy?"

"What way?"

"The simple life you spoke of and living around what is really important."

He shook his head. "No. I'm no different. I spend time thinking about what I don't have. For instance, other than my mother I'm close to no one in the family I was raised in. But that balances out when you see that I have Mabry and Nate. Heidi loves me dearly and her mother is still my best friend. So, no I don't live that way to answer your question," he said, before sighing slightly and adding, "I'm not sure that very many of us actually do."

"What was it like for you growing up?"

"Not good."

"What about your dad?"

Troy rubbed his hand briefly through his hair. "He always did and still does want to be the center of attention. He's a big showoff and it is embarrassing to nearly everyone but him. He doesn't realize how foolish he acts. He believes that he is simply charming and that no one can get enough of his act. He probably believes that he is a great father, when he has been anything but. I learned to never take anyone that I was dating around the family."

"Because of him?"

"Yes, and my brother and two sisters. Between his showing off and their demeaning remarks it is suffice to say that if I can't measure up than surely anyone that would choose to be with me must be lacking as well. On the other hand, if I was dating someone and I wanted to break it off I just took them to a family gathering."

She reached across the table and playfully slapped his arm. "You did not."

She looked at him, thinking of his words before he had stopped the serious nature of the conversation with a joke. He spoke without bitterness or regret. It was more of resolution.

He looked back at her and smiled. "Is this the part where you lean in and ask 'and how did that make you feel'?"

She smiled and said, "No. You don't seem to be bitter about any of it. Still it seems that you have given up. Maybe things will change."

He looked away from her. "Maybe I don't care."

She looked at him and started to speak but he interrupted her.

"As far as my family goes I did not say that I did not care about them. I did not say that if they needed something that I wouldn't do what I could."

"I would think that your dad would have been proud of you. Being a good athlete and everything?"

"My dad never gave any support of any kind except for a roof over my head and food in my stomach and he complained all the time about what it cost him to provide that. What he did best was criticize."

She hid how badly she wanted an answer to her next question with forced laughter. "Okay, now how did that make you feel?"

He looked back at her with his eyes squinted slightly. "I was a pitcher but I never could hit well. Even in Little League I struggled. Well he was a good hitter when he played and he would criticize me relentlessly on the way home from a game. It wouldn't matter if I had pitched a three-hit-shutout. I never heard a word about that. Never a positive word offered. I was ten years old when I realized that he was way off base. Maybe if he had backed up his criticism with an offer to help I would have felt different. Something along the lines of, 'son, you had a bad night. Why don't we go to the ball field in our neighborhood and I'll see if I can help you with your hitting.' The truth was he didn't want to be bothered. So, I tuned him out. After that nothing he said affected me much. Before surgery when my shoulder blew out, he said, I told you that that throwing motion of yours was going to ruin your arm. My pro career, my hopes and dreams exiting before my eyes and that was what he said as they were wheeling me in for surgery." He shook his head and laughed softly. "And the funny thing is he had never said anything about my pitching motion before that very moment."

"Did you tell him that?"

"Why? It wasn't as if he was going to say 'oh, that is right son'?"

"How do your siblings view him?"

"They listen to Mom and convince themselves that he is this father that truly loves them and deep down is this man just hiding his feelings because of the generation he was raised in where men were tough, and the breadwinners, while the wife raised the children."

"And you?"

"I think he is just a surface kind of guy. There are no deep thoughts hidden because that part of him failed to develop." He paused, and drank from his coffee. "Don't get me wrong. He is a good man. He assists people with things he is comfortable with like if they need help with an electrical problem, or a hand painting a room. Maybe that is how he shows he cares."

There was silence and then he softly chuckled. She looked at him and said nothing but waited for him to share. She was getting better at the quiet thing. It must be his influence.

"I will tell you a little story about Dad that shows his best side. Believe it or not I once owned a home. I had a patio that bordered the back of the house. I had a whiskey barrel fountain that flowed water out the spout continuously. The only drawback was the outlet was on the other side of the back door, and I wanted the fountain on the other side under my bedroom window so I could hear it flowing at night. I mentioned it to him and asked for his electrical help since I refuse to try to do anything electrical. He said, 'Why in the world do you want it on the other side? It is fine where it is at.' He shot my idea down as always."

"I thought this was a good story about your dad," she interjected.

"I thought you people were supposed to be good at listening."

She made a sweeping gesturing with her hand encouraging him to continue.

"The next morning the doorbell rang, waking me up before seven o'clock. It was my dad with his tools."

I opened the door and he said, "You ready to move that outlet so you can have the fountain under your window? We spent the morning doing the job and later he took me to lunch. Now, it is never anything much more than a diner, or fast food, but he never allows me to pay. So maybe in his way that is being a dad."

"And is that enough?"

"It will have to be."

"Do you love him, Troy?"

He shook his head slightly side to side and sighed. "I honestly don't know. Now, how much do I owe you for this session?"

She knew that he had said all that he intended to on the matter. She rose and said, "Thank you for listening. I don't get much of that at home anymore."

He looked at her and nodded softly.

"You are easy to talk to. I think I know that you won't judge me regardless of what I say."

"And how do you know that?"

"Maybe because of the way your family perceives you. Always expecting you to live up to some unachievable existence and putting you down when you fall short of the mark."

"Their version would be different."

"Maybe so, but I'm certain of one thing. You are honest about others and more importantly with yourself."

She paused for several moments and a peaceful look came over her. "Short of the mark," she said softly. "That is what the correct definition is of sin. We fall short and Jesus helps us make the mark. That is so much better than beating people down with their mistakes."

Troy smiled and said, "I know."

She eyed him curiously.

"You surprised I know that information, or are you forgetting who my minister is?"

"You really are close with David Lang, aren't you?"

"Yes, the preacher and the bouncer. We make quite the pairing, don't we?"

"I bet that you do."

She hugged him for a long time and had to force herself to let go of the comfort of being in his arms. She walked out the door slowing for a moment to rub Max one last time on his head.

14

THE NIGHTMARE WAS DISSIMILAR that afternoon but the message of death was not. There was no blood visible. Heidi, Carla, Alana, Nate, and Mabry were far out in the sea screaming frantically and beckoning to him for help. He swam furiously toward them. They were twenty feet away, and he was convinced that he would reach them. A large wave suddenly appeared impeding his progress and blocking his vision momentarily. The wave passed and when he regained his vision there was no one in sight. He called out hysterically but those lost at sea uttered no retort. He swam to the spot where he saw them last and dove repeatedly until he was too exhausted to continue. Every direction that he looked showed nothing but the vastness of the sea. The light of day left abruptly and it turned dark. Too fatigued he decided he would sink to the bottom of the sea with those he lost. He ceased treading water and began to descend into the shadows of the ocean.

He woke frantically in a cold sweat, his heart racing. He sat up and breathed deeply and slowly in an attempt to calm down.

Max was seated on the floor beside him. Troy rubbed his head, trying to assure him that everything was okay. Problem was things were not all right and the tender concern in Max's eyes told Troy that he was aware of this as well. Troy reached for the bottle of water on the nightstand and unscrewed the cap. He drank from it and set it back on the nightstand too close to the edge and it fell to the floor sprinkling Max with some of the contents.

"I'm sorry, boy," he said softly as he pulled Max to him and rubbed him firmly as they touched face to face. Max, leaning his wide snout into his master's face and pressing in firmly. He murmured softly.

Troy dressed and they walked to his Jeep. He opened the door for Max, and he climbed quickly to his spot. Minutes later he drove past the entrance of Carolina Beach State Park. He passed the Visitor's Center and took the next right where there were two campground areas marked A and B. Only A was opened this time of year and it contained only three RVs. He parked to the side of the barricade in front of sight B. They walked through a trail in the woods that stopped at the bank of the river. Max shivered excitedly in anticipation at the beckoning water.

Troy laughed softly at his companion. He bent down and got a stick and tossed it into the chilly water. Max bounded down the bank on to the narrow shore and leapt into the water. Moments later he was back at Troy's side ready to go again.

The game went on for several tosses and then they began walking back to the Jeep. Troy opened the back window of the Jeep and retrieved one of the towels he kept for just such an occasion. He rubbed Max vigorously with the towel. He heard a car approaching. Looking up he saw the white SUV that the Park Superintendent drove.

"Dog off the leash again?"

Troy smiled. "Now, Chris, you know we follow all the rules."

Chris merely chuckled. He was a jovial man and it seemed to Troy that he was always in a good mood. He was also a lover of Labrador Retrievers. He had three and he covered all the colors-- yellow, black, and chocolate. "You and Max have a good evening," he said as he drove away slowly.

The light was growing faint as he drove farther into the Park until the road stopped at the marina. He parked, left the engine running and the heat on for Max. He sat on the hood and watched the sun over the Cape Fear River. The array of clouds absorbed the orange and pink streaks of light and held them as if it was their home. He watched until night was inclusive. "How long God? How long my penitence for something I would do again?" He closed his eyes for several moments and asked God once again to forgive him his failures.

*

IT WAS SHORTLY PAST MIDNIGHT and the club was packed. Troy had anticipated a slow night with so many of the students gone home for the Thanksgiving holidays. The band was playing techno music and he could not stuff the orange foam earplugs deep enough inside his ears to escape the repetitious noise the band contrived. There were very few faces in the crowd that he recognized and he had an uneasy feeling that he could not shake.

Michael was working the door and Troy had instructed him to hold the line and to not allow anyone else in until some of the crowd left. They were close to capacity and Troy didn't want to push things with the local fire marshals that were known to show up when you least expected them.

There was a group of six guys that he had been watching closely. They were close to the band in the center of the floor and dancing with any girl that got near them. The problem was most of the girls were not receptive to their obnoxious manners. The ringleader was tall, probably, 6'7" and solid enough to make you think he played defensive end for the Carolina Panthers. His blond hair was cropped short on top and the sides were buzzed tight. He reminded Troy of the Russian opponent in Rocky IV.

Troy heard Michael calling to him. He turned and saw Stacey outside the door. She was wearing blue jeans, a dark blue Under Armour hoodie, and a red baseball cap. Her blonde hair was in a long ponytail that fell neatly out the hole in back of the hat. Michael waved her in and this brought on a storm of protests from those waiting in line.

Michael quickly informed the offended crowd that she was the owner's daughter and that if they hoped to get inside tonight they better pull back on the grief they were giving him.

Stacey placed her hand on Troy's arm. "I thought I would get out tonight. I was getting cabin fever. I thought that you said it was going to be slow tonight."

Troy's eyes had not diverted from the big man in front of the stage. "Stacey, I think it would be better if you went back to the hotel."

"Why, are you going to bash someone's head?" she said with a forced laugh.

He cast an annoying look in her direction and returned his eyes in the direction of the stage. He watched as the big guy in front of the stage came up from behind a small college girl with large breasts that fit snugly against her cream colored sweater. He was carrying two full mugs of beer and reached around her and tilted both against her chest. She screamed as he smiled drunkenly at her and then raised the mug toward his mouth and drained it quickly. He finished the other mug off in similar fashion.

Troy made eye contact with the two bouncers located on each corner of the stage. They had not seen the incident but were aware of the potential trouble from this crew and had been keeping an eye on them throughout much of the evening. Troy raised his right hand slightly with his thumb pointing slightly up. He tapped Michael on his leg and walked toward the stage.

Michael was familiar with the routine. He removed the cell phone from his waist. Troy had the phone numbers for most of the Carolina Beach Police officers stored in the contacts. Troy also verified the officers on duty before the club opened. This information was always shared with Michael. The text sent for help would simply read Mabry.

The practice was that Michael would wait for trouble to begin before sending the text. Troy felt that if they made too many calls on an urgent basis that turned out not to be an emergency that the response may get lax. Tonight, Michael knew that these guests would not leave without incident. He sent the text.

Stacey watched Troy nervously and her fear heightened when she heard Michael mumble, "This is going to be ugly."

Michael took her arm firmly and urged her to the door. "Stacey, get out of here now."

She went outside with little protest, though she had little choice since he nearly shoved her out the door. Next Michael did two things. The first act was standard operating procedure. He told the line at the door to back up at least thirty feet because they would be escorting people out of the club. The line backed up slowly.

Next, he made a move that might get him in trouble with Troy. He was never supposed to leave the door unattended. But tonight, with the holiday schedule and the projection that it would be a slow night, there were only two bouncers inside the club and Troy. Normally in anticipation of a night like this there would be at least six inside, excluding Troy and the person at the door.

Troy made his way through the tight crowd and approached the biggest source of the disturbance. He motioned him toward the door. He felt the others pressing in on him. The other two bouncers were on each side of the man in front of him who was grinning at being singled out. Troy also saw the look in his eye and he knew this one was not going to leave without force. The room became quieter and the band decided that it was a good time for a break.

Normally, it was an easy job. It wasn't how the movies portrayed it. He didn't know of any bar that was like the movie, *Roadhouse*. Really there were just a few simple rules. Do your best to keep potential trouble outside the door. React swiftly to trouble and with minimal debate. The objective is to remove the offending party from the club swiftly. If they choose to call you names as they are leaving that's okay. And last, but most important, hire bouncers who will fight if they must but do not come to work with a chip on their shoulder ready to spend each night parading around like they are a tough guy. That was the mistake that nearly every bar in the area made.

"Time for you to leave big man," Troy stated firmly without margin for debate.

"Why?"

"Let's go outside and I'll explain it to you."

He grinned tightly and snarled. "That might prove detrimental for you."

"We can see about that outside."

There are also rules within the rules. Never touch anyone unless it is necessary. Troy hoped to keep that rule intact tonight.

"Why do I have to leave?"

"That is not up for discussion. What is going to happen is that you will leave. You can choose the method. You can even push it to the point where the police remove you in which case you will spend the night in jail. Now, let's walk outside and we can discuss it."

He stood in front of Troy, refusing to comply. Troy nodded slightly to Geoff and Wayne, the bouncers behind the offending party. They quickly locked on to each arm of the antagonist before he could react, turning each one behind his back and began walking him forcibly toward the door. Troy stepped in behind them and turned to his buddies. "You guys come with him."

They defied him briefly with the look on their face but he knew they would follow. They hung out with this guy because it made them feel bad. They were going to follow him anywhere, even out the door.

The big guy struggled against his escorts. Grudgingly he was on his way to the door. Just when Troy thought that this might go smoother than he anticipated Geoff lost control of the guy's right arm and was thrown to the floor in the process. The man hit Wayne with his now free right hand.

The big man smiled as he felt the freedom of his arms. The smile vanished quickly as Troy suddenly locked his neck in a death grip. His forearm was jammed into his windpipe and the villain struggled to breathe. In a voice, hardly more than a whisper Troy said evenly in his ear, "So help me God, you are going out the door now or I will break your damn neck. Do you understand me?" The big man nodded briefly as he gasped for air.

Stacey had moved back to the doorway, unable to leave as instructed. It seemed as if she were watching a dream. Troy was moving the man toward the door. The man no longer desired to fight as he struggled to breathe. The fear that consumed her as she saw the brown beer bottle directed at Troy's head, swung viscously by one of the offenders behind him. The bottle was a foot from his head when she screamed too late. Suddenly, from nowhere a fist exploded in to the guy's face and the bottle fell harmlessly to the floor.

Troy never saw the bottle. All he saw was Michael, out of the corner of his eye, throw a quick short right and then he heard the bottle clank against the concrete floor, followed by its owner.

Stacey moved as Troy escorted the man through the door. Geoff and Wayne led the other four members of the group outside. Michael ushered the remaining associate outside with his hand gripped forcefully around the man's throat. The man was gasping for air but Michael did not seem to notice. His right hand remained clenched around the man's throat. Troy let go of the big guy just as the police arrived. Instinctively he turned behind him. Michael's eyes were glassed over in a silent rage.

Troy clamped his hand down firmly on Michael's arm. "It's over. Michael, let him go," he said as calmly as if he were telling a bedtime story to a small child.

The man gasped as he choked for breath. His eyes were unnaturally wide and filled with panic. They begged in complete and unqualified surrender.

Michael's eyes were locked in on his face. He seemed unable to hear. Troy kept his hand firmly on Michael's arm as he interrupted his vision and forced Michael to look him in the eyes. Troy smiled and nodded ever so softly.

Michael's eyes blinked and then softened as he looked into Troy's eyes. It took him a moment longer to realize that there was still some foreign object attached to his hand. He relaxed his grip quickly and the man fell limply to the ground gasping for air.

"Troy."

He turned and saw Billy C. He was a short, tough, Italian man in his mid-forties who had spent most of his adult life as a uniform cop. And he possessed no desire to be anything else. He had been on the force for ten years moving here from the city of Patchogue, New York, located on Long Island.

He was thick all over. For some reason, his build reminded Troy of a fire hydrant. Short, broad, and hard.

He was called Billy C., because his last name started with a C and ended with an O and had so many vowels in between that no one pronounced it correctly. The length of his last name also would not fit on the gold medal nametag on his blue uniform shirt. It simply read Billy C.

Billy C. liked Troy and respected him. That is why he had simply shaken his head no to the rookie officer that was drawing his baton to stop Michael from choking the man. Troy would handle the situation better than any rookie officer still wet behind the ears.

"Billy C. You got here pretty quick."

"I received a text at 12:13."

Now Troy had noted that it was 12:13 when he began his journey across the floor toward the trouble that was brewing. He always noted the time so that if there was a court case he could give accurate testimony. He turned and looked at Michael.

"I sent the text early. I had a feeling."

Troy nodded slightly his approval.

Billy C. removed his hat and rubbed his thick short black hair that was wet as always from the heavy concentration of gel it contained. "What do you want to do?"

"I want the big guy arrested. And I think Michael can tell you about the other gentleman he was holding."

Billy C. looked at Michael.

"He swung a bottle at the back of Troy's head. I stopped him."

The man had regained his breath if not his good sense. From his knees, he said in shortened breaths, "That's a lie. He hit me for no good reason, that n…" His voice trailed off.

Billy C. looked at Michael to gage his reaction. There was none.

The officer looked down at the punk on the street. "Suppose I let just the two of you go out on the beach strand and you can call him any vile name you so choose."

Michael knew that Billy C. was bluffing, even if the man on the ground did not. The man said nothing as the rookie officer and another officer handcuffed him and assisted him to his feet.

Michael looked at Troy and then back to Billy C. "That's okay, officer. There are only two things worth fighting over. Someone tries to hurt you or someone you care about. You don't fight over an overabundance of testosterone, or because someone such as this gentleman," he said gesturing toward the man, "lacks a proper vocabulary."

Stacey stepped forward. "I saw it officer. It was just like Michael said. That coward was about to shatter Troy's head with a bottle and Michael intervened."

"Anyone else, Troy?"

"No, the rest of those guys with them just possess piss poor taste in friends."

"Piss? They must have really got you worked up."

"Don't tell Mom. And I guess I should confess I told the big guy I would break his damn neck."

Stacey looked perplexed at Billy C.

He rolled his eyes at her. "Choir boy here does not curse. Just one more reason I don't like him."

Billy C. turned to the two other officers. "Okay, take those two morons to the station and book them. I'll get the details from here." The officers led the two away in handcuffs.

He turned to the other four men who were evicted from the bar. "I tell you what. I'll turn back around to talk to Troy. If I turn back and see you guys anywhere you will be joining your buddies in jail. You know that high-rise bridge that you crossed to get on this island?"

They all nodded their answer simultaneously.

"Get on the other side of it and feel very fortunate that you are given this chance. Do you comprehend meatheads?"

"We didn't drive," one of them answered.

"Do your legs work?" He turned back to Troy.

The smile on Troy's face and the noise of feet moving very quickly told him that the four men were exiting the Island as quickly as possible.

"Meatheads seemed kind of harsh."

"I didn't curse though. And which of your moms are you concerned about finding out you were cursing like a sailor tonight?"

"Both."

Geoff approached Troy. "I'm sorry, boss. He slipped away from me. This is on me. It's my fault."

"No, Geoff. It's my fault," Michael interjected. "I had a feeling that those guys were trouble and I let them in. Best way to stop trouble is to not allow it in the door."

Another thing Troy liked in his staff was not to be full of excuses. "Relax guys. This one is on me. I assumed it would be a slow night and I let some guys ask off; I should have had more staff working. Everything is okay. Nobody's hurt, right, Billy C.?"

Billy C. winked and nodded his head. "That's the way I see it boys."

"I appreciate you getting here so quickly," Troy said as he extended his hand.

"Just doing my job," Billy C. answered as he shook his hand. "Now, please tell me I can get this statement without that band cranking up again. I walked by earlier and that noise they were playing kept me from paying a social visit."

Troy looked at Geoff. "Tell the band to pack it in for the night. Give them a few drinks on the house." Geoff walked back inside without a word.

Billy C. looked at Michael. "I'll get your statement on the way out."

Michael nodded in agreement.

"You can handle things out here while I go back to the office with your boss and Ms. Storm, right?"

"I can."

"I know you can Michael." His eyes squinted at him when he said, "You are a good man, Michael. I bet I know who told you what the two things in life that are worth fighting about are."

Michael nodded softly. "Yes you do officer."

"Officer, after all this time? You are too polite young man. Let's use my name. Okay?"

"Billy C."

"Now, let's get this done. I would like to get home to my wife, the lovely Maria. I might even wake her up," he added with another wink and a smile, as he nudged Troy.

"She still allows that?"

Billy C. grinned broadly as he began walking inside. "Allows it? She encourages it my friend."

"Only in America, Billy C."

"And what does that mean, exactly?"

"That only in America could a cop shorter than Barney Fife land a beautiful woman that loves him."

Stacey tried not to laugh but she couldn't refrain. Billy C. looked up at Troy and lightly tapped his revolver. "Suppose I take one of those kneecaps out? Bring you down to a more appropriate height."

Troy laughed. "Please don't take your bullet out of your pocket, Barney."

Stacey laughed harder at the reference to *The Andy Griffith Show*. Billy C. cast an irritating glance toward her before turning back to Troy. His eyes tightened to the point of almost being shut. "It seems as if you would be a little nicer to me since I am always saving your bacon. Not to mention Sean McGill would have probably stomped your butt the other day and shot your dog if it wasn't for his fear of me."

Troy started to reply but Billy C. cut him off. "Please get Miss Storm and me some coffee and meet us in the office."

"Yes sir," Troy answered, saluted, and walked away.

"That's cute," Billy C. remarked.

Troy walked toward the bar to obtain the coffee requested. He watched Billy C. and Stacey walk to the office. There were not many people in this world he liked as much as Billy C. Over the sound of the jukebox he heard the steady barking of Max. Billy C. opened the door and Max nearly knocked him over racing out the door."

"Watch it, Max," Billy C. said loudly.

Max ran quickly to Troy, barking the entire time. Troy petted him and told him to sit. Max was obedient and his barking was quickly replaced by whimpers of love.

Troy turned to the bar. "Ginny, would you please get me three cups of coffee?"

Ginny placed the coffee on the bar. "You okay?"

"Sure."

She was a naturally pretty young lady. Long black hair, vivid blue eyes, and a smile that melted all the young men's hearts that came near.

"Troy, if I ever find a man who loves me half as much as that dog loves you I am going to marry him. I don't care if he is poor and ugly."

Troy said nothing and she continued. "You know while all the action was taking place it dawned on me that Max had been barking and scratching the door the entire time. There is no way he could have heard the trouble. Simply amazing," she stated with her trademark smile. She bent over the bar and looked down at Max. "You are such a good boy."

Max barked his agreement with her statement.

"Please don't do that," Troy said.

"Do what?"

He pointed to her more than ample chest that was partially spilling out of her loose black shirt. He picked the coffee up.

"Scared the college boys can't take it?" she asked as she straightened up, with a huge smile on her face.

"No. I am scared that I can't take it."

He proceeded on to the office where Stacey and Billy C. were sitting. He gave each of them a cup of coffee and sat down at Mabry's desk. He swung his legs up on the desk. He moved his neck side-to-side trying to rid it of the tweak it now seemed to have.

"Hurt yourself, big fella?"

"No."

"A little old for this line of work, aren't you?"

"I don't know. Are you too old to be walking a beat?"

"You want to join those meatheads in jail tonight?"

Troy smiled, and drank from his mug.

"Now for your statement please. That is if you are through with all of your clever comments."

Troy proceeded to fill him in on the events of the altercation. Occasionally, Billy C. would turn to Stacey and ask her if that coincided with what she witnessed.

They finished and sat in silence for a few moments. Billy C. closed his log and appeared to be deep in thought. "Troy, did you know my next door neighbor hired Michael to build a grilling area? He constructed it with stone. He also built a nice wood fence around his entire back yard. The kid is a whiz with stone, brick, wood, you name it. Now, I don't pry into your personal life. You do a good job here and you make my job easier. It's a rarity when I even need to do more than make a social visit." He rubbed his hand through his hair once again. "It just seems to me that Michael is just who you need if you ever decided to build courtyards and patios again. Okay, I know that it is not my business. And I know it would be hard for you to go back into the business without Kent. Oh, I know I should just mind my own business."

He rose to leave as he put on his hat. "Oh, what the heck, one more thing, while I am interfering into your life. That boy out there didn't fight for this club tonight. He fought for one of the only two reasons that you taught him that were worth fighting over. Somebody was going to hurt someone he cared about. What I am saying is that you would have a talented partner and a loyal friend. God forgive me, I know Kent was really special to you." He paused for a few moments before adding. "I think that Michael would be every bit as loyal."

He looked at Troy. "I hear you, Billy C. I'm just thick headed."

"That, my oversized friend, we can agree on. I'll talk to Michael on the way out."

"Thanks for looking after Michael and getting him that job with your neighbor."

"I never said I had anything to do with it."

"You didn't have to."

Stacey had watched with interest at the conversation. It filled in some answers to the questions that she had about Troy. She rose to shake the hand of Billy C.

He smiled at her. "Ms. Storm, a lowly beach officer does not often get a chance to be around a star. Would it be too much to ask for a hug?"

She smiled. "Only if you call me Stacey."

"Yes ma'am, Stacey," he said as they hugged.

He was to the door when she asked, "Billy C. do you often patrol a tourist hotel this time of year? I ask because I know that I have seen you several times before tonight near the hotel that I am staying in. You were not even in uniform some of the time."

"Stacey, a friend of mine told me about you and asked if I would keep an eye on you. As God above is my witness I told no one, not any other officers, not even my family that you are here."

"Mabry told you?"

"No, the big guy there," he said as he motioned his head toward Troy.

Stacey smiled, pleased that her guess was wrong.

Billy C. looked back at her. "I'd like to ask a favor of you if it is okay." He pressed on without waiting for an answer. "I heard my daughter, Marisa, playing your record the other day. She plays it all the time. Her birthday is next week. She will be thirteen. I don't have to tell her how or when I got it. I know that you don't want anyone to know that you are staying here." He hesitated, and then charged ahead. "Could I get a picture of you autographed?"

"Tell me about your daughter."

"Oh, God, don't do that," Troy said, feigning disgust.

"You shut up you oversized ox," Billy C. said sternly, as he looked at him, before returning with a smile to Stacey.

Troy watched in amusement as he proudly told Stacey about his daughter. How smart, pretty, mature and responsible she was.

"Would she keep a secret?"

"Sure," he answered proudly. His thick chest about to bust the buttons off his shirt.

"Does Troy know where you live?"

"He does."

"What day is her birthday?"

"Monday."

"How about if Troy and I come by?"

The excitement at giving his daughter such a present filled his face with delight. He seemed unable to find his voice. "You would do that?"

"Of course."

"You are not busy or something?"

"I'm here to relax. That is why I don't want it advertised that I am here. I want to be around people I like. I'm sure that I will like Marisa."

"Wow! How about if Troy and you come to dinner? We can do it about five, so you will have time to go to work, Troy. Okay, Troy?"

Troy recalled enviously what it was like to have a young daughter and to want to please her so desperately. "Billy C., you know that the club is not open on Monday."

"Hey, that's right. Let's make it seven." Billy C. was whistling as he went out the door. Troy felt like whistling with him.

"That was really nice of you," Troy said, as he stood.

Stacey turned and looked at him. Her eyes narrowed as she said, "Nice, I just wanted to get a date with you anyway I could."

He stood there looking awkwardly at her wondering if she was serious or not.

"Walk me out?"

"Give me a few minutes to write a couple of notes to Mabry?"

"Sure," she replied as she sipped her coffee.

They walked out into the bar. Michael sat on the stool by the door. The crowd had dwindled significantly.

They approached Michael. "Everything okay?" Troy asked.

"Sure, no more problems." He looked past them and his eyes focused on a drunk asleep on a table. "You want to take the stool and allow me to get the drunk off the table?"

Troy turned and saw a college student with his head down on the table asleep. The people around him were oblivious to him.

"Watch this, Stacey. The guy on the table is ready to go home. Removing him is easy but what you can count on is there will be a buddy who is not ready to leave. That's the guy who will tell you. "He's okay. I'll take care of him." But sleeping people make poor customers and the police don't like it. So, the choice is made. They both must go and the guy that was sleeping wakes up ill, and inspired by his buddy now wants to stay."

She watched as the scenario played out exactly as stated. Michael smiled as he walked both offenders through the door.

15

SUZANNE LISTENED TO THE GROUP, *Third Day*, as she drove in the direction of Carolina Beach. She had decided the previous morning that she would not be attending church. Certainly, Alan would hear about it and just as indubitably she did not care. She parked in front of Troy's house and walked around to the ocean side of the house.

She knocked on the door and waited a few moments. No one came to the door and she turned in the direction of the ocean and began walking.

The temperature was chilly, but the sun and lack of wind made for a pleasant morning. She smiled as she spotted Troy tossing a Frisbee and Max sprinting after it. He slowed as he neared the object of his attention and then plucked it from the air with a perfectly timed leap. Suddenly, she felt like an intruder and she started to turn around but Troy spotted her and waved.

She approached him and shrugged her shoulders slightly. "Are you getting tired of me just showing up?"

"Yes," he stated evenly.

She froze for a few moments and her face tightened in an almost distorted look.

"Hey, I was joking. Lighten up a little."

Now she felt foolish. "Thanks a lot."

"How are you?"

"Perplexed."

"You must be if your answer is to visit me." He paused and looked at the anxiety etched on her face.

She looked away from him and gazed out into the ocean. The absence of wind gave the ocean the calming appearance of a lake. It reminded her of a vast lake that she and her dad once fished on when she was a little girl.

He waited for her to continue.

"Alan comes home in two days. He called last night. I had nothing to say to him."

"Maybe you will be glad to see him. Maybe the time away will lend a fresh perspective for each of you."

"And maybe it won't," she answered swiftly.

She looked back at him and smiled slightly. "Are you doing okay?"

He moved his head slightly to one side. "Same old stuff. You deal with it the best you can."

She studied the weariness in his eyes. "I'm not trying to have an analytical session with you so please just hear me. You suffer with nightmares, don't you?"

"Who told you that?"

"No one," she replied softly. "Don't worry. I don't intend to pry."

The kindness in his eyes made her smile and then emotions inside her could not be held back any longer. She began to sob torrents of tears as she moved toward him, reaching and clinging to him.

Slowly he put his arms around her. He felt awkward. It was as if he was in a play and had suddenly forgotten his lines.

She cried softly for a few minutes. Her hands grasping handfuls of his sweatshirt. And then she abruptly pulled away and began walking briskly in the direction of her car.

He watched her unsure of what to do. He started to call out but refrained. The car started and he listened as car and driver departed. He was still rooted in the same spot. His shirt wet with her tears. Max sat beside him, wearing a look of uncertainty as well.

*

TROY ORDERED THE CLUB closed at eight thirty. There was a decent crowd for much of the late afternoon and early evening but nearly all of them departed as soon as the band played its last song.

Stacey was seated at the bar nursing a glass of red wine that she was served an hour ago. She studied him in the mirror behind the bar. She turned to him. "Where have you been all night?"

He looked back at her confused. "Here."

"Body yes, mind elsewhere."

Once again, his thoughts drifted back to Suzanne and how abruptly she left. He watched the crew restock the coolers and clean up in record time. No one wanted to tarry on Sunday night.

The bartender approached Stacey. "I can get you something else if you don't like that. It is a really dry wine."

She pursed her lips and said with a chuckle. "It's not that dry but if you were to light a match over it I think it might catch on fire." She laughed again at her own joke. "I don't care for anything else. Thank you." The bartender smiled and took the wine away.

Troy heard a song being whistled behind him. He glanced in the mirror and saw Billy C. walking toward them.

He sat on the bar stool next to Stacey and placed his hat on the bar. "Nice slow night. Just the way I like them."

Troy walked around behind the bar and poured a cup of coffee. He placed it on the bar in front of him.

"What, no smart comments, big boy? No? Do you want a donut with that Barney?"

Troy started to speak but said nothing. Stacey smiled at Billy C. and said, "Pay him no mind. He has been like this since I walked in three hours ago. Maybe he is just apprehensive about going out on a date with me tomorrow."

"If he cancels and disappoints my daughter I'll shoot him."

"I'm not canceling anything," Troy replied tersely. He left them without another word and disappeared into the office.

Billy C. looked puzzled at Stacey, who shrugged. "Something on his mind I suppose."

He drank from his coffee and a sour expression came over his face. "He put sugar in my coffee. Normally, I would assume he was picking on me but today I think that what passes for his mind is way out in left field." He retrieved his hat from the bar and put it on. "May I escort you home?"

"Might as well," she replied. "There is sure nothing happening here," she said in a frustrated voice.

They walked out into the cold night air. "Billy C., why do you like him so much?"

"What makes you think that I like that big ox?"

"Tell a girl the truth."

He nodded, smiled, and said, "Troy Dawkins is the most honest man I know, and if he cares about you there are no boundaries to his loyalty."

They walked in silence for a few minutes when Billy C. broke it with a question. "Stacey, do you mind if I share a cop story that involves him?"

She made a sweeping wave with her hand.

"It was Azalea Festival weekend two years ago. That is the biggest weekend in the city. Wilmington has a parade downtown. The Island fills with tourists. The clubs are packed with partiers.

"The boardwalk was littered with people. I got a call about a fight in one of the bars. I could barely move once I entered because of the congested crowd. I should have called for backup but there had just been a three car accident on the main drag.

"It turned ugly quickly. The people fighting each other decided it would be more fun to join forces and beat the hell out of me. I was thrown down on the floor, and I thought that they might beat me to death in their drunken rage. I could already feel my face swelling and I knew I had a couple of busted ribs. They just wouldn't stop. They kept pounding and kicking me."

"No one tried to help you?" Stacey interrupted.

"They were scared. It was six or seven big dudes doing the work on me. At some point I heard cheering in the background, so some were enjoying the show I guess," he said with a shrug.

"Through a narrow opening I could see the door. I kept hoping that I would see some officers coming to my aid. What I got was even better."

"What do you mean?"

"I saw Troy. He busted through the crowd like a linebacker. He hit the first guy with his Maglite on the head, shattering it into pieces. He then proceeded to beat the heck out of the other five guys. He was in a rage. I've seen a lot of fights in my time--been in a few as well, but I never witnessed anything like that."

"How did he know that you were in trouble?"

"He never would talk about what happened that night but Michael filled me in later. He said Troy and he were standing at the front door at Mabry's. Someone told them that I was in trouble. Troy shouted to Michael to watch the club and he ran to the bar I was at." He shook his head before adding, "You see all these phony action movies where something like that takes place. Well, I saw it for real.

You heard me mention the officer Sean McGill that does not like Troy?"

"Yes, I remember."

"I told Sean one day if he pushed Troy too far I certainly would not be the one to try and stop him. I am grateful that he is a good guy and even more so that he knows no fear if someone needs him."

They were at her hotel door now. "Thank you, Billy C. for everything."

"There is another part to the story." He paused. "The . . ."

She was startled to hear his voice catch with obvious emotion.

"Saving me was not the most meaningful thing he did that night."

"I don't understand."

"The paramedics came and took me to the hospital." He breathed deeply, bringing his emotions in check. "Troy went to my house. He refused to allow another officer to do it. You ring a doorbell past midnight where a cop lives and he is not home. Well, I'm sure you understand. Maria opens the door scared to death and the first thing Troy says is, 'He is okay. I promise you that he is all right.'

"He drove her and Marisa to the hospital. My two ladies," he said with a smile. His voice caught again. "They are who I live for."

"How badly were you hurt?"

"Three busted ribs, several stitches, some internal bleeding, and a wealth of bruises. I was laid up for a while."

Stacey shook her head softly.

"Don't ever ask him about that night or what he did. He will not discuss it. And he will be angry with me for telling you." He paused for several moments, deep in thought as he chose his next words carefully.

"He's such a big man. People in the club see him as this tough giant. The bigger truth is that what is gigantic is his heart. I will let you in on another secret. He hates to fight.

"You asked me earlier why I like him. I tell you void of any male, macho bullcrap that I love Troy Dawkins and if he ever asked anything of me I would do everything in my power to grant that request."

Stacey kept quiet feeling that there was much more to this story that he wanted to share with her. He did not disappoint.

"That night in the hospital he stood by my bed. It hurt me to talk because of the ribs and I was on some serious painkillers. I was trying to gather the strength to thank him for what he had done.

"Before I could he apologized. He said he was so sorry that he did not get there sooner before they beat me up so bad. He had tears running down his face. I will never forget that moment as long as I live. He probably saved my life and somehow he thought he failed me."

"Wow," she muttered under her breath.

"Maria would not leave me that night. She told him to go home, and she would call a cab when she needed to go home. He took over and told her in no uncertain terms no. He instructed her to make a list of the items that she would need from home. Next, he informed her that Marisa was going home with him. They would go to her house in the morning and gather what was needed and bring them to the hospital.

"Maria had never met him before this night. She looked at me, and I nodded my head as gently as I could manage.

"He did everything he said, as I knew he would. The next day he took my precious little girl to breakfast. Next, he took her home with him and spent the day playing with Max on the beach and later he took her to the video arcade. He told her that I was strong and that I would be home in no time. After that first day, he took her to school each morning and picked her up when school was out. And then he would bring her to the hospital to visit me."

He paused and looked off into the night air. "You know how when someone needs us we often look back and say I could have done this or that?"

She nodded.

"He could have done no more," Billy C. said, blowing air through pursed lips in solemn frustration. "And even with that he thinks he failed me somehow."

He turned and placed his hand on her arm. "I see the way you light up when he comes around. He does, too, even as much as he tries to hide it. You don't give up. You hear me? This is a man that does not come along often.

"My ladies they love him like he is family. His name is mentioned my wife crosses herself and tears up. My little girl lights up each time she sees him. Troy shows up at the door sometimes and asks if Marisa can go to the video arcade with him. He has even babysat before so Maria and I can go out. I trust him with who I hold most dear in this life. I can pay no higher tribute."

She kissed him on the cheek. "Thank you, Billy C. I look forward to meeting your ladies tomorrow."

He blushed and walked away.

*

AT TEN O'CLOCK, TROY AND MAX were riding toward Snow's Cut Bridge. The voice of Bob Segar sang wistfully, *We were running against the wind.* The trees on each side of the road were adorned with white lights. "Christmas," he muttered.

It was so long ago that Christmas was enjoyable. As a child he usually was awake by five and excitedly exploring the gifts under the tree. But as the years went by and one bad event followed another he came to truly loathe Christmas. It was a yearly reminder of what had escaped him. Not that he needed a yearly reminder when each day was a souvenir of all that had gone amiss in his life.

He thought of Kent as he did each day. He was a small, skinny man with an enormous sweet tooth and a perpetual boyish sense of humor.

His status within the family, at his own choosing was to be on the fringe of the proceedings that took place. Often he operated a video camera to capture events such as Christmas. And always after the meal was eaten he would sneak away outside and smoke his cigarettes in peace.

He had little family life to speak of growing up. His mother died when he was ten years old. He had no meaningful relationship with his father. They moved often, especially when the rent was due.

Despite his harsh childhood years, he grew beyond the environment that he was raised in. He was a good husband to Diane, and an even better father to his daughter, Kathy. He worked hard and provided well, and unlike his father he seldom touched alcohol.

They lived next door to Troy's parents. Kent spent a good part of each summer weekend taking care of not only his yard but his in-laws as well.

He was a high school dropout and yet he was the smartest man that Troy had ever known. He could fix anything from a broken stereo to rebuilding a car engine but it was working with wood that made him really come alive. Troy did not know if it was what he did the best or what he just loved doing the most.

In Troy's eyes, he was the most valuable member of the family. His intelligence and his willingness to help others kept him plenty busy during his time away from work. He never seemed to mind and if he did he did not let on. At times, Troy felt reluctant to ask him for help because he felt that Kent was asked to do too much for the family as it was.

"I miss you," Troy mumbled as he entered the neighborhood where Suzanne lived.

He found the street and drove slowly reading the numbers on each house. "Stay Max," he commanded as he left him sitting upright in the back seat.

The sidewalk curved easily to the front door. He rang the doorbell and waited. He could sense eyes on him through the peephole in the dark green door. He smiled slightly as he suddenly recalled a *Seinfeld* episode, in which, Kramer had reversed the peephole on his door.

The door opened and Suzanne smiled curiously at him. "How did you know where I live?"

"Since you haven't been here long enough to be in the church directory book I called my mom."

"Did she want to know why you wanted it?"

"No. Are you going to leave me out here or may I come in?"

"I'm sorry," she said opening the door all the way and stepping back. "Where's Max?"

"He is in the Jeep."

"Why?"

"I didn't know your policy on dogs."

She laughed lightly and moved past Troy. "Hey boy," she spoke softly, opening the door to the Jeep. "You are not going to stay out here. Come inside."

They walked inside the house. She was dressed in gray gym shorts and a tan sweater that time had nearly faded to white. She invited him to sit on the couch and she sat down on the beautiful hardwood floor beside Max. She began rubbing his back with long slow strokes.

"What brings you here?"

"I wanted to talk."

"Right," she said sarcastically.

"You left upset today."

Max was sprawled out now with his legs in front of his head. His head lifted slightly at the sound of his name before he quickly laid his head back down between his paws, soaking up the attention he was receiving.

She looked up from Max and peered into Troy's eyes. He was dressed in all black work attire. Suddenly her eyes drew in tightly and she looked impishly at him. "I guess since you are in my house than it is my rules. I get to ask questions and you answer."

"I could leave."

"Why did you come here tonight, really?"

"Because you were hurt this morning and I didn't know what to do. I wanted to go after you but I . . ."

She broke the awkwardness of the moment with a suggestion. "Hey, do you want a beer? I bought some Corona today."

"Sure."

She rose and walked into the kitchen. Max followed her. He heard the beers open and next he heard a lime being sliced on a cutting board. He heard water running and then the sound of Max lapping up water. He rose from the couch and walked into the kitchen.

It was a large kitchen with a middle island that contained the stove. The cabinets were bright white, the appliances all stainless. The floor was like black glass. "Nice place."

"Thanks."

Troy's thought drifted to a dream he had endured that afternoon. In the dream, a familiar one, he watched Kent die. The horrible thing about this dream was that it was an exact repeat of what had occurred that fatal day.

He could hear a voice but it seemed distant. "Troy," she said loudly. He looked at Suzanne and the concerned look in her eyes. "How did you know about the dreams?"

"Come with me," she said as she motioned with her hands that held two beers toward a small oak dining table. She placed a beer on the table in front of both chairs. She pulled out one chair and watched him sit down in the other. "Kitchen always seems to be the best place for talking."

She sat across from him and touched his hand briefly. "Tell me about the last dream."

His voice was even and his hand clutched his beer as he began telling her about Kent and the dream of that day, and how often that he dreamed the same dream with little variation.

"How do you feel when you wake up?"

He looked into her eyes and said, "Guilty."

"Why, you can't prevent a brain aneurism?"

He explained to her that the job was far away from medical attention and that he felt Kent might have lived if he would not have persuaded him into leaving his job and working with him.

She waited for a few moments and said ever so gently, "Tell me the rest of it. There's more."

He raised his eyes to meet hers. She nodded firmly.

There was an edge to his even voice that could not hide the anger that raged inside of him. "The truth is that every day I say, 'why God? Why him? It should have been me. He was so valuable to the family. He made his life good.' Something I have never been able to do."

He drank hungrily from his beer. "If you are going to tell me that it is wrong for me to feel this way, don't. And please don't tell me that there is a lesson in this. I'm tired of living with all these wonderful lessons that mean so very little at the end of each day."

She drank from her beer and chose her next words delicately. "Who else have you told this to?"

"The last part? God."

"I can't fix this Troy and you probably wouldn't want me to try. Believe it or not I don't want to examine this to death or more importantly analyze you. I would like to ask you two questions, if I may?"

He said nothing so she moved ahead. "Did Kent love you?"

"We never said it, but yes. We both did."

"What would he say to you if he saw you right now?"

He sighed deeply. "He would tell me to stop feeling sorry for myself. You know I never finished that job. I tried to go back and finish. The woodworking was nearly complete. The irrigation was installed. The landscaping was the only major thing left and that was what I do, or used to do. But I couldn't." He shook his head and forced an insincere smile. "And the owners sued me for not fulfilling the contract, and they won. Justice I guess."

"Asking for justice in this life is a waste of energy. You won't find it very often and when you do it won't be what you thought it to be."

"Life isn't fair, huh? Believe me I have learned that lesson."

"Do you ever think of trying again with maybe another partner?"

"I don't think so," he said with a shake of his head.

"Hey," he said suddenly. "I came out here to check on you. Maybe make you feel better."

"You have."

"How?"

"By being my friend and trusting me. Maybe most of all by making me feel useful. I haven't felt that way here. Maybe you and I both have quit on God in certain ways.

"You did not kill him and there is no need for two people to have died that day. Wasn't one tragic death horrible enough?"

The corners of his mouth moved slightly but it was his eyes that smiled sadly in agreement.

He rose from the chair. "Thanks for the beer. I better leave. We wouldn't want the neighbors to talk."

"Who cares?"

She walked with Max and him to the Jeep. He had his hand on the door handle when she said, "Hey."

He turned to her and she moved closer to him and reached her arms around his large upper body. He hugged her in return and they held each other for several moments and unlike earlier that day he did not feel awkward.

They released each other and she looked up at him with moist eyes. She kissed him delicately on the cheek. "You take care of yourself. You are a good man. Don't forget that. Give yourself a break."

"You might get an argument with people on that."

"Screw them."

He feigned being shocked at her language.

"I know. That is not the way a preacher's wife is supposed to talk." She turned and walked toward her house.

The Jeep door behind her closed and she heard the engine rumble to life. A neighbor to her right was peeping through her blinds trying to be discreet. Suzanne waved. The blinds abruptly closed.

Before she was inside she was already thinking of the missing part of Troy's trilogy of tragedy. And she knew without question that was where the darkest secret hid.

Troy drove home in silence. He thought of Suzanne and her words to him this night. "There is no need for two people to have died that day."

A memory from long ago visited him. Kent had borrowed tree climbing gear from a neighbor and spent a Saturday pruning broken limbs from the many pine trees in his yard. Troy felt queasy just thinking about how high up in the trees Kent was working.

At the end of the day they stood together as the sun faded on the day. One tree in particular caught Troy's eye. The tree was nothing but trunk for eighty feet up. Then at the very top, branches and the needles they contained formed what appeared to be a green puffy ball. It reminded Troy of a green tennis ball attached to a broom handle.

"What do you call that?" Troy asked as he motioned upward to the tree.

Kent hesitated and then his boyish face erupted with a wide smile. "Why that is a Sea Gate Palm Tree," he said, his white teeth sparkling against the grime and sap that nearly covered his face. "I thought you knew something about landscaping," he added, with a grin that seemed larger than his face.

Troy's almost constant anger toward God for taking the wrong family member subsided for the first time. He gazed up at the stars. "God," he called softly. "Did you really need another carpenter that badly?"

16

HE SHOOK AWAKE FROM the grip of another nightmare of death as the first light of morning filtered into his room. His hair was damp with perspiration. He reached beside the night table for the glass of water that rested on it. His hands shook as he raised the glass to his mouth. He drank all of it. As he attempted to return it to the stand, his hands trembled violently and he dropped it. The glass shattering on the floor. "Oh, God," he said wearily

He heard the clicking of Max's nails on the floor. "No, boy!" He called out sharply but it was too late. Max yelped and picked up his front left paw. Troy moved quickly and scooped him up in his massive arms. He sat him down on the bed.

He stroked his head. "It's okay, boy. I'm sorry." He gently lifted the inflicted paw for inspection. "Stay," he commanded firmly. He walked into the bathroom and retrieved the tweezers, alcohol, gauze and tape from the medicine cabinet.

He returned and sat on the bed next to Max. He bent down and kissed him on top of his head. "I'm so sorry, boy." Picking up the foot gingerly he removed three slivers of glass. He dabbed the rubbing alcohol on a piece of gauze and wiped his paw delicately.

Next, he wrapped it with gauze, securing it snugly with adhesive tape. Max laid his head on Troy's leg.

Troy rubbed him with long gentle strokes. "It was another bad dream, Max. They are picking up in intensity and frequency."

Max stayed in place listening intently to the soft tone in his master's voice.

"Do you know what this one was about?"

Max remained still, offering no answers.

"There were dead bodies everywhere. First, Alana asked me again why I didn't get to her sooner. There was blood all over her hands as she reached out to me. You know what happened next?

"The police showed up and they took me away in handcuffs. I tried to tell them that I didn't do it but they just laughed. They told me that I would die in the electric chair and they would make sure that I would suffer for all that I had done.

"I kept pleading with them to believe me. I'm innocent. I'm innocent. I kept repeating. They asked me why there was blood all over me. They locked me away in a cell." He shook his head softly. His day was only beginning and already he was spent.

"Maybe I deserve this Max because I am not innocent."

Max whined and nuzzled his head under his master's hand.

He thought about calling Carla but what would he tell her? Besides what could she do? He was a man haunted by terror and he could see no way out.

"Stay boy," he said firmly as he rose from the bed. He walked into the kitchen to get a broom and dustpan. He returned to the bedroom and diligently went about the cleanup of the broken glass.

He swept the floor meticulously. Max yawned and closed his eyes. Normally, he didn't allow Max on the bed. "What the heck boy. Sleep away."

He was returning the broom and dustpan to the kitchen when the phone rang, startling him. It was not quite seven o'clock.

He answered the phone and heard the softest, kindest, voice that his world contained.

"Dad, are you okay?"

He started to speak but his voice caught.

"Dad?"

"I'm here."

"Are you okay?"

"You have been out late," he said, attempting to change the subject.

"No, Dad. I woke and I could feel you in the room."

Tears rolled down his cheek. "I'm sorry that I haven't called. I knew you were mad at me and I just . . ."

"That's okay, Dad. I'm not mad. I just wanted you to spend Christmas with me. I miss you. I'm sorry that I was angry that day on the phone."

He sat down on the kitchen floor, cradling the phone. "That's okay. I deserved it. I miss you too."

"No, you didn't deserve it. I know that things are amplified for you this time of year. I should have understood that and not been selfish."

He wiped the tears from his face. "Heidi, you have never been selfish. You are the best daughter in the world. You always have been. I love you."

"Are the nightmares really bad?"

He paused, not wanting to worry her and at the same time he did not want to be dishonest. "I'll be okay."

"Do you want me to come home? I talked to Mike about it. He said he would understand."

"No, you stay there. It is always more peaceful for me when I get to the mountains. I'll be okay."

"But I hate you being alone, even if that is what you prefer."

"Max will be with me."

"Dad," she hesitated, unsure of her next words. "Dad, Mom and you told me about the baseball accident and I saw what Kent's death did to you. What it did to all of us. I've always thought there was something else that happened to you that was worse than either of these. I was little but I still remember Alana. What happened to her, Dad? She was here one day and then she was gone. I never saw her again. I asked Mom once and she answered that she just went away."

There was silence as Troy struggled to answer.

"Dad."

"I didn't even think that you remembered her."

"Come on Dad. I'm the kid that was reminiscing about the old days when I was seven."

He smiled slightly.

Her voice was even as she asked, "What is it, Dad, that I was never told. I always knew there was something. Something bad. Something really dark that has haunted you for a long time."

"You were always too smart."

"Tell me what happened."

"No. It is in the past and that is where it should remain."

"Maybe that is the trouble, Dad. It's a past never dealt with."

He was quiet as he heard her words play over in his head again.

"I love you, Daddy. I'll see you soon."

"I love you too, Heidi." He hung the phone up and crawled back into the bed and fell asleep instantly. Max snored peacefully beside him.

*

ALANA HAD LONG LIGHT-BROWN curly hair and eyes that carried a troubled look even during the happiest of times. And that was what that time with Troy was-- the best times in each of their lives.

They met one gorgeous spring day at a park playground. He was with Heidi and she was with her daughter, Amy. They began to strike up a conversation while their girls played together.

Never had he met anyone that he could talk so easily with. He talked so much that he thought that maybe he was making a fool of himself. He even talked about baseball and what had happened to him that day when the baseball gods cursed his right shoulder.

There was something about her eyes that enticed him as no one ever had. There was softness in her voice that lured him to hang on to her every word.

She explained that she was recently separated. She was new to the area and had lived up the road forty miles in the country with her husband, Larry. They operated a small hardware and feed store that was passed down by his family.

Her voice grew sad as she talked about how things had changed once they married. Larry discovered that she had a brief period of promiscuity during high school. It was a time when she foolishly believed the back seat whispers of love from teenage boys.

He became extremely jealous. Spying on her and attempting to control her every move. Where she went, what she wore, whom she spoke to, even though she had never done anything for him to be suspicious of. Finally, she could take it no longer and she left.

Larry tried multiple tactics to convince her to come back. He sent family members to talk to her, even their preacher. Somewhere along the line the community targeted her as the one at fault but then Larry always seemed to have two faces. The one he showed to the community as a hardworking family man who was a deacon in the church and then there was the manipulative evil person that he truly was.

She parted that day and Troy wondered if he would see her again. The next day he went to the park at the same time. After two hours of sitting he gave up and prepared to leave. That is when she appeared with Amy.

She smiled sheepishly at him as the girls took off to play on the swings. Troy was shy with women. Often, he would sense a spark with someone and he would not act upon it. Later he would be full of regret when he never saw them to get another chance. Today he would not repeat that mistake.

She had scarcely sat down before he turned to her. Slowly, he began to speak. "I know that you have a hard situation and if you say no I won't ask again. I would like to take you to dinner tonight."

She gazed at him for several moments. Finally, she nodded her head slowly. "Larry will be coming to pick up Amy later this afternoon."

He went to her apartment at eight. She answered the door and he could easily tell that his own nervousness was greatly surpassed by her own jittery emotions. "Could we talk for a minute?" she asked.

He followed her to the couch. She was wearing a long green dress and she was the most striking woman that he had ever laid eyes upon.

She sat back on the couch and tried to relax but quickly she was leaning forward, sitting on the edge of the couch. She started to speak but no words surfaced.

"If this is not a good idea."

She put a finger to his mouth gently. They sat in silence and then she broke the stillness with a slow even tone, her eyes never leaving his. "Troy, I was nineteen when I married Larry. I had Amy a year later. He was twenty-seven and everyone thought he was the catch of our little country town. For years I thought that this was the way my life would always be. I would be the good country wife and have children.

"We had Amy and being a mom took away from me desiring much of anything for myself. We both wanted more children but it wouldn't happen. We went to the preacher and prayed about it. I even suggested we go to a doctor to see if there was a problem. He refused.

"A few weeks ago, he hit me with his fist. One week later he did it again. I put up with a lot but I've seen women who become a punching bag. I refuse to live that life. I have an aunt here in Wilmington and she is the only family that has tried to help me. His family didn't believe me and if my family believed me they sure didn't support me. That was one month ago. I have never lived apart from my family or him. This is the first time I have been on my own. I have no idea where to go or what I'm going to do."

He sat there in silence trying to digest all the information and tried to think of what to say. He felt the delicate touch of her hand against his face and he wanted to touch every part of her as he had never touched anyone.

Gently she beckoned his face toward hers and she kissed him deeply and softly. They smiled sheepishly. "I just wanted you to know who you were taking to dinner."

"I already knew that," he replied. "I'm taking a beautiful lady to dinner. Someone I want to talk with for hours."

She tilted her head slightly to one side. "Beautiful?"

"Yes. Would you like for me to tell you why?" He did not wait for a reply. "First, you have the most incredible eyes that I have ever witnessed. The way your hair moves in the wind. Your every movement captured in such grace."

She studied him closely. "Do you talk that way to all your dates?"

"I've never talked this way to anyone." Somehow, she knew this to be true.

They fell in love swiftly. The next several weeks proved a wonderful and exciting adventure.

She woke one morning sick to her stomach and she knew that she was pregnant. A trip to her physician confirmed her suspicion. The time period so close to her first time with Troy and the last time with Larry, that mathematically she could not be certain of the father.

She never shared the news with Troy. The same day that she discovered that she was pregnant the leaders of the church visited on behalf of her husband and pleaded for another chance for Larry.

Larry confessed to them his abuse of her and swore before God that it would never happen again. The church leaders gently reminded her of past discretions and encouraged her to give her rightful husband before God one more chance.

Days later she called and told Troy that she was pregnant and that she was sure the baby was Larry's. She returned to Larry and months later gave birth to a son. A son that she knew in her heart belonged to Troy.

17

TROY STOOD OUTSIDE THE hotel door. He raised his right hand to knock. His left hand held flowers that were a mixture of bright yellow and lime green. He refrained from knocking. His heart thumping so loudly that he could not only feel the vibration in his chest but hear it as well.

Stacey had heard the footsteps approach the door and was watching his nervousness through the peephole. "Nothing but a big, bad, fraidy cat," she whispered.

Finally, he knocked. She waited a few moments and opened the door.

Troy smiled anxiously and wiped his sweaty palms on his jeans. She was dressed in a simple white dress that inched just above her knee.

"You look nice."

She placed her hands on her hips. "Nice, that is the best you can do?"

"Really nice," he added nervously.

She shrugged her shoulders and said, "I guess that will have to suffice." She took a black sweater off the couch and draped it over her shoulders. "Off to Billy C.'s house."

"We can walk. It's not far."

"The flowers are to take to Billy C's?"

Troy shook his head, remembering that he did indeed have flowers in his hand. "No. They are for you. They are Spider Mums."

"Where did you buy these?"

"On the main drag in front of the boardwalk there is a florist shop, Beach Blooms. A young couple, Aaron and Julie own it." He paused before adding, "You probably are used to roses."

"Please," she said as she rolled her eyes. "I find roses to be way too cliché for this girl. These are perfect. You did well."

"I mainly petted their Australian Cattle Dog, Charlie, while Julie put everything together."

She put the flowers in a vase she discovered under the sink and placed them on the small gray counter in the kitchen. She backed away and looked at them. She nodded her satisfaction. "Shall we go?"

The night air was nippy. A middling breeze blew in from the sea. The full moon was a brilliant orange as it hovered over the ocean. They passed the club and continued down the boardwalk. The wind increased for a few moments, rustling through a nearby cluster of palm trees offering a sound that Stacey found impossible to describe but soothing nonetheless. People were scarce as they usually were this time of year. The only exceptions were the lonely souls who worked the day and spent the night in the bar of their choice.

There was a small chapel off to their right. There was a sign on one of the heavy wooden doors. *Open daily for prayer.*

Amid the bars, video arcades, gift shops, and a donut shop, the little chapel looked strangely out of place.

"Ever been in there?"

"Once," he replied. "It's an Episcopal Church. The priest is a nice guy. The place is real small. There are maybe two dozen short pews."

"Do they hold regular services?"

"During tourist season."

"I didn't know God took most of the year off."

Troy chuckled softly. "Timothy, the priest, will meet anyone at anytime. It's more of a place for counseling and prayer. He is a good man, who once had a severe drinking problem. He tries to steer people to get help. He hosts weekly A.A. meetings, year-round."

They continued their stroll for six blocks until approaching a gray house perched atop pilings. They walked up the steps and rang the bell.

Billy C. was absolutely beaming as he opened the door. His wife Maria stood nervously behind him.

"Come in," they said simultaneously.

They exchanged greetings. Stacey observed Maria hug Troy so tightly that she appeared unwilling to let him go. She smiled at the warmness of the story she was now privy to. She observed the wetness in Maria's eyes as she released Troy. Maria crossed herself as music filtered from down the hall. Stacey's voice, aided by a young girl.

"Which room?"

"The second door on the left," Maria answered. Her English offered with a heavy Italian accent.

"Do you mind?"

Maria quickly replied, "No, no, not at all."

Stacey walked down the hallway, followed closely by everyone else. She tapped on the door.

A young girl with long brown hair, dark eyes, and braces opened the door nonchalantly. She looked at Stacey and her eyes grew in amazement. She tried to speak but could not find her voice. She pointed to a poster of Stacey on her wall, still unable to find her voice.

Stacey smiled warmly and nodded.

"Oh, oh wow!" She gushed, finding her voice. Billy C. stood by, his face glowing. It was a birthday present that his daughter would never forget. He was almost as proud and happy, as he was thirteen years earlier on this day when the nurse placed her in his arms. That day he had sobbed uncontrollably for minutes, washing his baby girl with tears.

"Would you like for me to sign your poster?"

"Would you?" Marisa shrieked. She scrambled through items on her dresser in search of a pen. She found one and gave it to Stacey.

"Why are you here, Ms. Storm?"

"Stacey, if that is all right with your parents," she stated, looking at them for their approval.

They nodded as the smiles remained etched on their face. Stacey turned back to the poster and signed it.

"I'm staying here for a few days and your dad mentioned that you like my songs."

"Like them? I love them!"

She hugged her daddy. "I love you, Dad. What a birthday."

Stacey looked kindly at her. "There is a catch to this. I don't want you to tell anyone that I'm staying here."

"That is very important, Marisa," Billy C. warned, as he waved his thick index finger from side to side.

She bobbed her head from side to side slightly. "Okay, no problem."

Stacey smiled at her. "Now, would you mind if your Dad took a couple of pictures of us?"

"Would I mind? Would I mind?"

Billy C. took at least a dozen pictures of a star and his exceedingly happy birthday girl.

They dined on tortellini and wine. It was a festive atmosphere and Troy could not tell who was smiling the most. The young girl or the father who delivered the perfect birthday gift.

Next, they enjoyed tiramisu and freshly brewed coffee. Stacey declared it the best dessert that she had ever tasted.

*

TROY AND STACEY WALKED quietly down the boardwalk. Stacey broke the silence. "She's a beautiful young girl isn't she?"

"Yes, she is," he answered softly.

A few steps later he said, "You were so good with her. She was meeting a star but by the end of dinner she saw you as a really good person. A person with good values that treats people fairly and honestly. I hope that is what she remembers the most."

"Thank you."

"I guess that initially I expected you to be this star that was probably accustomed to being catered to."

"Now, how could you think that knowing where I come from? If you would have made the major leagues and been a star would you have been that way?"

"Probably."

"I don't believe that. "I've observed you with people. You are kind and considerate. Nate and Mabry would have never let you stray far."

They walked in silence before she spoke again. "I think you just won't step away from the past."

"There's more to it than you know or need to know."

"So, you shut me out without a chance," she said her voice rising.

"What chance?"

"Please, Troy. Don't act like you are not a perceptive man. You know that I am interested in you, really interested. Is it because of this dang star conception that you refuse to give me a thought or are you just not interested?"

He remained calm. "I think about you," he said softly.

"Well, then do something about it," she demanded, her voice urgent.

Two men, sitting on a bench with cupped hats on their heads and nearly identical salt and pepper goatees looked up at them.

Her voice lowered. "I'm not asking for your hand in marriage. I like you. That is obvious and I think that you like me. There is chemistry in the air between us, right? Let's take a chance. No risk, no reward."

They were at the hotel when he answered her. "Don't come into my nightmare. You have way too much going for you, and I have nothing to offer. I'm an old bouncer for God's sake and you are a star."

She shook her head in frustration.

They walked in silence to her hotel door. She reached out and took his hand. "I am just a girl, Troy. I am not a star. Maybe we could chase the nightmares away. Will you come inside?"

He shook his head no, turned, and walked away. She watched him thinking that maybe he would turn around but he never hesitated as he made his escape.

He walked to his house thinking with each step that he must just be the biggest fool in the universe.

It was eleven o'clock and she was still stalking around her hotel room. She was packing her things hurriedly and wondering just how she would explain to Mabry why she would not be here for Christmas. "You have all these men who want to go out with you. But you are never interested so you come here and fall for some big dumb bouncer," she said as she flung a shoe into her bag.

Finally, fatigue set in and she sat down. And then she decided on a different course of action.

The first thing she noticed as she stepped out on to the boardwalk was that she had forgotten her shoes. She was still wearing the same white dress that she had worn trying to impress someone. It was cold now and she wished that she at least would have had enough sense to grab her sweater.

She walked hurriedly past a man who was moving awkwardly, obviously intoxicated. He smiled lustily and said, "Going somewhere?"

"Not your way, pal," she answered tersely.

She was out of earshot before he could gather a rebuttal.

She reached the cream-colored cottage. She approached the front door and tried to open it. It was locked.

The house was dark except for the light the moon offered. "Sleep you stubborn man. Sleep the night away while you cause me to lose all my bearings."

She was about to pound on the front door when she decided to go around back. She smelled freshly cut lumber and she recalled Troy speaking earlier of installing a pet door for Max. She squinted in the moonlight and saw the newly installed doggie door.

"Hope he built it wide enough for me."

On her hands and knees, she began edging through the door. At one point she thought she was stuck. How embarrassing would that be? She was almost through when she felt a wet tongue on her face. "I didn't think that you would bite me buddy," she whispered.

Troy woke to a slight sound but without worry sought to return to sleep. No intruder would ever get by Max.

He opened his eyes as she entered the room. In the moonlight that trickled through the window his eyes searched hers and saw the anger they held. She swept her hair behind her with a flick of her hand. She lifted the covers and crawled in the bed. He started to speak and she said quickly, "You are so good at not talking so try and maintain that."

In one quick move, she was on top of him and looked in his eyes. She touched his face delicately with her hands and then cradled as she lowered her head and kissed him long, gently, and with a smoothness that reminded Troy of a jazz song that he had once heard in New Orleans. She lifted her head back up and he saw a sad smile and a few tears trickle down her face. He put his right hand behind her neck and gently pulled her down kissing her with a passion he thought to be long ago dead.

*

THERE WAS A LADY PUSHING a stroller back and forth in front of his house. He sat on the front porch watching. She wore a hood that concealed most of her face, and he could not make out her identity.

He called to her. "Ma'am, are you lost? May I help you?"

She ignored him and continued to walk back and forth. Occasionally, she looked eerily at him. He felt fearful and unsure of what to do.

Then she pushed the stroller toward him. She stopped at the bottom step. She pulled back the hood and he saw that it was Alana. She removed the blanket from the baby. The baby was dead. He woke abruptly began to scream.

Stacey woke suddenly at the sound of his cry and moved to him. He pushed her away with his forearm knocking her off the bed. The thump of her body striking the floor woke him and only then did he realize that the demons had invaded his sleep once again.

He shook his head in an attempt to focus and then he saw her on the floor still clothed in the white dress. They never spoke after sharing the last kiss and she had fallen asleep soon after with her head on his chest. He had stroked her hair until he heard a slight snore and then he fell asleep.

"I knocked you off the bed," he said, shamefully.

"I'm okay," she said, as she crawled back into the bed. She touched his back gently. His back was soaked with perspiration.

He rose and walked toward the kitchen clad in an old pair of faded purple East Carolina gym shorts. She heard the refrigerator door open. He returned with two bottles of water, giving her one. He sat on the edge of the bed as they both drank quietly. Then he made a mock attempt at a toast. "Welcome to my world."

He studied her eyes looking for fear, rejection, or even doubt but there was none. There was tenderness and a concern that touched him deeply. "Don't get messed up with this. You have so much going for you."

"I don't have love in my life. Not until now."

He looked at her and said softly, "I'm a tired bouncer with bad dreams and nothing to offer you."

"How about your heart and a chance. We take the rest one step at a time?"

He looked at her and then at Max who as always stood closely by concerned about his master and these screams that haunted him.

She touched his cheek with the back of her hand and guided him back into her vision. "You care for me, don't you?"

He smiled and said, "You seem to have all the other answers, I'm sure that you have that one as well."

"Come back to bed," she offered gently. She laid her head on his chest and rubbed him as easily as if he were a delicate crystal. "Come on, boy," she called to Max. He jumped on the bed and laid his head across Troy's legs.

The three of them lay still. The quiet massaged by the ocean and its harmonic voice. And then another voice just as exquisite joined in.

Stacey's voice was low as she began to sing, *I took my love and I took it down. I climbed a mountain and I turned around. And I saw my reflection in the snow covered hills.* By the time she reached the end of "Landscape", one of her favorite songs by Stevie Nicks, Troy was sleeping peacefully.

She continued to lie there awake for over an hour, listening to his every breath, and praying to God that he would drive the demons away from the man that lay beside her.

18

THE SUN LEAKED INTO THE living room where David spent most of his time. He was reading the Word and praying. It was his quiet time with the Lord and each day began this way. He was reading in the Book of Joshua when he heard a slight knock on the door. He was not surprised to see his friend through the glass storm door. Troy was dressed in gray cargo shorts and a long sleeve white T-shirt, with Carolina Beach, written in cursive royal blue letters across the front of his chest. The boy had been on his mind since he woke before the sun was up. He smiled in gratitude of how his precious Lord prepared his heart for things to come, while motioning with his hand for his friend to enter.

Troy walked in and David signaled for him to sit. "I have been expecting you," David said with a warm smile.

"That is funny. I did not even know I was coming. I woke early and I was driving with no particular destination in mind."

"The Lord knew, Troy."

Troy breathed deeply and closed his eyes.

David looked at the fatigue on his friend's face and his heart went out to him. He felt blessed that such a man who bowed to no one considered him to be a spiritual mentor, even a father figure.

"Sleeping is still a problem?"

He nodded slightly without opening his eyes.

David watched him and prayed. He was silent for several minutes and at one point he heard Troy breathe deeply and he smiled as Troy drifted off to sleep. He continued to read his Bible.

"I fell asleep. It must be the peace I feel when I am with you."

"I have nothing that you can't have."

"Is Toni going to be upset that I am here so early?"

"She is visiting her sisters in Tennessee, but she would not mind if she were here."

"I feel like she gets tired of me coming here and nothing ever changes in my life."

"Troy, look at me." The two men looked each other in the eye. "That door is always open to you. You are not to think in any other way."

"I know, and I thank you for all that you have given me."

"What is it that you think that I have given you?"

"Slivers of hope, and to a drowning man, what greater gift?"

There was silence again and David waited for Troy to share. He would sit all morning if need be. He learned long ago not to be so tied to an agenda that he did not have the time to wait for open doors.

"I met a girl."

David looked at his friend and waited for more. "What is she like and might I add you do not seem overly excited and you are certainly not the type to settle." He rubbed his hands together. "Tell me about her."

"She is beyond any dream I ever had in a woman. I just don't want her to settle."

David rubbed his hands again, searching for the right words. He decided as he often did on silence.

Troy sighed. "She is gorgeous, kind, and she is a successful singer." He paused before adding, "Of course her judgment in men may be suspect."

"I don't want to hear that. You know it upsets not only me but our Lord to hear you put yourself down."

"The nightmares are gaining in intensity," he stated flatly.

David had prayed many times about the dreams that traumatized Troy. He knew that among many there was one incident stored away that trumped all the others. He did not know what it was but he sensed in his spirit that it was something so very dark.

Troy wanted to share with him about the undisclosed darkness but he had promised Carla. He was so tired of keeping this from his friend. Still, he would not break his promise to her.

As if reading his thoughts, David asked, "Why can't you share with me what it is that haunts you so?"

Troy rubbed his hands on his legs as his eyes remained closed. "I want to. You know that I trust you."

"I do know that, son. Whatever it is it will not leave this room. We need to get it out into the light, Troy. That is how we banish the darkness. We bring light to it. It is no different than turning the light switch on in a dark room. What do you have to lose by trusting an old friend?"

"My freedom."

"Troy, how free are you?"

Troy stretched the taut muscles in his neck.

"You promised someone to never share this dark secret."

David read the expression on Troy's face and knew that he was correct. He continued down that path. "You trust me. You know my word is good and if I tell you that whatever it is remains here with us and you still won't tell me." He paused, flicking his hand briefly through his hair. "I must suffice that you made a vow to someone not to share this secret. And a man of honor, such as yourself, does not break his word . . . ever," his voice trailing off.

Troy muttered, "Yeah, a man of honor like me. That is what people see, and not a tired broken down bouncer."

David rarely raised his voice, even when he preached, but he did now. "I don't care what other people see. I see an honorable man, wounded yes, but a truthful caring honest man. There is nothing broken in you that God can't fix." His voice softened, returning to his customary quiet manner. "Troy, how do you think God views you?"

He blew out a frustrated breath of air. "I don't know. He is so far away that I am not sure he views me at all."

"No," he said, with a shake of his head. "That is not true. I want you to close your eyes."

Troy looked at him with a peculiar gaze and David barely nodded. Troy obliged.

"This is my image of God, my father, our father," he added. "Picture a trail in the woods. There is forest all around. Gigantic towering trees, mixed in with every kind of plush plant life you can imagine growing in the natural floor of the woods. As it is with a forest there are pockets of thick underbrush. The path winds through the woods and it is clear and smooth. I picture walking along with my father talking easily. That is how it is when I am connected to his spirit without interruption. Now, like a small child, I stray off the path and I am caught in the briars, vines, and all of the dense underbrush of the forest. That is when I feel out of sorts until I return to the path and resume our walk."

"You feel disconnected at times?" Troy quizzed him, the surprise apparent in his voice.

"We all feel disconnected at times."

There was silence for several moments before David asked, "What is the image you have of God when I have stumbled off the path?"

"I guess he is angry."

"No. He stands patiently with his hand out waiting for me to recommence the walk that we were both enjoying so much. I want you to be clear he has never turned away when I stray off the path that he has laid out only for me. He still lives in my heart. My salvation secure in him."

"I can't imagine you straying off the path."

"I was the Shepherd of many churches. Do you think all my decisions were right? That I had the correct words for everyone? Of course I did not," he said, answering his own question. "It is not easy to stay in tune with the spirit at times and we can't work hard enough for it to happen. Do you know what gets us in the most trouble if we are truly a believer?"

Troy shook his head.

"During quiet times with no clear direction we try to go it alone. We don't know that is what we are doing. We just get antsy when God wants us to rest."

The next thing he said shocked Troy. "Carla."

Troy looked quickly at him. "What?"

"Carla is who you promised."

Troy's eyes opened larger in surprise.

"Can't you see God is pulling out all the stops to deliver you from what grips you?"

"Even if it means I go to jail?"

"God is powerful. He makes a way when there appears to be none." He paused for a moment and he looked out at the water and a thought came to mind. "Troy, I know you believe in God."

Troy nodded his agreement.

"That water," he said as he pointed. "You believe God created it?"

"Yes."

"How about the sun that rose a little while ago?"

Troy nodded.

"The oceans and all the mountains everywhere?"

"Yes."

"We agree that he is that powerful and that magnificent?"

"Yes."

"But you don't believe in his ability to help you regardless of your circumstances?"

"I want to."

"Call Carla."

"Excuse me?"

"Call Carla and ask her to release you from this promise so that you might be able to be free."

"She won't."

"Humor me."

Troy looked at him and did not move.

"Trust, Troy."

"I do trust you."

"God, Troy. Trust him."

Troy reached for the phone on the coffee table in front of him. He dialed Carla's number. David walked into the kitchen to gather coffee for each of them and to allow Troy space. He could tell the dialogue was one of disagreement as he had expected. He sat the cups of the steaming coffee on the counter and began to pray.

"She wants to speak with you," Troy called to him.

David gathered the cups and walked back to the living room. He handed one to Troy and sat down. He took the phone.

"Hello, Carla."

There was silence for several moments. "Yes, he can trust me, and not only that but you can as well."

Carla talked for several minutes and Troy could hear the animation in her voice as she tried every way to stop this hidden secret from being shared and then there was silence.

"Carla, it is obvious that you love Troy very much. He is the father of your child. He is your best friend. You don't want to see him hurt. I want you to ask Troy one question and we will leave this matter with your decision. Ask him if I don't love him every bit as much. Ask him if he is not like a son to me," the gentle man said softly, his voice breaking ever so slightly. "Ask him if I would ever do anything to harm him?"

Troy saw his friend's eyes well up with tears. He touched his shoulder. He thought the phone was being passed to him but David placed it gently down, ending the call.

"She said it was your decision."

Troy sat silently for minutes, occasionally drinking his coffee. David did likewise waiting patiently.

Troy cleared his throat and then he proceeded to tell all that led up to that night when he took another man's life.

19

ALAN SMILED AS THE JET touched down in Wilmington in the early morning light. He was home. Somewhat late due to flight delays but home nonetheless. Exhaustion consumed his body.

He felt confident that his absence had brought Suzanne to her senses. He would soon discover just how utterly erroneous his thinking would prove to be.

*

THE BAR WAS HALF FULL when Suzanne entered. She stopped to chat with Michael. "Where's the boss?"

"He's in the back with Stacey and Mabry. You can go back. Just knock on the door."

"That's okay. I'll wait." She paused before asking, "How is he?"

"He should be good. There is a rumor that he is keeping company with a certain lady."

She winced without thinking. She looked at Michael to see if he had caught her reaction. He played it off well if he did.

She dragged a barstool beside him and sat down. "How long have you worked here?"

"Two years."

"What was your first impression of Troy?"

"Aw, my infamous job interview." He chuckled softly. "He asked me at one point how I would feel being a black man working in a predominately white club. I corrected him and said, African American.

"He looked at me without emotion and said if you are looking for political correctness maybe you better seek employment elsewhere.

"Now, I could have been offended but I just had a feeling that this was a man I wanted to work with. He was direct, honest, and God knows I needed the money."

She nodded and looked off into space.

"You got troubles, Suzanne?"

"No, actually I have a new life. I just hope that I'm up for it. I'm going to leave. I'll talk to him later."

He watched her walk away and then he reached for the phone and called the office. Mabry answered.

"I need to see him. There's no trouble but ask him to hurry."

Troy was by his side in seconds. Max strolled along beside him. Michael explained about Suzanne, and Troy and Max took off quickly toward the parking lot in pursuit of her.

"Go get her, Max," he instructed.

Max caught her just before she reached her car. He sat down obediently in front of her. She knelt and began to rub his head. Briefly, she nuzzled his face, as she continued talking softly to him about what a good boy he was.

Troy caught up to them. "Good job, boy."

She stood and turned to Troy. The sight of him brought a much needed smile to her face. He was by the car now. "What's up? Why did you leave?"

"I thought that you were busy."

"Not too busy for a friend."

"I could use a friend right now."

"Come on back inside. We can talk in the office."

"This is private."

"They are leaving."

"Who?"

"Mabry and Stacey."

"Are you seeing Stacey?"

He moved his feet awkwardly. "That is another story. Let's talk about you first."

She reached in the back seat for a large envelope and they began walking toward the club. They were near the entrance when Mabry and Stacey emerged. Troy made the introductions. Stacey and Suzanne exchanged strained smiles.

Suzanne sat down on the couch and patted Max behind his ears. Troy sat across from her. He studied the strain and sadness in her eyes. His eyes fell to the envelope that was clutched tightly in her hands.

He motioned toward it. "I guess you want me to see that."

She passed it over without a word. He opened the clasp on the back of it and pulled out the contents. There was a letter and disc.

> *Dear Ms. Matthews:*
>
> *We thought that you might like to see the Rev. Matthews at work. You know how he loves to counsel young people about the danger of premarital sex.*
>
> *We wondered just how holy he really was. So, we invited him to our house for an emergency counseling session.*
>
> *Enjoy the disc,*
>
> *Brittany and Candice*

He looked up from the letter and saw the anger in her eyes. "Play it," she instructed.

"No," he said firmly. "I assume this video is incriminating for Alan."

"They played him pretty well. He had been there thirty minutes when Brittany excused herself. She returned to the room without clothes. He resists for a few moments but then Candice disrobes and well ... They were tanned, fit beyond most men's dreams, and cleavage to offer that would make forty of mine."

"That's no excuse."

She shook her head vigorously in agreement. "I know that and I know there is no defense for this," she said, her voice trailing off, as she pointed to the disc.

Suddenly her face lightened. "They did me a favor. I guess I should not view it that way. Lord knows those young girls need some serious help.

"I've been miserable for so long. This makes everything easier." She offered a forced laugh that was anything but a symbol of joy. "I had actually decided to give him, us, one more chance."

"What did he say?"

"He said they coerced him, trapped him, and that he deserved grace."

"I told him that he could receive grace from God and in time from me. But under no circumstances would I ever be his wife again."

"What will you do?"

"Go back to Tennessee."

She paused. "I need a place to stay for a few days. Will Mabry rent me a room?"

"Of course."

She laughed. "Money won't be an object."

Once again, he waited for her to fill in the blanks.

"We built quite a nest egg together over the years. We, or more correctly, I made quite a few good stock picks. I told him that he could have the house and everything in it, along with his pension but that he had one minute to call the stockbroker and tell him to liquidate enough securities to write me a check for $800,000."

"Did he argue?"

"Before he could open his mouth I held the disc up. It dawned on him that I might just play it for all the right people." She paused, before adding, "Maybe I will do it anyway. He has no business being a preacher anywhere."

"I don't know what to say."

"Like you ever did." She laughed.

"Do you want a beer?"

"Only if you join me? Let's toast to my new life."

"I can do that."

He returned with two Coronas with a slice of lime nestled on the neck of each. He handed her one and they forced the lime down into the neck and turned the bottle upside down briefly. Their thumb pressed securely against the opening.

"To your new life."

They tapped their bottles and drank slowly.

"Will you be okay?"

"Tough, strong, independent woman like me, are you serious?"

"Sorry, I forgot how tenacious you are."

She drank again. "Tell me about your girl."

"You would think someone as successful as she is would have better taste in men."

"How do you feel about her?"

"I'm trying not to."

"That is the wrong answer, idiot."

He smiled warily at her. "I'm sure that with your charm you will have no troubles attracting men."

"Very funny."

"I'll get us another round and then I will call Mabry about your room," he said, rising and walking toward the door. "Best I don't go but Michael and a couple of the guys will go with you tomorrow to get your things."

He was in the doorway when he turned back. "Do you know what kind of man that you will want when you have healed from all this and are ready to begin fresh with someone?"

She smiled and said nothing. He was through the door when she whispered, "Someone just like you."

20

Mabry's favorite part of the beach house was the deck. She particularly loved in the early morning as the sun ascended out of the Atlantic. She sat in one of the high resin chairs that allowed you to look over the rail without obstruction. There was steam rising slowly from the coffee housed in a purple ECU mug that sat on the small round white table beside her open Bible. The sky was faultless and the air crisp. She was comfortable in her jeans, white T-shirt, and a purple and gold ECU hoodie.

It was the last weekend for the club before it closed for the season. She thought about Troy and if, as usual, he was preparing to take off for the mountains to escape the holidays. She was not one to see the devil behind every bush, but she did think one of his greater schemes was to isolate people. She had nothing against time alone and this time right now in the early morning was a favorite for her. Still, to be isolated too much was not a good thing. She knew Stacey was very interested in Troy and perhaps had fallen in love with him. She thought of Nate and while they had their share of disagreements through the years they were truly partners in everything. The truth was the man spoiled her rotten. On cue she heard the door open and he was by her side refilling her coffee mug.

"Thank you."

"You are welcome."

"Not just for the coffee. For everything," she said, reaching and touching his weathered face.

"Something troubling you?" When she failed to respond he said, "It is the last weekend of the club and you think Troy is going to take off to be alone in the mountains."

She still did not respond and he added, "And you worry not only about Troy but Stacey as well because she has obvious feelings for him."

"You know me well, Nate."

He kissed her cheek and said, "And you want to fix all of this and you can't."

"Troy looks so weary and I can tell the nightmares are tormenting him. I can't help him. His mom called last night to ask if he was leaving for the mountains. We both cried over him. Neither of us with any answers for him other than our prayers."

"I know there is a wound so deep in him that only God can heal it and that will happen when Troy lets it go."

"Do you ever think he will?"

Nate smiled warmly at her. "Honey, prayer is one thing, and faith another. Let's hang on to both."

She nodded at him as she studied the kindness in his eyes. He was a tough man, small in stature, but big in all the things that mattered. "You and Troy always jab at each other but you really care about him, don't you? And not just because he means so much to me."

They heard footsteps on the stairs and looked at each other. Nate said, "It is early. Stairs and not the elevator. It is too light of foot for knucklehead so I guess I will get Stacey a cup of coffee."

Stacey emerged moments later. Mabry smiled at Stacey, admiring how she could wear jeans, a long sleeve T-shirt that appeared about three sizes too big, and a Carolina Beach ball cap and looked absolutely striking. "Have a seat young lady," she said as she gestured toward the empty chair beside her. "Nate is bringing you coffee."

Stacey sat down and the two women looked out at the ocean. The door opened and Nate sat the coffee on the table, kissed Stacey on top of her ball cap, accepted her thank you, and returned inside.

"What are you reading, Teach?" she asked, pointing to the open Bible.

"Reading about the prodigal son."

"Do you read the Bible every day?"

"Pretty much every morning. It is a rare occasion that I don't. It tends to put me in a better perspective for the day to come."

There was quietness for a few minutes, save the gentle waves breaking near the shoreline. "When the song first hit I felt more than joy, a relief that my parents were not right about me." She paused, searching for the remainder of the story.

"They never were right about you, Stacey. You did not need a hit song to disprove their foolishness."

Stacey nodded softly as she continued to watch the ocean. "At first I felt this angry satisfaction toward them. I did not like that about myself." Stacey pointed toward the worn Bible on the table. "I began to read the New Testament last year. I read the entire New Testament in four months and most often in the morning like you. I went to church some with neighbors growing up, and I went with you guys some when I lived with you, but it never took root. You know what I mean?"

"Yes."

"There was a time I was not certain that my music taking off was the best thing for me. I sure needed the money and it was an artist dream to acquire that break. There are many more talented than me that never made it. But I began to make questionable decisions and one day I snapped at this young Hispanic lady at the hotel we were staying in because my room service breakfast was not exactly the way I wanted it. She had limited English vocabulary but meanness is translated in every language. She looked wounded and I was responsible for it. I think it was that night I began to read the Bible. I read all of Matthew in one sitting. It was three a.m. when I finished. And then I knelt beside my bed and prayed, really prayed for the first time in my life. I poured my heart out and asked God to search it and remove the ugly parts." She stopped and drank from her coffee mug.

"What happened?"

Stacey's voice choked slightly as she spoke. "It felt like it does when you are cold and you slip into a warm bath. The way the warmth soothes you inside and out displacing the chill in your body. I began to cry and I felt for the first time ever that God was not distant, not angry, not disappointed but truly loved me as his child." She wiped her tears away and said, "I have not been the same since that morning.

People with the tour knew something was different but no one really asked. I never felt the need to explain. I did get some strange reactions when I insisted on singing "Amazing Grace" at the end of some of the concerts. The fans seemed to appreciate it. I guess most of us believe in God. We just don't walk the path with him. I decided I would. I have been more at peace and I am not angry anymore, well with the possible exception of that obstinate man-child of yours."

Mabry placed her hand on Stacey's arm. "Why Troy? You must have a list of men a mile long asking you out."

"I decided I would not date for the sake of dating. I wanted to feel God's hand in it. I am not saying he sits up there and plays matchmaker for everyone. But I do believe if we give that part to him he will let us know if it is a good path and whether he will bless the two people. I feel peaceful with Troy even while he is so haunted by darkness." She drank from her cup. "Maybe two people falling for each other is not just about today and tomorrow. Maybe they also can help heal past hurts." She sipped her coffee again. "I have spent the night at his place and he has the worst nightmares. He wakes and he is so ashamed. This big tough man and he wears the look of a small boy caught in a bad act. It is heart breaking."

"Why become involved in a situation that may never resolve itself?"

She shrugged her shoulders and whispered softly, "Maybe I am the angel God has sent for Troy and he just does not know it yet."

There was silence again. "I am not sleeping with him, Teach. Well, let me clarify that. I am not having sex with him and he has not tried."

Mabry chuckled and said, "I don't recall asking." She thought for a few moments before adding, "He is afraid that if he lets you into his life it will only hurt you. That is how you can tell Stacey that he does care deeply for you. Just please be careful."

"Careful with my head or careful with my heart?"

"Both."

*

IT WAS EARLY FRIDAY MORNING. Troy sat studying the ocean. Max laid in the sand in front of him with his snout placed on Troy's black high top Converse shoes. He eyed his master and knew once again that something was awry.

There had been a lot wrong lately and sleep alluded Troy and when he did manage to dose off the nightmares began with unbridled intensity. He had tried to keep his distance from Stacey the past few days and he had refused to allow her to stay the night.

It was moments like now he thought maybe it was best to call the authorities and tell them what ensued that night. He did act in self defense but he also lied about any involvement. The truth was they may convict him of murder. At least everything would be out in the open and maybe he could sleep at night. He looked up at the sky and asked, "What do you think God?"

Max rose and laid his head in Troy's lap and began to whimper. He cupped Max's face in his hands. "You look tired boy. I think I am keeping you up at night. Have you been standing watch over me?" He knelt and kissed him on his nose and rubbed his face gently.

Max settled back at his feet and Troy knew the decision he had just made was not going to be received well. He and Max were going to leave for the mountains as soon as the club closed tomorrow night. "Let's go, Max. It is time to pack the duffle bag."

21

IT WAS SATURDAY, THE LAST DAY of the season for Mabry's. The club opened at three in the afternoon and as was customary they closed the doors for the season at nine o'clock ushering the remaining customers outside. There were three bands that had played ninety-minute sets. Troy smiled wearily. He turned back to the staff. Mabry was present for the last night as always.

Mabry toasted the staff for a very successful season. She looked around and speculated as to who would be back the following spring if the doors opened once again. They had been approached recently with a very generous offer to purchase their property. The truth was that they were both ready to sell. Nate wanted to sail away for months at a time while they were young enough to do it. Her eyes fell on Troy and she knew that she could not sell anything until she was sure that her boy was going to be okay. It would not do for him to discover that she had refused to sell the property primarily because of him. He would quit on the spot and probably move away, leaving her no way to watch over him. She had to feel good about his future before they could depart. God bless Nate, who chose to understand this. She felt like she had gotten her way too much in their life. She wanted to give her husband the things he so richly deserved.

Troy seemed to grow wearier with each passing day. She had hoped, had prayed that Stacey would help him find his way to happiness. But it would take an answer more powerful than Stacey's love to drive the demons out that consumed his life.

Troy felt her eyes upon him and he gazed at her briefly, before turning away. The dreams were worse than ever. They seldom rested. Each one collectively seemed to be a gathering of all the bad things that had frequented his life. He knew that Mabry hoped that he would not depart to the mountains for Christmas but his decision was made. His bags were packed and he was leaving tonight. Part of him hated to leave and he knew there would be hurt involved, but he reconciled that it was for the best, especially for Stacey.

The door swung open and Stacey entered. Her face captured in anguish. Her cheeks stained with old tears. Max trotted to her side. "I went by your house. I had a feeling. The Jeep is packed and ready to go. You were not even going to say good-bye."

All the eyes in the room turned toward Troy. He shifted nervously on his feet. What could he tell her? That he wanted to love her, to be with her, but it was best for him to move on. And more importantly for her to leave and forget the foolish notion that something could work between them.

"Is that true?" Mabry asked softly.

He looked at her and then at Stacey but he did not reply.

"You've never been anything but honest with me and now is not the time to change," Mabry said, the anger etched across her face.

His head moved slightly up and down. She looked at him sternly and his head dropped lower.

"I'm sorry," he said. "Max, let's go." He started toward the door but Max held firm by Stacey's side.

He turned back and commanded slightly louder, "Max, let's go."

Max looked up at Stacey and then slowly began walking toward his master.

The door closed and Stacey's head fell to her chest."

*

THE SUN WAS BRIGHT AND FULL, hovering just over the ocean. Stacey had been unable to sleep even for a minute. She walked down the beach and stopped at his house, hoping upon hope that the Jeep would magically be present but it was not.

She walked toward the club. She thought about the night that they had walked to Billy C.'s house, and the night that she sneaked into his house. Why did memories that were once so precious hurt so badly now?

She rubbed her eyes wearily and when she opened them again she saw his Jeep parked awkwardly in the corner of the bar parking lot. She raced toward the door of the club and began pounding on the door. No one answered.

She ran the several blocks to Mabry and Nate's house. She sprinted up the stairs, almost falling on the last one. Nate was sitting out on the deck sipping coffee. He smiled at her and said, "Good morning."

She barely acknowledged him as she swept past him and into the house. "Mabry," she called loudly.

Mabry was jarred awake by the strain in Stacey's voice. Her eyes were barely open when she saw Stacey standing at the foot of her bed.

"His Jeep is at the club. Let's see if he is there," she pleaded.

She started to advise her to let him go but she saw that glimmer of hope in her eyes and she couldn't do it. She smiled kindly at her and nodded. "Get a cup of coffee for each of us and give me a little time to get dressed. We will take my car."

Minutes later they were inside the club. Stacey flung open the door to the office fully expecting to find him asleep on the couch but the room was silent and barren.

"Do you think that he has just had enough? A few nights ago, he woke screaming and since then he has refused to allow me to stay over." She rubbed her hand harshly over her hair. "Maybe he found the only way he could escape."

"No," Mabry stated firmly. She wished that she believed what she had just said with as much conviction as the tone of voice indicated. Always a woman of action, she picked up the phone and called Carla and asked if she had heard from him. That proved to be a dead end as well.

Mabry's thoughts drifted back to Stacey's questions. She wondered if he had indeed decided to swim far away from the dreams that haunted him. "Let's go to Suzanne's room. Maybe he went to talk to her."

They walked briskly to the hotel. Mabry knocked on her door. The door opened and Suzanne stood there dressed in running attire.

Stacey grabbed her arm in desperation. "Is Troy here?"

"No, what's wrong?"

"We can't find him. He was going to leave last night but his Jeep is in the parking lot."

Suzanne saw the fear in each of their eyes. "I'll help you look. Let's go," she said.

They walked the boardwalk checking the breakfast house first. Next they walked to the Crush & Grind. No luck there either. They doubled back to his house where they found Carla standing in the driveway.

She looked at them and asked, "Any luck?"

The three of them shook their heads no.

"Let's keep looking. What about Max, any sign of him?"

"No," Mabry answered.

Suzanne looked at Mabry who seemed unwilling to look her in the eye. "Mabry," she asked firmly, "you think that he did something, don't you?"

"Did what?" Carla interjected.

It was the fear in Stacey's face that told Suzanne exactly what dark thoughts they shared were.

Suzanne took Stacey and Mabry by the hand. "Absolutely not."

Stacey walked over to a wooden bench and sat down. Her shoulders slumped and she began to sob without restraint. Her voice choked and Suzanne could barely make out her words. "You don't understand. He can't sleep. The nightmares won't leave him alone. He is worn out." She leaned her head down to her knees and wept. "It is my fault. I kept pushing him to live. I was selfish and I should have just let him be."

Carla sat on the bench beside her and held her in her arms. Mabry stood over both with her hand on Stacey's shoulder. Suzanne walked over to Stacey. "There is no crime in loving that man. You gave him a chance and your heart. Don't be sorry about that and stop thinking that he is gone because I refuse to accept that. He is here somewhere and we are going to find him," she said, leaving little room for debate.

It was Carla who spoke up. Her eyes lightened with a sudden thought. "Suzanne is right. We are missing something. Since Max is nowhere to be found either, that means only one thing. Max is with him. Troy would never allow anything to happen to that dog, right?"

Suzanne and Mabry nodded with new found belief. Stacey raised her head. Her face a shade of pinkish red, covered with tears. She looked at Suzanne and she wanted so desperately to believe. Suzanne nodded one time firmly. "Let's go find him, okay?" Carla stood up first and helped Stacey to her feet.

One hour later they sat on a bench by the boardwalk. The four of them were wracked with despair. Suzanne was even wearing down.

She bowed her head and silently prayed. *God, please show us the way. Send an angel to guide us. Please Lord, please.*

She lifted her head and opened her eyes to a sight that shocked her and at the same time sent cascades of goosebumps throughout her entire body. David Lang was walking slowly on the boardwalk and his eyes were intently searching the area.

She rose and called softly to him, "Rev. Lang."

He turned toward her voice and he walked gingerly to her. "Please call me David."

His easy going humble demeanor was so endearing and she certainly could understand why he was loved by so many. She met him briefly but her husband had refused to reach out to such a beneficial resource. It was one of many of Alan's mishaps. The truth was her husband would never be able to touch what David Lang had and maybe that was why he shut him out. He knew David was a mountain that could not be scaled, though she knew from all she had heard that the man in front of her was in competition with no one. It was too bad Alan believed he must be the lead in everything.

The ladies stood and greeted him. Mabry knew him from the times Nate and she attended church when he was the senior pastor at Portside. She hugged him and said through her tears, "He is lost and we can't find him."

He let go of her and looked at Stacey. "You must be Stacey and I wonder are you the woman that I have prayed for so long?"

Stacey gazed at the softness of his expression. There was a light that seemed to radiate out of him. She recalled something Troy once said. "David and my mom are two people that I feel like I am in the presence of God when I am with them."

"I certainly hope so."

He turned to Carla and said without doubt, "You are Carla, Heidi's mom. It is nice to meet you."

She had never met him and she was puzzled that he knew her. David said gently, "Troy used to bring Heidi with him sometimes when he visited. She looks so much like you."

She hugged him and said with broken voice, "Troy loves you so much. The way he talks about you. There is no one he respects more."

"I am blessed to have him for a friend. Now, why are we all gathered here this morning?"

Mabry spoke first. "We are looking for Troy. We thought he left for the mountains. That was his plan but his Jeep is still here and we can't find Max either." She paused before adding, "Why are you here? Did he call you?" she asked hopefully.

"No. I woke early this morning and he was on my heart and I knew something was amiss. I called and when I received no response I felt the urging of the spirit to come here."

"Wow," Stacey muttered. "You are really connected but . . ."

He smiled that grandfatherly smile of his and asked, "Do you believe in a spirit like that?"

"Yes," she said calmly. "I just have not experienced it personally," she said, her voice trailing off.

"There is nothing special about me. The advice I would offer to anyone that wants a fully blessed spiritual life is to place God above all else and reduce as much clutter as you can in your life so that you can hear that small, still voice. And begin each day with quiet time with our Father. He is not distant and he longs to have an intimate relationship with us."

Suzanne interrupted. "This is all great conversation but we can't find Troy. We need to focus on that right now."

David reached out and touched her shoulder. "I am concerned but not fearful. Jesus did not wake me this morning to drive here on a lost cause. Troy is here. We just have to find him," he said assuredly.

"All of you form a circle and hold hands." He waited until they did as instructed. "Close your eyes," he instructed and he began to pray.

"Father in the name of your precious son Jesus we are all gathered here concerned about Troy. We need your help. Holy Spirit direct our steps so that we may find him and when we do help us to have words to help him. Amen."

They looked back at him and his expression appeared to be searching for something he did not understand.

"What is it?" Mabry asked quickly.

"He is sitting somewhere in a dark place. Max is at his feet."

"You saw that?" Stacey asked.

He smiled at her.

"Do you know what it means, or where he is?" Carla asked, her words coming in a rush.

"No, I don't," he answered gently before adding, "But he is not sitting in a chair."

"That doesn't make sense," Carla said.

"Yes, it does," Suzanne stated firmly. "I know where he is," she said decisively. "Follow me."

They walked along the boardwalk until Suzanne approached the door of the little chapel. She read the sign over the door. Open daily for prayer. "He is inside."

The women looked at her wanting to believe but they were all uncertain. David just nodded.

"Not a chair because he is sitting in a pew," she said.

She walked toward the huge wooden door and pushed it open. The room was dark except for scant rays of light from the morning sun, filtering through a tiny window. She searched the room as she waited for her eyes to adjust to the darkness. She saw nothing and was about to accept that she might be wrong. It was then that she noticed a smell. It was a smell that was out of place with the other aromas of aged wood, carpet, dust, and burned candles.

She smiled and she knew what it was. Max was here. She took another step and then she saw Troy. He was seated on the first pew in the far corner. There was a huge wooden cross at the front center of the church. His gaze was fixated on it.

She held her hand out behind her, signaling her companions to not follow her as she walked slowly toward him. They heeded her instruction and they sat quietly in a pew.

Troy did not turn at the soft sounds of the intrusion. She sat down on the same pew several feet from him. Max lay quietly across Troy's feet.

She sat in silence for minutes as Troy sat without movement gazing at the enormous cross. And then he turned to her and said softly, "They never lock the door. Not even at night. I came here to talk to God. Do you think that he hears me?"

Gently, she nodded her head. His eyes seemed to be far away in another place. She worried that the strain had finally broken his mind. "Have you been here all night?"

He stared ahead, offering no reply.

"What have you been talking to him about Troy?"

"Why I can't sleep? Why do I lose everyone that I care about?"

"Is that why you want to run away? So, Stacey won't get hurt?"

He remained silent.

"Life just happens sometimes, Troy. Sometimes people, good people, catch more than their share of bad breaks. It doesn't mean the bad will continue. I do know that there is a woman who loves you and would help you through any difficult times. And what is hurting her right now is that you won't give her a chance. Give the two of you a chance."

She slid down the pew gradually until she was close enough to touch him. She gently took his hand. "Tell me, Troy. Tell me about the other part of the trilogy of tragedy."

"I can't," he offered.

"Tell her, Troy. It is time," Carla said firmly, without hesitation.

He nodded softly and continued to stare at the cross. Maybe it was time.

Slowly he began to speak of the darkest night of all.

"I was at Carla's when Alana called. She told me that she wanted me to come and take her away. She swore that she would never leave my side again and that it was my child, my son. Her husband was away at work and she wanted me to come quickly. She was afraid of him. He took her car keys away and he was beating her again. I told Carla that I was going and she insisted that I take her pistol just in case.

"I was filled with adrenaline. I was going to be with the woman I loved and my son. I was so full of life, of hope, as I drove to receive what was mine. There were woods surrounding the house. I parked on the edge of the woods as she instructed and walked a trail to her house.

"The door was open and I walked inside. He was standing in the middle of the room with this long bloody knife in his hand. He smiled at me with this evil grin. I have not ever seen anything like that. It was then that I saw to the right of me their daughter covered in blood on the floor. I looked around and saw my son lying in a pool of blood in the far corner of the room.

"I was numb as I walked toward him. He motioned with his head behind the couch and that is when I saw Alana. She was lying behind the couch on the floor and her white dress was covered in blood. I knew that she was gone.

"He just stood there grinning. He was out of his mind. And then he says, you know, I will probably get away with all of this. You are here. I can blame all of it on you, either that or they will think that I am crazy.

"I walked toward the door unsure of what was real and what was not and then he said, your bastard son is dead. He was gloating. He was so full of pride over such an evil act of violence. He took so much that night.

"He waved the knife at me and said, 'Maybe I will be the hero in all this. I came in and I killed you in self defense after you murdered my family. That is it. I will frame you. Yes, that is what I will do.' He said this agreeing with himself as if he were having a two way conversation in his head.

"He began walking fearlessly toward me. I was frozen for a moment and I barely reacted when he swung the knife at my face. The tip of it came so close to my throat that it seemed I could feel the breeze it produced.

"I had almost forgotten the nine-millimeter tucked in the back of my jeans. I reached for it and slowly raised it. He was still grinning at me as he began to swing the knife for a second time and that is when I shot him in the chest.

"I drove to Carla's and told her what happened. I was going to the police but she said no. We had a daughter and we could not risk my going to prison. We cemented the gun in the bottom of a bucket. The next morning, we took Carla's boat out miles from shore and I tossed the bucket overboard. The police came a few days later and questioned me but no one ever saw me there and Carla told them that I was at her house that night. His family kept pestering the police to investigate me. They were convinced that I killed him. And they were right," he added, his voice barely more than a whisper. "The police knew that he killed everyone there but they never put together the puzzle of who killed him. Maybe they did not care about catching his killer considering he murdered an entire family." He looked up at the cross. "I couldn't even attend my own son's funeral."

"Are you sorry that you killed him?" Suzanne asked.

His eyes narrowed and the focus returned to his eyes. "Only that I didn't kill him sooner," he replied. "He was evil, a son of the devil."

She put her arm around his shoulder. "Then why are we here? Let's move on. No one is coming to take you away."

"Why are the dreams worse than ever?"

"Guilt, fear, and the devil himself. I don't have all the answers but that doesn't matter. Let's think about what is important and let's give God the past. The future is that there is a wonderful woman back there that loves you and wants to share your life. Some people are not blessed with one mother that loves them. You have two. Your father may have missed the mark in your life but David is here and he loves you like a son."

He turned, seeing Stacey, Mabry, and Carla sitting a few rows back with David. Tears were streaming down their faces as the women held each other tightly. David smiled and nodded gently. "My friend," Troy said with an ever so slight nod. "I'm sorry that I hurt and scared all of you," he said, searching all their faces.

"Stacey," he mumbled and then he shook his head and said nothing else.

She rose from the pew and walked slowly toward him. She dropped on her knees before him. "I know that you ran away to protect me but I don't want to be protected. I want love. I'll love you through whatever you want to do. Please put away the past. Let's think about today and maybe even tomorrow."

"Troy, you have never told anyone about that night since you told Carla?" Suzanne asked.

"It's never been discussed since that night even between Carla and me until the other day when she gave me her blessing to tell David."

"I think that the dreams will leave now."

His head cocked at her and his face asked why, but no words emerged.

"I just believe it. You don't want a lot of analytical babble. Trust a friend, okay?"

He nodded softly. He looked at her, and then at Stacey. He turned to David. "Do I have to turn myself into the authorities and make this right?"

David rose and walked to him with Mabry and Carla. He grasped his friend's arms tightly with both hands. "Look at me," he demanded.

Troy raised his eyes to meet David's.

"You acted in self defense and there is no reason to open this up. You opened it to God, so let's allow him to be the judge. Let it all go Troy. Let it all go now, son."

He smiled and something inside of him broke unabated and tears rushed forward. He would never recall how long he cried that day. What he would remember is that people who loved him dearly held on to him and wept with and for him. And somehow, he found in his heart the faith to believe that the demons were cast away, never to return.

22

IT WAS THE FOLLOWING SATURDAY afternoon. Troy, Stacey, and Max were lounging at the cottage watching *Field of Dreams*. Stacey bought him an early Christmas present. A very nice 42' flat screen television. He tried to reject the present and she told him in no uncertain terms that she was a movie buff and that was going to be one of their simple date times. He relented. She also bought him a cell phone and told him sternly, "I want to be able to call the man I love and not have to hunt for him."

Troy could have never imagined he would be watching anything to do with baseball but the pain of a torn labrum had found a place of rest in him since that morning in a worn chapel. He was no longer afraid to sleep. Stacey encouraged him to read the Psalms every night at bedtime and he followed her instruction.

Stacey's head was lying on his shoulder and he heard a slight snore followed by deep breaths. She was asleep and he smiled at how comfortable she was with him. She was indeed a simple lady with simple tastes and desires. It was erroneous of him to ever envision her as someone who thought they were a star.

The phone rang and Stacey lifted her head quickly and rubbed her eyes. "Wow. I guess I fell asleep."

"Yes. The snoring gave that away," he said with a smile as he reached for the phone.

"Hello," he answered.

"Hi, son." The sweetness of his mom's voice warmed him.

She barged ahead with conversation as she was apt to do. "I know you don't want to attend church anymore but I thought you might like to know that David is speaking tomorrow."

"The king of egos decided to share with him?"

She sighed and responded, "There is more to it than that. I don't know what happened but Alan is taking a leave of absence. It is all very hush hush but I get the feeling that he won't be back. The elders asked David to take over on an interim basis. He agreed to do that but he told them it was to be for a very short time and he would liberally be sharing the speaking on Sunday mornings with the associate ministers.

"Your dad is still not feeling well, but I am going and I was wondering . . ." she said her voice trailing off.

"Yes."

"Good, and maybe you will take your mom to lunch after church?"

"I have a better idea. Come home with us after church and I will cook."

"Will you make that barbeque chicken I like so much? What is that sauce that you use?"

"George's."

"So?"

"Don't I always spoil you rotten, Mom?"

"Funny, your siblings always say that is what I did to you." She regretted saying that and waited for his retort. But there was none so she continued. "And the grilled asparagus you made the last time?"

"I will make that as well."

"Wait," she said. "You said us. You mean Nate and Mabry?"

"No. I love you, Mom. I will see you tomorrow. Bye."

"I love you. See you tomorrow morning, son." Ruth placed the phone in the receiver and said, "Us . . . umm."

*

IT WAS SEVERAL MINUTES BEFORE eleven o'clock and David was resting in his old office. He looked around at all the achievements of Alan plastered all over the walls and shelves. *"Pride goes before destruction, a haughty spirit before a fall,"* he whispered. He took a moment to pray for Alan and that through his fall he might be restored to what God desired him to be. It was easy when people spoke of you as a great minister to develop an ego that leads you to lean on your own understanding and not seek God for clarification. After the search for Troy that morning Suzanne had asked if they could have coffee together sometime. He agreed and she shared the story of Alan and his demise. He told her that he would pray for Alan but he had no business being a minister at this time. She agreed and David set up a meeting with the regional supervisor of the area. He also went with her to lend support.

David never lost sight that he was an instrument that could be replaced at any moment. God surely was not dependant on him for anything. He blessed him with a powerful ministry but he was not indispensable. It did not mean that he did not deal strongly with matters of the church at times because he certainly did. He viewed his role as a Shepherd and he thought each member of his flock vital. Sometimes this attitude was met with opposition from the perceived more powerful members of the church. Sometimes people thought that if they tithed more it entitled them to be in on more of the important decisions. It played out in a lot of churches in his observation over decades of ministry but he would have no part of it.

He sensed someone filling up the door frame and he smiled at his huge friend. "Good morning, Troy." His friend looked lighter as if a huge burden had been removed, which is exactly what had occurred.

"Have a seat," he said, gesturing to the chair on the other side of the desk.

"I heard you were speaking and I thought I might come. Do you think I will be evicted?" he asked with a slight smile.

"Not on my watch."

"Is it your watch?"

"For a season."

"Suzanne told you about Alan?"

He nodded gently. "The matter has been taken care of."

They heard hurried steps outside the door. Bill entered, his mouth moving almost as quickly as his footsteps. "I saw that man that threatened Alan and . . ." his voice trailed away as he realized that David had company and from the size of the man's back he realized that it just might be the man he was speaking of.

"Can I help you, Bill?" David asked pleasantly.

Troy started to speak to the man that bullied his mom but David gently shook his head.

Bill stood frozen and tried to speak but all that emerged from his mouth was an undecipherable stammer.

"Bill, did you have a reason for wanting to speak with me?" David asked. "My time is short before the next service so if you have something to share, I ask you to address it quickly."

Bill discovered his voice. "This man is barred from the church."

Troy watched in amusement as David rose to the task as senior pastor once again. "Under whose authority was he banned from this church?"

Bill struggled for an answer.

"Well, as chief elder."

"There is no chief elder. And you have one vote just like the rest, no more, no less, and I might add on a matter that has not even been brought forth through the proper channels."

"He should not be here after what he did."

Troy began to rise from the chair. "I can leave. I don't want to be somewhere that I am not welcome."

"Sit back down right now," David said sternly. Troy smiled thinking that this was the only man in this world that could speak in such a firm manner to him and he consent to it.

"Bill, you may push this if you so desire but I don't think you will receive the needed votes under the best of circumstances, especially when I inform the elders that if Troy goes, I go."

"You . . ." Bill stammered again. "For him, why?"

"He is my dear friend, Bill."

Bill turned in defeat to leave.

"Bill, have you spoken with your daughter, Linda, this morning?"

Bill turned and his eyes narrowed at he looked at David. "No."

"She will no longer be on the worship team. Not for a season at least."

"You can't do that. She is the most talented singer in the church."

"Is that what is important?"

Bill struggled for an answer and failed to respond.

"Anyone who is on the worship team should be actively involved in this church."

"I don't understand," Bill said, finding his voice.

"When is the last time that your daughter attended church here when she was not on the stage singing?"

"I don't know."

"I do. It has been almost one year."

"Still . . ."

"Don't you see the problem, Bill?"

He shook his head.

"Anyone on that stage should be a worshipper, not a performer, and quite frankly I don't care how talented they may be."

"How do you know all of this?"

"The associate pastors are comfortable sharing with me."

"That is just gossip," he angrily responded.

"No, I don't believe that to be the case. The situation with Linda has caused dissension among the worship team."

"They are just jealous that Linda is more gifted."

"I believe they desire the rules to be applied evenly. Fairly," he added.

"But, you can't."

"It is done. I have met with our worship leader, Don, and Linda this morning. They both agreed that this is right."

"Is this because Linda got divorced this year?"

"No."

"My daughter was baptized in this very church when she was seven-years old. She has been a member for twenty-five years. But you don't see her as a part of the church."

"A name on a membership role does not constitute being part of the church."

"Perhaps my family will leave this church."

"That will be your decision, Bill."

He angrily exited the room, closing the door firmly behind him.

David turned back to Troy. "I hope you attend church somewhere regularly and I hope it is with that pretty young lady who looks at you like you walk on water, but you are welcome here anytime."

"Now David, only Jesus walked on water."

"That is not true. Peter did until his faith gave way to fear. He could have walked on that water all day as long as he believed."

"I should know better than to get into a biblical debate with you." He paused and said, "I am still afraid at times. I am fearful the dreams may come back or I may have to answer to law enforcement one day for what happened that night." He stopped, searching for the right words. "But I am not going to surrender to fear any longer," he said determinedly.

"One day at a time Troy, and sometimes even one moment at a time. Do you remember the path I told you about?"

"Yes, I do."

"Walk the path and allow God to sweat the details. He won't let you down."

Troy thoughtfully considered all that David was sharing. "Do you know that Stacey is a Christian?"

"Yes, I do know as a matter of fact. I could see the light of God in her right away. It does not come from religious behavior, or following a set of perceived rules. It derives from relationship and that comes from having that supernatural moment of being born again. It differs for some and certainly not many are as extreme as it was for Paul on the Road to Damascus, but it happens. It happened for me when I was eighteen. I never knew I would be called to be a minister."

David glanced at the clock on the wall. It was five minutes to eleven. "We can talk about this anytime you want. I think you know what to do and I believe this young lady is your gift from God."

Troy studied him and saw as always that unflinching assuredness in him.

David pointed his crooked right index finger. "Do not think for one second you are not worthy."

The two men embraced each other. Troy wondered how he could ever have found such a friend and what he did not know was that David was thinking the exact same thing of him.

David let go of him and grabbed his two arms firmly as he so often did. "Son, you look ten years younger and miles happier than I have ever seen you. Take that and run with it. And if you decide you want a life with God and Stacey I would be honored to marry the two of you. Well, let me clarify. I would be honored to conduct the service, but I like to think that God would preside over that."

"I had a dream this week, David."

"But not a nightmare?"

"No, not a nightmare. I dreamed that Stacey and I were getting married on your dock in front of your house. The water was so calm it was lake-like and the sunset was shooting these magnificent colors across the sky. You were dressed in a white robe. Your wife was by your side. My parents, Nate and Mabry, Michael and his little girl. Carla and her husband and son. My friend, the police officer Billy C. and his ladies. It was so vivid."

"What about Heidi?"

"She comes rushing in at the end of the dream and her smile mirrors the sunset."

"Son, you did not have a dream. You had a vision. Now let's get out of here before they fire me," he said with a broad grin.

They entered the packed sanctuary together. David put his arm around Troy as they walked toward the pulpit area. David turned to him and hugged him strongly. He walked up the three stairs to the pulpit area as Troy returned to his seat between his Mom and Stacey. On the other side of his mom sat Nate and Mabry.

His mom whispered in his ear. "I love her," she said gushing.

He put his arm around her and softly said, "I do too, Mom."

David kept the message short. Troy never felt the need to look at his watch when David spoke. It was probably at least fifteen minutes but no more than twenty. David spoke about the path and how he envisioned walking with his Lord on that path. He also spoke of friendships and how sometimes they come in unlikely packages and that was good because it is not good for us to be so comfortable.

It was at the end that David addressed what he knew he must. "I will take over the senior pastoral duties on a short time interim basis. There is a lot of talk this morning about what has happened. Let's not partake in gossip, rumor, and innuendoes. Let's focus on praying for our church and for each other. Pray for me during this time. Those of you that know me know that I take my role as your Shepherd quite seriously. I need your help.

"My last words of advice this morning for all of us is this wonderful scripture. *Proverbs 16:18 Pride goes before destruction, a haughty spirit before a fall."*

Troy could not help but notice that David's eyes seem to fall right on Bill who sat on the first row with the other elders. He chuckled softly.

The elders walked to the front of the church to be in place for those seeking prayer. The music leader, Don, and the worship team sang *Amazing Grace.* Troy sat calmly and thought about the conversation that David and he shared in the office a little over an hour ago. It seemed readily apparent that God was calling him. He had felt the tug before but never like this. He always resisted before but he felt so peaceful at this moment that he could not describe it. He heard a whisper. *"I do a new thing."*

He turned to Stacey who was kneeling in front of the pew. He turned to his mom who was doing likewise. Who said that? He thought if not them, who, and then he understood.

The song was winding down and most of the people who had walked to the front for prayer had returned to their seats. He breathed deeply.

He rose without additional thought. He walked up the left side and made his way to the center, bypassing elders as he did. He meant no offense but this had to take place with his friend, his very dear friend that he loved so much.

He made it to the center of the church but he was late. David was already on the stage area, his back to the congregation. I have come this far, Troy thought. Three more steps will not prevent me but he never had to make them. His friend sensed his presence, or so he thought. Later, much later, David would tell him that he heard a voice in his spirit and it said, "David, turn around. Our son has come home."

David walked down the steps to him and saw tears rolling so gently down this big man's face. Troy tried to speak and no words would come out. "Take your time son. I will wait all day with you. Everyone else can go home."

Troy breathed deeply. "I want to walk on that path with both feet for the remainder of my life." And then he sobbed into his friend's chest.

David gave a small cut sign with his right arm and Don took his cue, bringing the music to a soft ending, and then prayed the prayer of dismissal. Troy cried on his dear friend's shoulder for several minutes. Stacey and his mom, along with Nate and Mabry walked to him and surrounded him with their love and tears.

Early the next morning David, with the help of his wife, Toni, baptized Troy and Stacey in the cold water of Banks Channel beside the dock that Troy knew he and Stacey would be married on in the coming spring.

23

IT WAS CHRISTMAS EVE NIGHT and Mabry's dinner table was surrounded with happy people. Stacey smiled each time she felt Troy's hand touch her leg under the table. She wondered each time how such a powerful man could possess such a delicate touch.

He was sleeping solidly through the night now. He was a new man and the past no longer ruled his life.

Mabry looked at her friend, her student, her son, and saw clearness in his eyes and best of all, happiness. She looked across at Suzanne and they exchanged smiles. They tipped their glass to each other slightly.

She recalled the first day that they met. She had wanted her banished from the island. But now she thought that none of this would have happened if she had not intruded into Troy's life. Brought here by a letter, a foolish letter written by a man who had lost a treasure.

She patted her husband on the arm. He smiled at her as he sipped from a glass of red wine. "Our boys will be here early in the morning and they are staying till New Years."

"I am aware," he said with a smile. "I am their Dad, by the way."

Billy C. was present along with his two ladies. Michael sat at the end of the table with his daughter on one side of him, his mother on the other. None of them knew about the night that ended in a small rustic chapel.

Each person at the table was drawn into the joy and peace that was as present as the food spread before them.

Troy studied Michael from across the table. Michael sensed his eyes on him and looked up and met his gaze.

"Something on your mind, Boss?"

He rested his hands on the table. "Michael, I don't think that you will be working at the club next year."

"Oh," Michael said softly.

"I have a plan."

Michael said nothing and waited patiently. He was still reeling from the news of losing his job.

"I need a partner to build courtyards and patios. There is a job already lined up after the Holidays."

"You want me to work for you, Boss?"

He shook his head. "No. I do not want you to work for me. I want you as an equal partner. We share. We split everything right down the middle."

"I don't have the cash to start."

Mabry interrupted. "Nate and I would be pleased to be investors."

Troy smiled warmly. "Thank you, but I need to do this on my own."

She nodded her understanding.

"I have enough money to get us started. We can get by initially with equipment rentals. Later we will buy our own equipment. Billy C. has a friend in Wilmington." He smiled at Billy C., who smiled broadly in return.

"He is quite wealthy and he wants an outdoor paradise to look at while he basks in the hot tub with his young wife. Actually, she is his fourth young wife. We can net 50k on this job and be done before March if we bust our behinds. We take fifteen each and put twenty back into the business. Are you interested or do you want to spend your life working as a bouncer?"

He shook his head in disbelief as he looked down at Tomeika. He looked up and locked eyes with Troy. "Are you serious? Fifteen grand on the first job. Wow."

"Is that a yes, Michael?" Troy asked firmly, unable to hide the slight smile that crept into the corners of his mouth.

"Yes. Absolutely. Yes, Boss."

"Troy, not boss, Michael."

Michael nodded. "Troy."

"There is one thing you have to promise me."

"Name it."

"You keep working toward your degree until you get it."

Michael smiled his agreement. "If you will make one promise to me."

Troy nodded his concurrence.

"That when I take my graduation walk you will be there."

"You have my word."

Mabry watched the interaction with much amusement and then she chose the time to share Nate and her plans. "We are selling the club and the hotel. Nate and I are going to take off in a sailboat for a long trip."

Troy knew in that moment that they had been ready for this move for quite some time. They had kept the club to make sure that he was okay.

Suzanne looked at Stacey. "What about you? Back on the road?"

She took hold of Troy's arm. "No, not for a while. I don't want to do records for the money. It's nice but that is not enough. I'm going to live here and wait until I have material that meets my demands before I tour or release the second record. I am sure it will drive my agent crazy, but I think I would like to do a worship album. I keep having these songs come to me."

They all looked at her for explanation.

"I want to do a worship record with original material."

The people at the table raised their eyes and smiled. Suzanne broke the silence. "I think that would be great. I will be first in line to buy it."

"Thank you, Suzanne," Stacey said with a glowing smile. She continued her smile as she turned to Mabry. "Mabry sold me the cottage that Troy is living in. He and Max are getting a new landlord and maybe some company, unless of course they desire to live elsewhere."

Troy's look of surprise gave way to a smile. Max rose from the floor and walked around to Stacey, sat politely, and looked up with adoring dark eyes. He barked once firmly.

"Don't worry boy," she said. "You always had a place to stay. Your master was the only one in danger of being evicted." The people at the table laughed together.

There was a pause and the eyes around the table seem to rest on Suzanne. She smiled at them. "I will be fine. I am going home to Tennessee and remind my sons that they have a mother. That is the first step and then who knows."

"What did you tell them?" Mabry asked.

"I told them that their dad was a low down good for nothing . . ." Then she laughed. "No, I told them that we were splitting and that it was for the best and they agreed. They are smart boys."

Troy looked around the table. How blessed he felt. "Mabry and Nate, I am happy for you guys and your next adventure, but there is an event that will require your attendance."

"We will be in touch for you always, son," Mabry said.

"And you would come home for a wedding?"

"Yes," they answered together. "We will wait until the waters warm a bit and Nate has a lot to do to prep the boat," Mabry said. "It will probably be May before we leave."

"Good. I am certain that the wedding will take place before your departure."

"Billy C., Michael, you guys would be in the wedding?"

Michael smiled brightly his answer. Billy C. raised his glass and nodded.

"Tomeika, would you want to be the flower girl."

"Yes," she said, with a huge grin.

"Wait just one minute," Stacey interrupted, as she cocked her head at Troy. "Nobody asked me anything. Better make sure you got a bride in place before you go inviting people."

He turned to her and smiled with unshaken confidence. "Don't you think that it is time for new beginnings?"

She gazed up into his eyes and waited for words she dreamed of.

"Will you marry me, Stacey?"

Stacey rubbed his arm again and nodded. "Yes," she whispered. Pushing back her tears she said, "Nate when the time comes will you give me away? You are my real dad."

Nate looked at Stacey and then at Troy. "It would be my honor."

Quietness settled over the table but it was as if you could hear the smiles and the sheer joy that permeated the dining room.

Troy stood, towering over the table. He raised his glass of wine. "To Christmas, and new beginnings."

They rose together and touched their glasses. "To Christmas and new beginnings," they all said as one.